M000189663

NO RESERVATIONS

STEPHANIE ROSE

NO RESERVATIONS

STEPHANIE ROSE

That's What She Said Publishing, Inc.

Copyright © 2020 by Stephanie Rose

All Rights Reserved.

No part of this book may be reproduced or transmitted on any form or by any means, electronic or mechanical, including photocopying, recording, or by any information storage and retrieval system without written permission of the author, except for the use of brief quotations in a book review.

This book is a work of fiction. Names, Characters, places, and incidents are either the product of the author's imagination or used fictitiously. Any resemblance to actual persons, living or dead, events, or locals is entirely coincidental.

Except the original material written by the author, all songs, song titles, and lyrics contained in the book are the property of the respective songwriters and copyright holders.

Cover Design: Najla Qamber Designs (www.najlaqamberdesigns.com)

Editing: Christine Allen-Riley

Proofreading: Hawkeyes Proofing

021622

To Beth,

for allowing me to pillage references from her life for details in this story, and for making every day better with her friendship.

To Jodi,

for getting me through quarantine with her fierce spirit and endless string of TikTok links, and for always being the friend I need.

SOUNDTRACK

Tightrope - Sara Bareilles
Make It Real - The Jets
Stand by Me - Weezer
I'll Never Get Over You Getting Over Me - Exposé
Make You Feel My Love - Adele
Wonderwall -Oasis
Goodbye - Debbie Gibson
If You Only Knew - Shinedown
Hesitate - Jonas Brothers

Playlist can be found on Spotify

PROLOGUE
DOMINIC - FOUR YEARS AGO

"Dᴏᴍ, honey, stop moving around so much. I'm getting dizzy," my mother said. Her hoarse chuckle still reverberated around the room even though she was too weak to raise her head.

"You need to eat. The nurses are too busy socializing to answer the call bell. I'll go get it."

She grabbed my wrist with her bony hand when I popped off the chair next to her bed. "You pressed the button two minutes ago. I'm not the only patient." A half-smile ghosted across her pale lips. Whenever I'd throw a tantrum as a kid or freak out as an adult, she'd give me that same look. The "are you done, yet?" smirk of amusement that always seemed to bring me back to reality. We'd laugh and I'd calm down, but this was the first time it didn't work. "A package of stale graham crackers isn't the magic cure, Domenico."

"Domenico?" An unexpected chuckle fell from my lips.

"It's the name that I gave you, so I can still use it whenever I want."

A tiny smile crept across my lips. "Whenever I'm in trouble, right?" I brought her hand to my lips, stifling a cringe when I glanced at the bruising along her wrist.

She let me change my name to Dominic in school because I'd hated Domenico. She set me on a path but always let me be who I was.

Without her, who was I? I had no clue. I was still outwardly denying it, but I knew she was never coming home.

"Hi, Linda. What can I do for you?" Luanne, one of the nurses we'd come to know all too well, came up to my mother with a warm smile.

"Is there juice or a package of graham crackers lying around?" Mom croaked out. "I didn't feel like eating dinner but I'm—"

"If there isn't, I'll find some. Appetite is a good thing." Luanne's eyebrows raised in pleasant surprise. There were no more good things or good signs, but I wasn't ready to admit that out loud yet—or ever.

"Dom," Steve, my stepfather, called from the door. "Can you step outside for a minute?"

The minute I met his eyes, I already knew this wouldn't be a conversation I'd like. He was as tired as I was. Mom and Steve were high school sweethearts who'd parted before college. Mom met my father and had me, then divorced him when I was only a baby. She ran into Steve one day at the grocery store, and the rest, as they say, was history. He'd lived with us since I was seven but had only married my mother a few years ago. They'd always joked about not wanting to ruin a good thing, but he was a great stepfather and loved my mother with all he had. On the rare moments I saw past my own pain, I felt sorry for the guy. He looked as if he was dying a little bit each day, too.

"Go," my mother lifted her hand to shoo me out the door.

I trudged outside to where Steve was leaning against the wall with somber defeat in his eyes that made my skin prickle.

"What?" I rushed over to him in a panic. "What did they say?"

"Nothing I wasn't expecting. Dominic, we have to move your mother out of the hospital."

"We're taking her home? Good."

"No," he sucked in a breath before raking a hand through his hair. "There's a good facility in the Bronx. They specialize in caring for end stage cancer patients. They have a really nice staff, and they'll focus on keeping her comfortable."

"What—like a hospice?" If we took her home, it would have meant the same thing, but the thought of actually checking her into a place like that made my heart free fall into my stomach.

"Yes. I hate the word as much as you do, but she's going to need more care than you and I can give her, even with the daily visits from the nurse she'd get at home. I drove over earlier today, I didn't want to talk to you until I'd checked the place out. You can go, too, before I tell them—"

"No, I trust you." I dragged my hand down my face. "When would she go?"

"If I tell them yes now, probably tomorrow afternoon. Dom, trust me, if there was anything else we could do, I—"

I squeezed his shoulder and brought my cloudy gaze to his. "You don't have to tell me that. I know." A lump in the back of my throat was choking me, and I needed air. "I'm going to take a walk outside. If the truck is there, do you want anything?"

He shook his head before slapping my arm. "Go. I needed a minute after the social worker suggested this, too."

I nodded without lifting my head and moped outside. Her

prognosis had never been good, but now, we were officially out of hope.

Plopping down on the concrete bench in front of the entrance, I rubbed my eyes with the heels of my palms. Until now, I'd managed to hold in any crying until I arrived home from the hospital, not wanting to make my mother worry about me anymore than she already did. This time, a tear escaped.

"Dominic!"

The click of my girlfriend's heels echoed in the silence as she came closer. It was dark and quiet, sort of eerie for a place always so busy during the day.

My head drooped before I raised my eyes. The tiny smile curving one side of her mouth was part sadness, part worry, and all love—and too much for me to handle right now.

"It's late, Thea. You shouldn't be here alone."

Thea fussed over me all the time and, although I loved her for it, it also drove me nuts. She was a caretaker and fixer by nature, but death couldn't be fixed. The closer we came to the inevitable, the more I wanted to be left alone.

"I worked late, or I would have been here sooner. And figured you hadn't eaten. Lucky for you, Wendy's is open late." The corner of her mouth lifted before she held out the white bag to me. "We don't need to speak, but you need to eat."

She shook it a couple of times after she sat next to me before I finally grabbed it.

I kissed her cheek and rested my head against her shoulder, breathing her in as she rubbed my back, making circles with the palm of her hand. I took that as her acceptance of my wimpy, wordless apology.

We stayed silent as I ruffled through the bag and pulled out the foil-wrapped burger.

I huffed out a sad chuckle after taking a bite. The grease flooding my taste buds turned my stomach. Most of our conversations lately were arguments about my lack of sleeping and eating. Although I was bone tired, I couldn't sleep more than an hour or so, my mind and body on edge for the phone call I dreaded but now expected. Nothing tasted good, so food didn't appeal to me.

"How is she today?"

Rather than answer Thea, I peered up at the night sky, illuminated by the street lights surrounding the hospital. Not that you could ever get a clear view of the stars in the city, but it looked off all the same. It was because *I* was off, a stranger in my own skin.

"We're moving her into hospice tomorrow," I said, forcing down another bite even though each mouthful turned into a brick stacked into the pit of my stomach.

"Oh no," she gasped, grabbing on to my arm. "I'm so sorry. What do you need, babe? Tell me."

Concern glistened in her gorgeous hazel eyes.

"I need to go back in time and throw my mother's cigarette pack in the garbage." I straightened on the bench, my nostrils flaring with my slow, angry breaths. "Or drag her to the doctor the second she started that deep cough." I dropped my face to my hands and pinched the bridge of my nose.

She'd stopped smoking years ago, but unbeknownst to us, the damage was already done. As much as I'd bitched at her to quit, I never thought we'd really be here right now.

"You can't blame yourself." She leaned closer, planting a kiss on the top of my head. "You've done everything you could for her—"

"But it wasn't enough," I snapped. Thea flinched, and I winced as guilt clenched my stomach. "I don't know how to do this, Thea. She's—"

How do you explain an impending loss that great? My mother was the nucleus of my whole damn life. Everything I did, everything I was, was because of her. Even though she'd never forced her own will, she colored every decision I made. I always considered her reaction before anyone else's.

She deserved better after taking care of me for my entire life. Her life with Steve was over before it had barely begun. The unfairness of it all made me want to scream.

"Sweetheart, you need to go." I said, finally meeting her gaze. "It's late, and Steve and I aren't going home for a while." They didn't like us to stay all night, but I planned on camping out in the chair next to her bed until they kicked me out.

Thea's eyes filled with tears. "I don't want to leave you alone like this."

"I *want* to be alone, Thea."

Her jaw quivered as she shook her head. "Babe, please let me be here—"

"I know I sound like a dick right now, but the only way I can process this tonight is by myself. Please understand that."

She nodded slowly and pushed off the bench. I stood and took her face into my hands resting my forehead against hers as thick tears cascaded down her cheeks.

I was hurting her, and while I felt like shit for it, my energy was too depleted to do anything about it.

Grabbing her hand, I led her back into the parking lot, spotting her car right away in the nearly-empty space.

"Drive safe," I told her before pecking her lips.

"Call me tomorrow?" It was half question, half plea.

"Sure," I whispered, too exhausted for actual sound.

A sad, half smile curved one side of her lips before she kissed me, her hand drifting across the week's worth of stubble on my cheek.

"You need to shave," she said as her nails scratched through the long bristles at my chin.

"I'll do that right after I eat and sleep. Happy?" The hint of a smile tilted my lips, and my chest squeezed at the quiver in her jaw.

"I knew my wiseass boyfriend was in there somewhere." Her hand feathered down my cheek. "Please finish the food in the bag." Thea's chest rose and fell with a heavy sigh. "For me." She didn't wait for me to answer before she climbed into her car and drove off.

I wished we could go back in time to a place where we were so high on love we didn't come up for air, before the lingering loss I hadn't even fully experienced yet, sucked the life out of me. Mom had been in and out of treatment since her diagnosis a year ago. Each time it hadn't worked, the more I'd withdrawn from Thea—along with everyone and everything else.

I dug my buzzing phone out of my pocket after I threw the rest of the food into the trash. I felt awful doing it but I couldn't swallow another bite without the threat of it coming back up.

Joe: *Hey, my dad just told me your mom is back in the hospital. How are you holding up?*

My best friend had just moved from Queens to a small town on the Jersey Shore to open his own restaurant. He'd been saving every penny he'd made since we were in college and found a good price on an old dive bar in need of an overhaul. It was a huge undertaking, but that was Joe. I had no doubt he'd have that place up and running by the end of summer.

Dominic: *Like shit. How's the place coming along?*
Joe: *Slow. I'm a one-man show, but I'll get by. Tell me what's going on.*
Dominic: *She's not coming home. Moving her into hospice tomorrow.*
Joe: *I'm so sorry, man. What can I do?*
Dominic: *I wish I could tell you. After... I don't know what to do or where to go.*
Joe: *You could come out here for as long as you want. Remember you said I'm in the middle of nowhere. Could be perfect.*

I was surprised to hear myself snicker. I had teased Joe about the tiny, obscure little town he'd moved to. I vaguely remembered calling him a bumpkin before asking if the new place had running water.

Joe: *Go tell Linda her favorite son loves her.*

I smiled at the memory of Mom referring to us both as her boys when we were kids since Joe had always been over the house. I didn't know how to say goodbye to the most important person in my life or figure out my place in a world without her.

1

DOMINIC

PRESENT

"Look," Joe started before running his hand down his face as he leaned on the edge of his office desk, "you both need to stop this." He snuck a glance at me, and I could only shake my head, marveling at the stupidity of having to call one of our waitresses and waiters into the office to scold them like children and tell them to get along.

Up until this point, we were waiting out whatever was going on between them, but the fighting in front of customers was getting out of hand.

"Well, maybe you could tell her to stay at her own damn tables," Tommy said while giving Jordan a scathing look that almost made me laugh in both of their faces.

"If you served them quicker, I wouldn't have to." Jordan crossed her arms and shot Tommy a snide grin.

"If a customer at one of Tommy's tables asks you for anything," I said as I motioned to Tommy, who was still looking Jordan over with a disdain far too intense for this ridiculous discussion, "all you have to do is find Tommy and tell him rather than take it over. Joe and I will take you at your word that you're just trying to help and not take his tips, but let's make sure there's no confusion the next time."

Both of them lifted their heads, scathing from the dissatisfaction over the compromise I'd proposed. I reared back in Joe's chair, fighting a laugh. I had zero doubt I'd find them making out instead of duking it out one of these days. Infatuation made people do crazy shit.

"I think that's a great solution. Don't you agree?" Joe had that intimidating edge to his voice that even made me stand straighter sometimes. I was second in command, so I was allowed to break everyone's balls as we comanaged The Beach Pub, the bar and restaurant I'd helped Joe build from almost the ground up four years ago.

I lost my cool a few times, but Joe never had to yell. He reminded me of when we were little and his dad would make us stop whatever we were doing with a look. Until I'd met Mr. Hunter, I'd thought old Italian ladies like the ones in my family cornered the market on the glare of death.

They both exhaled in defeat and reluctantly nodded.

"Good!" Joe pushed off his desk and made his way toward the closed office door. "It's getting busy out there. Glad to know I don't have to babysit anymore." He jerked his head to the side, his polite but firm way of saying get out.

Jordan was the first to leap off the couch with Tommy stalking behind her.

"I think we handled that well." I stood as Joe shook his head with a chuckle.

"I think those two need to get on top of each other before they kill each other."

"Ah, and therein lies the problem." I raised a finger. "They were getting close when Jordan broke up with her boyfriend. But now that she's back with that tool, Tommy's pissed off, and she's confused. I feel for the poor bastard."

"Yeah, that's tough. I don't remember a girl twisting me up like that back then." I followed Joe back into the dining area.

"Because Caterina was the first. You were the cool, unattainable cucumber until she walked in here."

"Very true," Joe agreed with that same goofy grin playing on his lips whenever he talked about his wife. "Now, you're the cool cucumber." Joe smirked as he made his way behind the bar, where he usually stayed.

"Nah, I just don't have time for that."

"Right." Joe snickered as he wiped down the bar. "That's why you've been in a mood since February."

"What do you want me to say?" I sighed and let my head fall back. "Thea deserves to be happy, and I'm happy for her."

"You *seem* happy," Joe raised a brow at me.

"I'm the one who fucked up and pushed her away. However miserable I am right now is on me."

When I found out, a few months ago, that she was engaged, it dug into my gut like a constant thorn—but why? Did I expect Thea to be alone and pine for me for the rest of her life? I always hoped she'd find someone to make her happy, but I'd underestimated how *un*happy that would make me when it happened.

"When I meet someone I want to make time for, I'll figure it out. All right?" Since I'd heard about Thea, I couldn't focus on dating anyone—not that I'd ever really been able to. Lately, she was all I saw, and it was driving me up the wall. I claimed not to have time, but I yearned for some kind of distraction to keep me from obsessing about my colossal mistake.

"All right." Joe raised his arms in defeat. "I wanted to talk to you about something else, anyway. Business-related, not the early twenties angst of the wait staff."

I coughed out a laugh. "I'd welcome a change in subject. Shoot."

"What do you think about expanding?"

My brows pinched. "Expanding? What like buying the lot across the street? I thought the town wasn't selling it."

"They aren't. Let me rephrase that." He splayed his hands on the bar. "What about a second location?"

"In Ocean Cove? I don't know about that, Joe. Wouldn't we be just competing against ourselves?"

He cocked his head from side to side. "We would, but not if the location was in a different town. Like Pentier Beach."

"Hmm. That could work. Close enough to go back and forth when we needed to, but far enough away to not eat into the profits here. Aren't they building a new hotel there?" Pentier Beach was a smaller, more residential town than Ocean Cove. In fact, I couldn't remember seeing any hotels at all whenever I drove through it.

"Yes. That's exactly why I'm asking. They're looking to lease out the restaurant space and Bella dropped our name. Her company is investing in the hotel."

"Your sister's company wants to invest in a hotel at the shore? I always thought they were more upscale." Joe's sister, Bella, was a financial whiz, and had been my crush for a short time when I was a teenager, but I'd never tell Joe that. I remembered Joe's sister as beautiful and brilliant. And that brought my mind back to Thea, again.

"They see an opportunity, I suppose. And that town is prime real estate, but isn't a tourist attraction. Not yet anyway. We can maybe grow a consistent customer base without standing on our heads in the off-season."

We both chuckled. Caterina was our marketing guru, and through her efforts on social media, and getting us involved in local promotions, we stayed profitable during the year. But our bread and butter was still the summer crowd.

"Let's do it!" I slapped the counter. "What do we have to do?"

"The reps they have on site are supposed to come here to meet with us tomorrow morning. Caterina and I were talking about it earlier, and she already has a ton of ideas. This week's marketing meeting is going to be full of more data and stats I can't understand."

"So this week's meeting isn't going to be the two of you stumbling out of your office all disheveled and pretending no one notices, which, we always do." I lifted a brow and cracked up when he scowled at me.

"We have a six-month-old baby who still hates to sleep at night. Don't judge."

"What was your excuse when she was pregnant and you guys had 'meetings'?" I raised my fingers in air quotes.

Joe's lips pursed, yet he didn't utter a peep of denial. "This is why we need to get you a hobby. For someone who's supposed to be so busy, you sure as hell find time to be nosy. "

"Hey, it's a good plan. If you have enough kids, in a few years we won't need busboys."

I caught the towel he threw at my head and ambled into the dining area. Although I teased the shit out of him, I was nothing but happy for Joe and his wife and the family they'd started. Hell, I'd pushed him toward that life, because I knew what it was like to live with regrets.

As much as I tried to cover it up, I was too tired to pretend that it didn't suck.

2

THEA

WHAT DO you wear to a business meeting with the man who destroyed you four years ago?

I pursed my lips out in disgust at my reflection in the mirror. The pile of clothes strewn haphazardly on my bed taunted me from behind.

I'd spent my morning practicing faces in the mirror. The urge to jump out of my skin was visceral, yet I had to find a way to appear relaxed and professional. My attempts at aloof, bored, and overly enthusiastic appeared just as fake as they felt.

I'd heard through the grapevine that Dominic was still helping Joe run his new restaurant on the Jersey shore. I suffered through stories of how much a change of scenery and a new life helped him deal with his grief.

He'd said he was staying at the shore indefinitely, but what he'd meant was permanently.

No matter how much it killed me to admit, leaving healed him in ways that I never could.

Not able to stand myself anymore, I left the mountains of

dresses on my bed and headed into the kitchen to force down some breakfast.

My company had provided me with a modest rental for the next couple of months with a sweet view of the beach. I'd been thinking of my new assignment as a semi-vacation, until my boss mentioned the restaurant we'd be working with.

My phone buzzed across the kitchen counter as I set up the one-cup coffee machine. Smiling at the photo of my best friend, Sue, drifting across the screen, I pressed the accept button and exhaled, yearning for a friendly voice.

"You're up early. I didn't think teachers woke up before nine during the summer."

"Teachers with two-year-old sons don't get to sleep in, no matter what season it is. How are you holding up?"

"Fine," I lied as I leaned against the edge of the kitchen counter. "Not exactly the relaxing beach getaway I'd antici-pated, but I'll deal."

"Of course, you will. You're a badass boss lady."

"Oh yeah. I feel really badass right now. Would you believe I practiced faces in the mirror for a good twenty minutes this morning and changed dresses three times? I'm going to be too busy at this new hotel to entertain this nonsense on a daily basis." I shook my head as I poured creamer into my steaming coffee mug.

"You're seeing the man who broke your heart for the first time in four years. You're allowed to be a little shaken up. After today, it will just be business as usual." I heard Jared, Sue's son, babble into the phone. "Stop J, I need to give Aunt Thea a pep talk."

A laugh bubbled out of my chest, relaxing me if only for the moment.

"I'm fine. Honestly. Good job on the pep talk. Lots of affirming words."

"How's this? You're gorgeous and Dominic Gallo is going to eat his heart out. Go back to the mirror, and tell yourself that."

"I'm not very believable, but I'll try," I sighed. "Thanks, Sue."

I hung up, swirling the last drops of coffee in my mug. I had a job to do. This hotel and restaurant would open on budget and without a hitch.

I'd be badass even if it killed me.

"THEA, OVER HERE!" Violet, the Halston Hotel manager, waved me over to her table. My heart pounded in my ears, and I had to put a ridiculous amount of effort in keeping my breathing even after I'd stepped through the door of The Beach Pub. The hostess gave me the go ahead to sit when I pointed to Violet's table, and I made my way over, eying my surroundings for the familiar face I'd dreaded seeing for weeks. Sue was right, once the initial shock wore off, I'd get used to seeing Dominic again.

Hopefully.

When my boss first told me the details of my new assignment, I'd been thrilled. As relationship manager, the investment group I worked for sent me from project to project to ensure everything stayed on schedule and on budget. Some locations were nicer than others, but I thought I'd lucked out with an assignment on the Jersey Shore. When I sifted through the folder he'd given me and looked over the plans to rent the restaurant space to a local and successful establishment, it seemed like an excellent idea, until I read the name of said restaurant.

I knew that Joe's restaurant was named The Beach Pub

and it was based in Ocean Cove, not even a thirty-minute drive from Pentier Beach. All the numbers made sense, and The Beach Pub was a perfect choice. They had a great reputation and growing customer base. Leasing the restaurant space was supposed to be the detail I worried the least about.

"Was it my imagination, or did I spot you running on the beach early this morning?" Violet lifted an eyebrow when I sat down next to her. In her early forties, she was older than I was, but she seemed nice and easy going. Some hotel managers were neurotic maniacs until opening day, and thankfully she'd shown no signs of that yet.

"No, it was me. I'm used to going to the gym in the mornings, but there isn't one close enough. I figured I'd take advantage of Halston's prime location." I tried to give her an easy smile as I rested my purse onto the seat next to me. My attempt to work off my nerves hadn't quite panned out. Butterflies still filled my empty stomach and sped up with each passing second. Scanning the room, I sighed softly, wishing they'd come out to greet us so we could get it over with.

"You said you were friends with Joe and Dominic, right?"

I scanned the dining area. The place felt like Joe. Understated, modern, not too beachy but it still incorporated some of the spirit of the small shore town.

"I should be honest with you." I grimaced and scooted my chair closer to the table. "I used to date Dominic."

She raised a brow before she propped her elbow onto the table and rested her chin on her wrist.

"What do you mean by date?" She raised her eyebrow again.

Date was a weak word for what I'd had, or what I thought I'd had, with Dominic. Before his mother got sick, I would have said, with certainty, that he was the one. But that explanation wasn't exactly appropriate considering I was about to take a business meeting with him.

"We were together for a while, but there's no animosity. I promise you that it won't be any kind of issue."

"Okay, I believe you." Violet looked me over with narrowed eyes. "And I trust that you'll tell me if that changes."

"I will, but it won't. I can assure you." I said it more to myself than to Violet. In fact, I'd repeated it in my head a thousand times this morning, when I drove out here from Queens, and again, after I parked my car and headed inside. I hoped the repetition would somehow make it stick and catch on.

I'd stalked all their social media sites over the past week and still felt the sucker punch to my gut when I checked their Instagram page. A picture of Dominic standing in front of the entrance, his smile wide and beautiful like the Dominic I remembered and adored before it had all fallen apart, had been seared into my brain ever since.

I was actually happy that he seemed content in his new life but still sad and angry that it didn't include me. That was something I needed to finally get over. I considered suggesting another restaurant to rent the space, but other than having regular contact with the ex-love of my life, there wasn't a plausible reason.

"Violet, sorry to keep you waiting." I recognized Joe's voice behind me.

"I haven't been here more than five minutes, and Thea just got here. Nice to meet you in person, Joe." She rose from her seat to shake his hand, and I followed, gulping down the lump in my throat as I pulled up my proverbial big girl panties.

Joe blinked his widened blue eyes a couple of times before his mouth fell open.

"Thea? No way!" He pulled me into a hug. I relaxed and hugged him back, feeling both relieved and disappointed that Dominic wasn't with him.

"Hi, Joe." I squeezed his forearms as I pulled back. "Congratulations on a successful business, but I can't say I'm surprised."

He lifted his shoulder in a humble shrug and glanced wistfully around the room. Joe was always a great guy; nice to a fault and very driven. He'd wanted his own restaurant for as long as I'd known him, and I was truly thrilled to see how well he was doing.

"Thanks. As many hopes as I'd had for this place, I'd never thought about adding another one. It's a little crazy to me."

He drifted his hand across the short bristles of his beard as a grin stretched his mouth, the silver band on his left ring finger catching a glint from the sunlight filtering in from outside. Joe never struck me as the marrying type, but I guessed things could change quite a bit in four years.

The tiny hairs on the back of my neck stood straight up as I sensed a presence behind me. I didn't have to turn around to see who was there.

"Thea?" Dominic's greeting was a whisper of disbelief. Taking in a sharp, and hopefully unnoticed breath, I turned to face him.

"Hi, Dominic."

3

THEA

We locked eyes for only a moment, but the deafening silence made it seem like hours.

He looked the same, yet completely different. A short beard dusted his chin and cheeks and his hair was a bit longer than I remembered. It was slicked back but a stray lock draped over his eyebrow. His shoulders seemed bigger than the last time I'd seen him, when worry and grief had left him a shadow of himself. His black T-shirt pulled across his broad chest and black lines from a new tattoo, new to me anyway, peeked out from under his sleeve.

Dominic's olive skin was a rich bronze like it'd been every summer, always a laughable contrast to my Casper the Ghost paleness, but all the color drained from his face as his eyes widened.

"What...what are you doing here?" he stammered, looking me up and down as if I were some kind of illusion.

"I'm the relationship manager for the investment group funding the hotel." I said the words slowly not to give away the quiver in my voice.

His brow furrowed before I caught him sneak a quick

glance at Joe. Joe replied with a tiny shrug in my periphery, and I would have laughed if not for the adrenaline coursing through me. They still had their own silent code.

He took a shaky step toward me, blinking a few times before his gaze slid back to mine. His dark eyes were hazy, but intense. In those last weeks we were together, it was as if he hadn't even known I was there, and now, the very sight of me left him speechless.

If I'd seen Dominic on the street, I wouldn't know whether to run up and wrap my arms around him or cross to get away from him. His arms raised slightly at his sides as he inched closer then plopped back down, almost defeated. I wondered if he had the same confusing inclination.

I didn't know what to expect from him today. Part of me thought he'd pull me into a hug like we were old friends. Like he was completely oblivious to breaking my heart. But I never thought I'd get this kind of reaction. It was almost as if he couldn't handle my presence any more than I could handle his. The longer our eyes locked, the thicker the air was between us.

I couldn't deny all the feelings I still had for Dominic. They ranged from hurt, anger, and a soft spot of love I couldn't will away. There was more than tension radiating off of him as we stared at each other, that connection we had still pulsing between us. That same connection I'd never found with anyone else. Combined with the rapid flow of blood to my brain, the plethora of emotions caused the room to spin around me.

Both of us were rooted to the floor, unable to move. Our reaction to each other wasn't what I expected, and I was embarrassed to be at a loss as to how to move on from it.

"Hi Dominic, I'm Violet. I heard all about you from my call with Joe yesterday." She stepped between us, extending her hand for a few awkward seconds before Dominic took it. He muttered a "nice to meet you," while his eyes remained fixated on me.

"Thea said you all were old friends." I spied Violet's narrowed eyes as she looked between us.

"Yes, old friends." I nodded, running my hand over the sweaty nape of my neck before I sat back down. "Let's talk about the new space." I tilted my chin toward the empty seats on the other side of the table, now using the energy I was exhausting to stay upright to crack a tense smile.

"I'd like my wife, Caterina, to join us," Joe said as he slid into the seat across from me. "She handles our marketing."

"Of course," she told Joe, still giving me a side eye. I promised her my history with Dominic wouldn't be an issue. But as soon as we saw each other all the oxygen sucked out of the room. As I slid my damp palms over my dress under the table, I hoped I could recover and prove that it wasn't a lie.

"Sorry I'm late!" A pretty woman with long dark hair rushed over, pulling one of the chairs from the other tables and placing it next to Joe's. "I'm Caterina."

Violet and I stood to shake her hand.

"Is this everyone we need to speak to?" Violet asked as she glanced around the table.

"Yes, this is it." Joe smiled at his wife before extending his arm along the back of her chair. "I'm the owner, but Dominic runs things around here with the staff and events. Caterina takes care of all our social media and promotion."

"It's a simple offer," Violet started before handing Joe a folder of paperwork and pricing. "Halston is an independent hotel and can lease out any of the spaces inside without needing higher level corporate approval. The restaurant would be separate from the hotel kitchen and essentially be your property to set up as you wish. Pentier Beach has seen the same upturn as Ocean Cove in recent years, and we have investors who believe in the property and opportunity."

"Which is where I come in," I said, forcing a smile. "As I mentioned earlier, I work for the investment group sponsoring the hotel. And for the next eight weeks..." *Good lord, eight weeks.* My body almost folded from the inward cringe. "I'm the company's eyes and ears on the ground so to speak. I'll be working closely with Violet to set up permits, finalize decor, and all that fun stuff."

Joe and Caterina nodded while Dominic sat stoic, leaning back in his chair. If I could, somehow, ignore the tingle of his stare for the rest of the meeting, I'd be just fine.

"The hotel is mostly finished, but the restaurant space is empty for the moment. We were waiting on the new tenant's direction on what equipment they'd need and how to wire accordingly."

"We actually took a drive over there yesterday." Joe smirked. "We have a few questions, but I think I can speak for all of us when I say that we're definitely interested, for the right price of course. Right, Dom?"

Dominic didn't answer, trapped in the same trance he'd seemed to be in when he'd laid eyes on me. In all our time together, I'd never seen him so unglued. If he felt a fraction of what I was feeling, I understood. But he left *me*, so in my silly jilted mind, I was the only one who had the right to be so unnerved. To stop my hand from shaking, I had to slip it between my knees and squeeze them together, but he looked catatonic.

"Dominic!" Joe scolded, as if to verbally slap him across the face to snap out of it.

"Yeah, sure," he stammered. "We're interested."

"I'm sure you'll be happy with our proposal." Violet reached into her purse and handed out her business cards to all three of them. "And Caterina, we're actually looking for a part-time social media manager as we get ready to open. If you have the time, maybe we could cross promote when the lease is official. It sounds like you're already taking care of that here, would you be willing to talk about maybe working for the hotel?"

"Sure. For the right price, of course." Caterina's gaze darted to Dominic, and I spied a tiny grin drifting across his lips, his first sign of life.

I sipped my water, hoping the cold liquid sliding down my throat would make it easier to breathe.

This was about to be the longest eight weeks of my life.

4

DOMINIC

FIVE YEARS AGO

"Dominic, you don't have to make my birthday a big deal. I told you that before."

Thea lounged on my bed, her legs tangled with mine, nothing between us but one of my T-shirts. I loved it when she wore my clothes, even when I never got them back.

I pulled her on top of me and cradled her face. Her smile was wide, her lips and chin chafed from all the attention I'd given her with my mouth, tonight. She laughed as I tickled her side, her golden eyes twinkling as the ends of her tousled chestnut hair tickled my shoulders. She was all lean, mouth-watering curves. It was impossible for me to be in the same room without touching her.

"What if I said ..." I trailed off cocking my head to the side. "That I already made it a big deal?"

She narrowed her eyes at my quirked brow.

"What did you do?" She sat up, straddling my waist. The reminder of her being naked under my shirt almost made me lose my train of thought.

I grabbed her hips and pulled her closer, a slow smile pulling at my lips. "We leave for Florida on Friday. My friend has a timeshare in the Keys, and wouldn't you know, it's available right now," I said as I sat up, brushing her tangled waves off her shoulder. "Just you," I dropped a light kiss on her jaw, "me," I pressed my lips to the crook of her neck, loving when she shivered in my arms. "And miles of water and sand."

Her gaze averted mine for a moment. "You planned all of that for me."

"If you don't want to go, I'm sure I could find someone else to share that big king-sized bed with, but I'd need to know by Wednesday."

She pushed against my chest until I fell back. I cracked up when she crashed her mouth into mine, but stopped laughing when her tongue grazed my bottom lip. I was so high on this girl, I couldn't see straight. My mother and stepfather always teased me about how *bad I had it* for Thea, but what I showed barely scratched the surface.

"Wednesday? I could let you know by then." A wry grin tilted her lips as she rested her chin on my chest.

"Good, because I'd have to start making my way down the list, you know how it is," I teased.

"I do." Her smile faded as she roped her arms around my neck. "You're crazy." She kissed me slowly as she settled on top of me. An entire weekend with her all to myself would be heaven. Almost every night, she was either in my bed, or I was in hers, but I always hated parting ways in the morning.

No woman before her had owned me like she did. We talked all day long and never ran out of things to say. I always wanted more of her. We'd only been together for a year but I couldn't remember a time before her. It was as if my life started the random night I ran into her at a bar. Before then, she was someone I knew in passing during high school.

I remembered thinking, was she always this beautiful? And what the hell was wrong with me that I didn't notice? I took her in that night as if I was seeing her for the very first time, and in a lot of ways I was.

"I'm crazy about *you*," I murmured against her lips before I flipped us over. I settled between her legs and cradled the back of her head. "I wish I could do better for us than just a weekend but—"

"A weekend is perfect. I hate when one of us goes home the next day." Her bottom lip jutted out in a pout.

"About that, maybe when we get back, we can talk about one of us *not* having to go home the next day?" I quirked a brow to see her reaction. Her eyes widened, but I hoped in a good way.

"Like move in together?"

"Maybe." I lifted a shoulder, as if it was just a suggestion, not something I wanted so badly I was afraid to come out and ask for it. It had been on the tip of my tongue to propose for weeks, but I was terrified she'd say no. Moving in together was my wimpy way of testing the waters.

"Don't you want to give a vacation together a try first? See if I annoy you?" She kissed my cheek before I shook my head.

"You'd never annoy me. More like you'll get sick of how needy I am." I ran my hand along the collar of the T-shirt hanging off one of her shoulders. "I'm getting this one back, right?"

"Maybe, maybe not." She lowered her head and breathed in. "Mmm, smells like you." She shut her eyes, opening one and raising a brow. "I think that's a no."

My chest rumbled with a laugh. "If you lived with me, you could steal my shirts anytime you wanted. Especially if you wear them like this," I pulled at where it drooped the lowest and dropped open-mouthed kisses along the swells of her breasts. She giggled as she writhed beneath me, rolling us over before she straddled me again. My greedy cock thickened underneath her, despite having been inside her for most of the night.

I had a hunger for Thea I knew I'd never satisfy.

She leaned forward and kissed me, slow and hungry, sucking my bottom lip before she straightened to peel off my shirt and let it fall somewhere behind my bed.

"Is that better?" Her full breasts swayed a little as she laughed. My eyes fell on her rigid nipples, still red from being between my teeth earlier. I grabbed her by the nape of her neck and kissed her, licking inside her mouth and swallowing her whimpers as my tongue stroked hers.

"You naked is always better." I moved her hips down just enough to tease her, the head of my cock grazing against her clit and drawing out a loud moan. I stifled a smile, thinking of the looks we'd get from my neighbors if we saw them in my hallway tomorrow. Thea could be loud, and I loved it.

She moved down one glorious inch and took me inside her. My hips lifted off the bed to get as deep as I could, and it still wasn't enough.

When it came to Thea, it never would be.

5

DOMINIC
PRESENT

As MANY TIMES as I blinked, Thea didn't disappear. Walking into the dining area and watching her talk to Joe as if a lifetime hadn't passed since the last time I'd seen her, I was sure my imagination had conjured her up. She raced through my thoughts all the time lately and had even snuck her way into a couple of dreams—my subconscious taunting me and reminding me of how much of an asshole I'd been four years ago.

The dreams hadn't done the real-life Thea justice. She was so beautiful, all the air had drained from my lungs. The second I saw her, I wanted to wrap my arms around her and tell her how much I missed her and beg for the forgiveness that I'd never deserve but still craved. My arms hung at my sides as I lost the ability to speak with any kind of coherence.

I'd thrown away the best thing that ever happened to me, and even though I'd come to that realization years ago, seeing her again made the loss barrel over me and hurt so much I could barely breathe.

Joe rattled off all the questions we'd come up with together since I struggled to say my own damn name.

As she spoke to us about the proposal, I focused on the absence of a ring on her finger instead of the details I was supposed to be paying attention to. Did she just not wear a ring, or was she not engaged, anymore? The burning need to know distracted me from anything else.

"Before you make any final decisions," Violet lifted a finger and pulled out her phone, "we'll take you on a tour of the space on Monday. I know it may be hard for the three of you to be away at once, but maybe we can do something early, like 7 am. Will that work?"

"Works for me." Joe leaned his elbows on the table. "We'll probably have to bring our daughter with us, but hopefully she'll be asleep in her stroller." Joe squeezed Caterina's hand and she nodded in agreement. "And if it looks like a definite yes, I'd like my lawyer and my financial advisor to give the contract a once over. Is seven all right with you, Dom?" Joe lifted a brow at me, as if to say, "Answer this time, asshole."

"Yeah, that works for me. We open at eight on Mondays, but Pentier Beach is close enough, so that shouldn't be an issue." I searched Thea's face for, well, I wasn't sure what. Other than our awkward greeting, she didn't look my way again.

I thought the dreams had been torture. Thea not giving me a second glance was a far higher level of punishment.

"We'll let you guys get back to your day." Violet stood. "Thea and I have a lot of places to see in Ocean Cove today, so we need to get going."

"Where are you off to?" I asked her while my eyes stayed on Thea.

"I'm meeting with a few vendors to see if we can get a little more local help. As I'm sure you know, Pentier Beach is a nice area but on the sleepy side. I think many of the residents come to Ocean Cove for restaurants or bakeries. As we prep for the hotel's opening, we're trying to bridge the gap a bit."

"Well, Maria's is the best bakery we have. I hope you're making a stop there." I stood, a sudden urge to step in front of Thea and stop her from leaving before we had a chance to talk alone.

"I am," Violet said. "We're just taking a look at the different properties and area as a whole. It's a slow afternoon as far as work at the hotel, so I suggested we take advantage of the nice day to divide and conquer. Thank you for your time, and we'll see you on Monday." Violet shook all our hands before turning to Thea. "See you back at the hotel later."

Thea nodded before Violet headed out the door.

"It was really nice to see all of you. I'm excited to meet your little girl." Thea pulled her purse strap over her shoulder. A weak smile tickled the side of my mouth when my eyes landed on the freckles covering her arm. Whenever she caught a little sun, freckles would break out all along her skin. She'd leave the shore in eight weeks covered in them.

"Hopefully she'll be asleep," Caterina said. "She's a nosy little thing, so I'm guessing probably not." Her brows pulled together. "The site isn't dangerous is it? From the construction?"

"No, just empty space and drywall. I'll let you get back to your day."

"See you Monday," Joe said, looping his arm around his wife's shoulders before making his way over to the bar.

Before I knew what I was doing, I grabbed Thea's arm as she turned to leave.

"Seeing Ocean Cove would be better if you had a tour guide. I could come with you, show you the highlights."

Her eyes fell to where my hand rested on her elbow.

"I appreciate the offer, but I already have a list of places. Thanks, anyway."

"But I can give you the inside track. Can't get that off Google, right?"

She stiffened before she shook her head. "I'm sure I'll be able to manage." She backed away and jerked out of my hold.

"How about we go somewhere and talk? I'm ninety-nine percent sure we're leasing that space, and maybe we could figure out a way to make the next eight weeks not awkward as fuck."

She shrugged, again. "It's a job to me, Dominic. Nothing more. I'll be fine."

But I wouldn't be. I was losing it already.

"Meet me at the coffee shop at the end of the boardwalk at one. If you don't want me to show you around, then give me a half hour. I know it's more than I deserve, but...please."

"Finley's Coffee Shop? The one with the huge chocolate chip cookies?" She folded her arms and narrowed her hazel eyes at me. I almost hadn't recognized her at first with the blonde ends of her hair, but her profile gave her away. I couldn't tear my eyes away from the full lips that had always been on mine or the graceful slope of her neck. Her beauty both enraptured me and tormented me at once. Again, nothing I didn't have coming, but I couldn't just let her leave.

"Okay, show off. You've done your research. And yes. I'll buy you a frozen mocha or whatever you want, and we could talk."

The beginnings of a smile ghosted her lips before she cleared her throat. "One it is. See you then. And Dominic, there's no reason we can't handle eight weeks together. I'll meet you if that's what you really want, but it's not necessary. We..." she trailed off, gnawing at her bottom lip as she always did whenever she became flustered. "We were a long time ago."

"See you then." I stifled a grin at her huff before she stalked out the door.

I watched her leave, only turning around when the click of her heels faded into the distance.

We may have been a long time ago, but everything I was feeling was current. And if the fire in her beautiful eyes was any indication, it wasn't all in the past for her, either.

6

THEA

FIVE YEARS AGO

"Are you planning to run for mayor out here or something?" I played with the umbrella straw in my drink as I tilted my head, keeping my gaze on Dominic as we settled at a table.

"Why because I'm friendly? Since when did you become so antisocial?"

"I'm not antisocial, but you're a lot chattier in Florida than you are back at home." I took a slurp and narrowed my eyes. "This is only our second day here, and from last night you already made friends with the host and know two of the waiters by their first names."

"I'm in a good mood. No harm in being nice." He shrugged and moved his chair closer to mine. I winced from the sting when he stretched his arm across my shoulders. Although I'd slathered sunscreen all over my body, my upper back was fried.

"What's wrong?" His brow crinkled as he leaned in.

"My back is on fire." I squirmed closer to the edge of the seat for some relief.

"Just like the rest of you," he whispered before taking my earlobe between his teeth.

I laughed and elbowed his side. His mood was infectious even though I teased him about it. Between laying on the beach all day and tangled up in each other at night on a really comfortable king-sized bed, our mini-vacation had been perfect.

But every day with Dominic was like that. Time always flew by whenever we were together, and I always dreaded when it ended. But when we came back to the city, maybe it didn't have to.

I hissed out a painful breath, cursing my bra strap for drooping and aggravating the sting. When I turned my head, the smolder in Dominic's gaze heated my skin even more.

"You're doing it again," I said, leaning forward to drum my fingers on the top of his wrist.

"What's that?" He gingerly slid his arm off the table and looped it around my waist to pull me closer.

"Staring." I kissed his cheek, and his lips stretched into a shy grin. It was almost as if he'd had something to say for the entire weekend, but for some reason, he couldn't come out with it.

"Can I help it if you're too beautiful to take my eyes off?"

"Laying it on a little thick, aren't you, Gallo?" I cupped his cheek. "You can tell me anything, you know that, right?"

He turned to kiss my palm. "I know. I'm just enjoying having you all to myself. No crime in that, is there?"

"No, I'm enjoying having you all to myself, too. Mostly." I heaved a dramatic sigh and rested my elbow on the table.

"Aw, sweetheart. You never have to fight for my attention." He dropped a kiss on my temple. "You have all of me. Here, and everywhere."

When I turned my head, his playful smile was gone. His dark eyes bored into mine and stole my breath. I never blamed anyone for gravitating toward Dominic, he had a pull no one could resist, and I was forever under his spell.

"Hey, nice to see you back." The waiter from last night came over to our table with a big smile and handed us both a menu. "It's open mic night if either of you sing."

"No, thank you," I said with a chuckle. "No one wants to hear me sing."

"It's been a long time since I got up there. I'm probably rusty as hell."

My head whipped toward Dominic. "You used to sing? How did I not know that?"

He shrugged as he flipped through the menu. "A couple of cousins would drag me to the stage at weddings. I used to kick everyone's ass at karaoke. My voice wasn't half bad, but like I said, it's been awhile."

The waiter smiled at us before he walked away.

"So, you're shy all of a sudden? You have all these new fans here."

Dominic laughed at my quirked brow. "No, not shy. I'll tell you what, if *you* want me to sing, I'll do it."

"I think I do." I rested my chin on my hands, a slow grin curving my lips.

His eyes widened as he leaned back on the chair.

"If that's what you want, you got it. Just let me know if you're trying to live out a rockstar fantasy, so I know how to play it off later." He threw me a wink and stood.

I spotted Dominic already laughing with one of the guys in the band as weak applause still lingered from the woman leaving the small stage. When he made his way to the microphone, my heart pounded in my ears. The jerk didn't look the least bit nervous. I shook like a leaf, and I wasn't even up there. He gave the crowd an easy smile before the beginning chords of "Stand by Me" started to play.

He looked over at me as he sang, swaying back and forth like he owned the room as much as he owned me. When his eyes met mine, they twinkled and stirred up a ton of different feelings. There was a little mix of shock and awe, as I had no idea he had a voice like that. It was sweet and husky, and he even held the long notes without a single crack. He was adorable and sexy on that stage, and I wanted to hear more. I wanted more of everything from Dominic.

I'd dated my share of guys, maybe even thought I'd loved a couple, but I'd never felt like this. I loved every second we spent together this weekend, but what I really wanted was to go home and find out if he was really serious about us moving in together. He'd only brought it up once, but I thought he was trying too hard to be casual about it at the time.

But what if he *was* casual about it? If he asked me, I was an easy yes. I'd move in with him and follow him anywhere because there was nowhere else I wanted to be. Being this much in love with someone was both thrilling and terrifying all at once.

Clapping and cheers broke out when he finished. He slipped the mic back into the cradle on the stand and stepped off like it was all nothing.

"So, what did you think?" he asked, as he slid back into the seat next to me. "I told you, I'm a little rusty—"

I grabbed the back of his neck and kissed him before he could finish. He laughed against my lips as I pressed harder.

"Are you hungry or do you want to leave now?" he rasped in my ear and dragged kisses down my neck. "If you want to be my groupie tonight, I'm all in."

I swatted his arm and dropped my head to his chest.

"You're amazing," I told him when I raised my head. "I think I want you to sing more often." I sifted my hand through his hair, his eyes fluttering a moment when my nails scraped along his scalp. "In fact, when we get back to the timeshare, can you sing 'Stand by Me' with your shirt off? That's more in line with my rockstar fantasy."

I leaned in to kiss him, giving his bottom lip a little nibble as I pulled away.

He shot me a crooked grin, nodding slowly as he gently slid his hand over the nape of my neck.

"Your wish is my command. Maybe we can hijack the timeshare for a few months. I'm not ready to take you home, yet." A bashful smile tilted his mouth. "I've always had that problem."

My home was Dominic. All he had to do was say the word.

"Let's get dinner and get out of here." I ran my nails up and down his arm and quirked an eyebrow.

Dominic waved our waiter over. "I have a shirtless concert to prep for, we can eat in the car on the way back."

We grabbed takeout and piled into our rental car. I made Dominic sing every song that came on the radio, but made sure to lower the volume enough to hear his voice. He nailed every single one.

"Stop laughing at me," I yelled, holding back the twitch of a smile as I pushed Dominic away once we stepped inside. I rummaged through my bag for the big green bottle I knew I'd need. I couldn't take the steaming of my skin anymore.

Ignoring his snicker, I squirted the aloe into my hand and winced at the cold sting when I slathered it onto one crisp shoulder.

"You look like someone threw sun rays at you." He chuckled, grabbing the bottle from my hands and squeezing the green goop into his palm. "Turn around and take your shirt off," he rasped, triggering a breakout of goosebumps down my neck.

I lifted my tank top over my head and crossed my legs under me on the bed.

"You saw me put sunscreen on. This is what happens." He massaged the relief into my skin, his strong hands cooling one part of me and burning up the rest. My eyes rolled back as I succumbed to both sensations.

"So many freckles," he kissed down my arm. "Look, this patch is like letters, I can almost make out a word."

"Oh yeah, what does it say?" I said, my voice now a breathy whisper.

He gingerly turned me around pushed me back on the bed, climbing on top of me with a wicked glint in his eye. "I think I can spot my name...right here." He trailed his finger down my chest and traced a circle around my belly button. I'd caught sun there too but only burned the skin on my back.

I cocked my head to the side, my cheeks sore from the wide smile spread across my face. This man was exhausting in all the best ways.

"My freckles spell your name? You're a cheeseball."

"It's true, see?" He licked a straight line down my stomach and then swirled his tongue in a half circle. "That's a D." My hips bucked off of the bed when I felt the curve of the O. I shot up, grabbing both sides of his face and crashed my mouth against his, the anticipation of the M too much for me to handle.

He laughed against my lips and settled between my legs, his erection grinding into the ache at my core and making me forget the sore skin on my sticky back.

"Looks like I'll have to claim you another way." We both stopped laughing when he brought his lips back to mine, kissing me long and deep.

I pulled back and shook my head.

"You don't have to claim what's already yours."

7

THEA

PRESENT

As MUCH AS I hated to admit it, Dominic was right. If we were going to be seeing each other for the next two months, simply ignoring each other while we were in the same room wouldn't work. Especially, since *neither* of us could ignore the other, if this morning was any indication.

I'd forced myself to be professional while everyone was around, but when it was just Dominic and me, the hurt I'd been trying, and hoping, to ignore bubbled to the surface. If all we were capable of was skittish eye contact and stilted conversation, it would make an already uncomfortable project torturous. Addressing it was the best chance I had to move forward.

I took a long stroll down the boardwalk before I met Dominic, spotting a family eagerly awaiting an ice cream shop to open. The little boy had a mess of dark hair, his adorable Spider-Man bathing suit dripping from a dip in either the ocean or a ride at the nearby water park.

I couldn't help the smile pulling at my lips when he clasped his hands under his chin as if he were praying they'd start serving. And my heart cracked right down the middle when his father scooped him up and pointed at the menu.

I tore my gaze from him and kept walking. He looked three or four years old, my brain doing the all too quick math equation it did whenever I encountered kids who looked about that age. Before I made it to Finley's Coffee Shop, I inhaled a long breath and slowly let it out. There were enough ghosts messing with my head today. I needed to focus on one at a time.

"Hey, you made it." Dominic sauntered over, his lips stretched into a wide grin. His blinding, gorgeous smile used to be my favorite thing in the entire world. In those last months we were together, it had vanished. Seeing him today, reminded me of how much of an empty shell he'd been before he'd left. It created another conflict in my already troubled mind.

If Dominic was still that distant and sullen man, I would have still hurt for him. But the selfish parts in me, the ones that had never fully healed from losing him, were pissed off plain and simple. I'd wanted to be the one to help him, to give him back that beautiful spirit that had been drained from him when Linda had suffered for what seemed like forever.

The first year we were together was wonderful. After his mother was diagnosed with cancer, nothing was ever the same. I wanted to be there for him so badly, but little by little he pushed me away. I'd hung on in the hope he'd eventually let me back in, and we'd move in together like we talked about. But it never happened. The sicker Linda became, the more he slowly pushed away from me until he was gone.

I hadn't been enough or what he'd needed. As much as I wanted to deny it, it was that simple and that hurtful. I needed to finally swallow the bitter pill that had been choking me for all these years and move on.

"I did. Half an hour, right?" I fiddled with my purse strap. His smile dimmed as he nodded. Unexpected guilt crept up on me for being so abrupt, but since the moment I'd known I'd see him again, my guard had been raised so high, it was impossible to relax. We stood a few feet apart, and even this was too close for my comfort.

"I found us a table already," he said, motioning with his hand to a spot in the corner. I made my way past him, feeling his eyes on me with every step.

"I don't know if you've had lunch yet or just wanted coffee. They have a good chicken Caesar wrap, if you still like that." His eyes darted from mine as a sheepish smile pulled at his lips.

"I do. I'm surprised you remember that." I slid into the seat as a warmth I hadn't expected flooded my chest. It was one thing to be guarded, another to be mean. He did have a point: for this all to work, we needed to clear the air and figure out how to be around each other without us, and everyone around us, feeling awkward and uncomfortable.

"Really? You had a rating system for the croutons places used." He rolled his eyes before he sat down. An unexpected laugh fell from my lips.

"I wouldn't mind lunch. Do you have to order up front or does someone come to the table?" I reached into my bag to pull out my wallet when Dominic leaned over to grab my wrist.

"On me, since I asked you here. Wrap and an iced tea? They have a sweet tea that's good."

I nodded. "Sure. Sounds great."

A slow smile crept across his lips. "You got it."

I watched him make his way to the front and speak to the women behind the counter. Both of them smiled as he approached, one bursting out laughing at whatever he said.

The first thing I'd ever noticed about Dominic was his disarming swagger. He owned every room he walked into, but not in an arrogant way. He was charming, funny, and loved to poke fun at everyone around him, including himself. No matter how bad my day had been, whenever we were together my cheeks would ache from laughing.

I couldn't tear my eyes away from him while he waited for our food. His movements were still so damn familiar. The hint of a smile at the corner of his mouth right before he'd teased me just now brought back so many bittersweet memories. He was like an old song I hadn't heard in a long time, but once it started to play, I knew every word and note.

I remembered other things, too. The serious Dominic who only I saw. The Dominic who would whisper in my ear how much he loved me while he moved inside me. I'd heard of muscle memory and how your body could still go through familiar motions even though your brain didn't quite remember.

The heart was a muscle. Maybe it did the same thing. Mine wasn't supposed to love the now stranger before me, but the motions were too familiar to stop.

8

THEA

Dominic thanked the cashier and turned back to our table. I straightened in my chair, grabbing my phone to pretend I'd been fiddling with it the entire time he'd stepped away. Judging by the wary eyes he gave me as he placed our food on to the table and sat across from me, he'd sensed me staring.

"Thank you," I said as I unwrapped my lunch. As anxious as I was, my stomach growled as I lifted the wrap to my lips. I stifled a groan when I bit into the perfectly toasted crouton and the tang of the dressing hit my tongue.

"Told you." Dominic's lips curved. "They have the tiny croutons you always used to like."

I nodded, happy my mouth was full as I didn't have a response to that. The fact that he remembered something so trivial about me made my heart seize a bit. You only recalled the little things about someone when you cared enough to notice.

Dominic leaned back in the chair with a heavy sigh. "I guess it's lame if I ask how you've been, right? I actually do want to know how you've been but...Jesus," he sighed, running a hand through his thick inky black hair.

"You never thought we'd have to struggle for a conversation starter." I put the wrap down and laughed to myself before taking a sip of tea. "Honestly, neither did I." I rested my elbows on the table. "I've been good. Busy with my new job, but it's been great, so far. I'm glad to see you and Joe doing so well."

I spotted his chest deflate a tiny bit. It was nice to know I wasn't the only one holding a tense breath. "We are. Ocean Cove is a great town, and each year, the restaurant gains more regulars. Summers are the busiest time, as you can imagine, so a second location in a more residential town would be perfect." He took a long pull from his water bottle and squinted at me after he set it down.

"You must travel a lot." He kept his eyes on me as he unwrapped his sandwich. My eyes drifted to his wrist and forearms. Even though his skin was darkened from the sun, I still could see the dusting of hair and remembered how soft it felt when I'd run my nails back and forth every night before he fell asleep.

I'd never imagined we'd be on opposite ends of a table making tense small talk.

"Not that much. Usually, the spots are in or around the city with only a few overnight stays. This is the first assignment that seemed more like a vacation." I took another bite of my lunch, but Dominic's attention remained fixed on me.

"Does your fiancé mind that you're away so much?"

I stopped chewing and fell back in the chair.

"My fiancé?"

His gaze darted from mine for a moment. "My aunt told me back in February she heard from someone in your family that you were engaged. I forget who she said, I know she runs into your cousin Carron a lot."

I finally managed to swallow. "Of course, she did."

"My Aunt Netta is still the original TMZ."

Despite all the tension, I burst out laughing. Netta was a sweet little old Italian lady who was the nucleus of all gossip in Queens and parts of the Bronx.

"Well, to answer your question, no. I'm not engaged anymore, so it's of no one's concern if I travel a lot."

"Oh," he whispered, seemingly more to himself than to me. "I'm sorry, I didn't know."

"It's fine." I waved my hand at him. "Not a big deal."

The sin of that explanation was that it really *wasn't* a big deal to me: the engagement or the breakup.

"So, how have you been? My parents see Steve sometimes and said he's doing well. How's your dad?"

"Steve is fine. He usually comes out here for a weekend or two during the summer. Dad is good. He likes to come in the off season and read the racing form at the bar for the day. His idea of quality time."

I returned his smile before I could help it.

"The Beach Pub is doing well, you seem to be..." I trailed off, a wave of hurt and anger making me sit straighter in my chair. "I'm glad you got what you needed when you came out here."

"Well, it wasn't immediate." His mouth turned down. "You can ask Joe. When I got here, there were days we didn't speak at all. I'd just go to the restaurant and paint or plaster or scrub something and then head back to the apartment I'd rented to pass out. I was in a bad place for a long time, and I didn't want to take anyone with me."

"I get it. Look, maybe we should find a change in sub—"

"Losing you is the biggest regret of my life." His whiskey-colored eyes were glassy and wide as he leaned in closer. "I need you to know that."

The air drained from my lungs as I squirmed in my seat.

How many times had I dreamed of him saying that? There had been a time when I'd prayed for the words that just fell from his lips, but instead of leaping out of my seat and into his arms, all I did was nod while I bit the inside of my cheek to will back the tears clouding my eyes.

It was too late, and I needed to make myself whole on my own, not wait for him or depend on someone else to press the broken shards of my heart back into place.

"When I finally came to and realized how much I screwed up, I tried to call you, but I knew it was too late. And that's something I'll always have to live with."

With everything in me, I'd wanted to answer his calls back then, but I couldn't. He may have come to, but I'd still been broken in every way.

"I was sick and in the hospital around that time. After I came home," I exhaled a long breath, "I didn't have it in me to talk to you or anyone."

A sad smile curved his lips. "I understand. Trust me, I never blamed you for not answering me." His eyes thinned to slits as if he just registered exactly what I'd said. "You were in the hospital? For what? I never knew that."

"I had surgery. Appendicitis. They caught it in time, but it was a long recovery." I forced down the last bite of half the wrap and rolled up the rest in the paper, now having lost my appetite at the story I'd told so many times I didn't even have to think about it. It was the one instance in my life practice had enabled me to lie.

Bad enough his regret was making me stumble. His concern had me itching to run for the door.

"I'm sorry I didn't know you were sick. I'm sorry for all of it, Thea. Even if you can never forgive me, I hope you believe that." He reached across the table and draped his hand over mine. The sincerity in his eyes was laced with pleading, the feel of his skin on mine triggering goosebumps down my arm. It was too much, already.

He still lured me in, and I hated it.

I cleared my throat. "I think we'll be fine for the next few weeks," not able to offer any other reply than a dodge. "It'll go by fast once we get busy with renovations."

"Well, I can help with that. You know I worked in construction before I left, and I did a shit ton of work building up the restaurant. One of us needs to always be at the pub during the busy season, but I can be the point person if you need one."

"You would be able to get away enough to do that?" I ran my finger up and down the side of my glass, making tiny lines with the tip of my nail as I considered what Dominic was suggesting.

"Once the contracts are approved, I can help you and your boss plan it out and be there to help," he continued. "Wouldn't it be better to have one of us there the days you need decisions made about set up? Just a thought."

Violet had suggested just that last night before we'd left work. Instead of getting used to seeing Dominic once in a while, I'd have to acclimate to dealing with him almost every damn day. I both looked forward to and dreaded the idea.

"I certainly appreciate the offer." I cleared my throat, searching for a professional tone. "Once you guys officially sign, we can go over the particulars."

"Are you sure you can handle a whole summer at the beach?" he asked, his lips spreading into a grin.

I was still getting used to his beard, and the more I stared, the sexier it was. As if he could read my thoughts, he ran his hand along the bristles on his chin, studying me with an amused gleam in his dark eyes.

"What do you mean?" I pressed when his lingering stare made me shift in my seat.

He jutted his chin to my arm. "You've already got a ton of freckles, so I bet you'll be covered with them by the time you leave."

His mouth, the mouth I now couldn't peel my eyes away from, curved into a smile.

"I still have the Irish girl curse." I shrugged. "I've learned to live with the freckles. They always come, no matter what level of SPF sunscreen I buy."

"I didn't think they went higher than 100 before we went to Florida. When you'd squeeze the bottle, I always expected a sweater to come out."

A real laugh fell from my lips, relaxing me for only a second before I caught the flash of heat in his gaze.

I shook off the chill, and the heat, from the intrusive memory of the best vacation I'd ever had. Our weekend in Florida was the happiest I'd ever been, and I'd never expected it all to crash so easily.

Maybe he was thinking of it, too. I always wondered if I should've fought harder for Dominic and for us, or at least checked on him more. Maybe I should have answered his calls and told him the real reason I'd spent a weekend in the hospital.

"Thank you for lunch. I should go. I told Violet I'd meet her back at the hotel around two, and there are some emails I have to reply to." I took a long sip of the tea, trying to cool the swirl of emotions inside. I both couldn't wait to leave and didn't want to go. This would be a dangerous summer if I wasn't careful.

"My pleasure." Dominic stood as I rose from my seat. "This was nice." He ran his tongue over his bottom lip.

I held back a smile. In the rare moments that he became nervous, that was always his tell.

"Maybe we could even be friends. I missed you, I've actually been thinking about you a lot lately."

There it was again: the heat and the pleading in his eyes that made me want to forget all the nights I'd cried myself to sleep and the shameful moments I'd tried to fake it with someone else and only ended up feeling worse.

We'd never be friends, but in order to do my job, I had to pretend.

"Sure. While I'm here." My hand shook as I slipped my phone inside my purse. "See you Monday morning?"

He nodded, and I turned to leave. I stilled when his hand slid around my arm.

"Thea?"

Why did he have to whisper my name like that? It brought too many things back, some wonderful, some plain excruciating.

"Yes?" I swallowed, my mouth too parched to form any more words.

"Thank you." He leaned forward and pressed a kiss on my cheek. The familiarity of his lips singed my skin. The urge to cinch my arms around him and bury my head into his neck to cry again for the loss I still couldn't get over washed over me, almost making my knees give out.

I rushed outside, taking big gulps of salty, humid sea air to get my breath.

Regardless of what either of us could have or should have done, it didn't change what was. Here, in the present, we were possible business associates who had to navigate around a shared, sad past.

And as always, Dominic would be my biggest weakness. It was up to me to not let that weakness break me. Again.

9

DOMINIC

"So, what are we thinking?" I asked Joe as he reached into the back of his truck to unlatch Ava's car seat from the base. Her mouth was full of a squeaky, plastic ring that Caterina had said was for teething. When her blue eyes met mine, a wide grin split her mouth as she squirmed in her seat.

"Look who's up. Ready to take a tour, pretty girl?" She giggled, kicking her legs and wrestling with Joe as he tried to snap her seat into the stroller. Ava was a slobbery ray of sunshine and went nuts whenever I walked into a room. It had been a long time since a woman was that happy to have me around.

"Yes, I know you love Uncle Dom. You must see something we all don't," Joe said as he adjusted the straps on Ava's seat.

"That's not true, we all love Uncle Dom." Caterina came up to me, dropping a hand to my shoulder. "Are you okay? You seem a little jumpy."

"I'm not jumpy," I denied a little too loudly. Truth was, I wasn't looking at this expansion as objectively as I should have been. As long as the tour didn't uncover any mold or asbestos, it was an easy yes for me. This was a great opportunity for us, and I'd do whatever I needed to build it up, just like I had with the original restaurant.

But instead of using it as an escape from my life as I'd done back then, I had another vested interest in this place.

"Our lawyer told me the contract checks out as far as terms and liability, and I had my dad give it a once over, and he said, from a financial standpoint, it's a good offer." Joe leaned over to kiss his daughter's forehead. "All in all, it seems like a good investment, as long as the inside looks decent, and you can handle yourself." He lifted a brow as he ambled over to me with Caterina wheeling Ava behind him.

"Thea and I are adults; we'll be fine." I said, narrowing my eyes at Joe. "I can handle myself."

"Dom, when you saw each other, the entire room stood still," Caterina noted with a chuckle. "It was almost like a movie, where everything goes into slow motion, and music starts to play when two people make eye contact."

Joe snickered as he followed his wife to the side entrance.

"The both of you have a lot of jokes for this early in the morning."

"Look," Joe started with a heavy sigh. "If this is your way back to Thea, that's great. But it may not be. You're going to have to figure out how to handle that. If you say you're okay with it, either way, Caterina and I will drop it."

"I'm fine, Joe. It's business." I shrugged, a dumb attempt to cover up the hope I had no business entertaining after all I'd put Thea through.

"Ah, right on time." Violet greeted us the second we stepped inside. "Let's get this tour going."

"Good morning." Thea came up behind her, greeting us with a huge smile that stole my damn breath. Somehow, she'd become even more gorgeous during the past four years. With the green dress hugging her perfect body, I couldn't look away. She mouthed a hi to me with a tiny wave, causing my chest to swell a bit.

Maybe we made some progress at lunch? She still didn't really look at me, but she was, at least, acknowledging my presence.

I didn't deserve her forgiveness, but I wanted it. Fuck, I still wanted *her*. But Joe was right. This lease was a big deal for us, and I couldn't give up my focus over what was probably a lost cause.

"What a cutie," Thea crooned as she peeked over Caterina's shoulder at Ava.

"I told you she'd be up. Too nosy." Caterina chuckled and tickled her daughter behind her knee. "This is Ava."

"Hi Ava," Violet crouched over Ava and shook her chunky hand before motioning behind her. "Not much to see yet, so we'll be fast, I promise."

We followed Violet and Thea around the space. It seemed clean from what I could tell, the walls bare, with the lingering smell of fresh paint. The interior was much bigger than I'd expected it to be. When they led us to an outside courtyard that overlooked the beach, I threw a glance at Joe. He nodded slowly when he met my gaze. I was sure he was thinking of the live bands we had from time to time or parties on the beach in the back of the restaurant. I'd need to measure the area inside and outside to be sure, but it seemed almost as big as the pub.

Getting the place ready in eight weeks would be tough, but we could do it. In fact, it would be the perfect transition after the summer was over. When the tourist crowd waned, we could focus on this area and push promotion hard. Caterina stood next to Joe, her eyes wide as I guessed her mind was overrun with possibilities.

"And, per your request, here's the inspection report." Violet handed a file to Joe. "If you're good with the terms and the offer, we can talk about signing later this week, if you're interested, that is."

"Oh, I'd say we're very interested." Joe flipped through the papers in his hand. "Let me give this a read and let you know if I have any questions. I'll be in touch tomorrow, if that's okay."

"Totally fine." Thea said. "I already have some estimates from contractors. When you sign, we'll go over what you'd want or need."

"I could come back and discuss that," I blurted out. "Once, I mean, if we sign." I stuffed my hands in my pockets and shrugged, as if somehow that would make me appear aloof and not an overeager moron. "Like I told you, Thea. I'm happy to help."

"Thea mentioned you may be interested in coming on site to help oversee the construction." Violet nodded as she looked between us.

"Wasn't that nice of you." Joe turned his head toward me with a raised brow.

"Having one of you here on a regular basis would definitely keep things moving. I'd say being open for the summer isn't possible but we'd love to be fully operational by October. You're free to wander around a bit if you'd like. I have some calls to return, but the door is unlocked when you're ready to go." Her mouth stretched into a wide, sincere smile. "I think this could be a great partnership. Hopefully, we can start things off soon."

Violet shook all of our hands and made her way back into the main hotel area.

"Looks bigger from the inside, doesn't it?" Thea said, as she came closer to us. "I'm sure you guys have a ton of ideas."

"We sure do!" Caterina said, as she scanned the space. Joe laughed and looped his arm around her shoulders.

"I guess we'll be in touch. Nice to meet you, Ava." Thea smiled down at the carriage, Ava gave her a gurgle and leg kick in return. A wistful smile ghosted her lips for a moment. "If you'll excuse me, I have a meeting in a few minutes. Feel free to keep looking around as much as you like." A wry smile pulled at her lips when her eyes met mine. "I guess I'll see you soon."

"Yes, looks like it. Sorry about that." I pretended to wince and drew a chuckle out of her.

We had a couple of moments like that during lunch. The familiarity and ease of how we used to be peeking out, but then we were right back to being strangers.

I didn't want to be strangers anymore. Even if I couldn't get her back, I wanted us to be at least more than that.

"You know," Joe said, breaking me out of my trance. I was still fixed on the path Thea had taken before she left. "Before I knew Thea was involved, I was going to recommend that you oversee this place." He ambled closer. "We have an assistant manager at the pub now, so we wouldn't need to depend on each other so much, and you deserve something of your own. There's no one I trust more than you."

"And now you *don't* trust me." I took a step closer, linking my arms over my chest.

"I trust you. I even trust you to keep a level head if things got messy between the two of you, which, judging by the tension between you whenever you're within a couple of feet of each other, is most likely inevitable."

"Joe—"

He raised his hand to cut me off. "You've been in a funk since February over this woman, and," he sucked in a breath before he continued, "now that you know she's not engaged anymore, you're even more fixated on her. Whether you're admitting it out loud or not—"

"I'm fine. Like I told you."

I turned to see Caterina's sad smile as she rocked Ava's carriage back and forth.

"Let's get back, we need to look at that report," I said before I stalked back to the parking lot.

I said nothing on the drive back, because Joe was right. Hell, I worried about me, too. I couldn't go back in time and undo my biggest mistake, but I also couldn't pass up the chance to make it right in the present.

"Your job sent you to the beach for a summer." My sister, Moira, shook her head as we ambled down the short boardwalk. "There are worse things in life." She nudged my arm until I shrugged with a reluctant nod.

When she'd driven in this morning, the first thing my sister asked for was an Italian ice. The closest place I knew of was in Ocean Cove along the beach. We spent the afternoon strolling up and down the wooden path, her constant attempts to drag me out of my own head, unsuccessful.

"You invited me here for the July fourth weekend because you claimed you wanted to have a little fun and relax before the construction started at the hotel. I didn't drive three hours to watch you mope until Sunday afternoon." She stopped, arching an eyebrow and tapping her foot. "I did that for close to sixteen years before I left for college."

A laugh escaped me before I could help it. "I'm not moping. I'm just, thinking is all."

"You could get reassigned if you wanted to, right?" Moira asked as she led us to the wood railing and leaned back. "Make up something about Mom and Dad and stay close to home. You don't have to deliberately torture yourself every day."

She was only three years older than me, but I'd always seek her out before anyone else if I was upset, even before our parents. She'd seen me at my worst after Dominic left, and if I did bail out of this project, she'd be the only one to really understand.

"No, I'm fine. I can't let this beat me." I rested my elbows on the rail next to her and focused on the crashing of the waves.

"It's not a matter of letting it beat you, it's self-preservation. I always liked Dominic, and while he didn't hurt you on purpose, you're still not over it." She looped her arm around my shoulder. "I'd like you to live a little, baby sister. Enjoy your life."

"I enjoy my life," I countered, the statement sounding hollow even to my own ears.

Moira said nothing, leveling her blue eyes at me.

"Have you seen enough boardwalk?" I asked her. "If we're going to argue all afternoon, I'd rather do it with a wine cooler on the beach by the rental."

"Wine cooler?" She chuckled. "Sorry, I stand corrected. You really are living it up out here."

She snickered when I elbowed her side.

"Thea!" My eyes clenched shut at the sound of Dominic's voice.

"Hello to you too, Dom," my sister teased when we turned around.

"Moira? Hey, how are you?" He came up to us and pulled her into a hello hug and her eyes widened at me over his shoulder.

"Good, visiting my favorite sister for the weekend and dragged her out for an Italian ice."

"Best part of summer, right?" Dominic beamed at me, and I hated it. I hated his easy smile and how his polo shirt pulled across his chest, my eyes unable to tear away from any of it.

"It is, and this was the closest stand I knew of." I resented the lick of heat in my belly as his eyes did a quick perusal down my body. The eyelet coverup showed enough of my black bikini underneath to feel exposed under his stare.

"Pentier Beach doesn't have much—yet." He laughed, his wide grin more blinding than the July sun. "What are you guys doing later? You should come to the pub. We have a band coming that plays old covers. Like the one we used to go see in Rockland, remember?"

"I remember." I remembered too much, that was my problem. "We don't know what we're doing, yet."

"Oh," he said, his smile fading. "They come back a few times usually during the summer so if you miss them tonight, you can always catch them next time. I better get back. I had a pick-up to do, but I like taking a walk down the boardwalk during lunch if I can get out. We're getting busy, so I won't get many lunch breaks." His eyes lingered on mine. "I'm sure you know Joe signed the lease this week. Looks like we're partners."

"Yes...for the summer," I stammered, forcing a smile in hopes of appearing relaxed.

"About that, I figured I'd come by the hotel around ten on Monday. We could talk about what you have out for estimate and go over what else we would need. Is that all right with you?"

He ran his hand over his chin, the bristles of his beard longer than when I'd seen him the other day. It brought my attention back to his mouth. This almost felt like a teenage crush—the awkwardness I felt in his presence and the need to both be close to him and as far away as possible.

In only a few days, the interactions between us had stirred up more old feelings—feelings that never went away and now taunted me whenever he was close.

"That's fine. Come to the hotel, and we can meet in the office."

"I'll do that," he said, his voice was soft before he backed away, his gaze still fixed on me. "Very nice to see you, Moira. You ladies have fun this weekend." He smiled, waiting a long minute before finally turning around and heading in the opposite direction.

"Don't," I told my sister as I tried to get a handle on my breathing.

"Don't what? I don't even know where to start, Theodora."

"Ugh," A gagging noise erupted from the back of my throat. I hated my full name and my sister loved to invoke it whenever she wanted to prove a point. "It's fine—"

"It is *not* fine. He couldn't take his eyes off of you and you can barely look at him. And crossing your arms doesn't stop your hands from shaking. You've done that since you were a kid." She pointed at the table on the corner. "Sit."

I slid onto the concrete bench without a word.

"Hear me out. And this is going to sound like an odd suggestion, but did you ever think about clearing the air with him a bit? Like getting it all out there between the two of you before you have to attempt a business relationship?" She kicked my ankle until I lifted my head.

"We did. Sort of." I cocked my head from side to side. "He wanted to have lunch so it all wouldn't be so awkward."

"Well, that didn't work. Did you *really* talk or was it the same painful conversation I just suffered through with you?" She drummed her fingers on the table.

"He talked for the most part. He said losing me was his

biggest regret and he wanted to be friends while I was here. I told him while we were here we could be friends, but..." I trailed off, knowing what she was going to say.

"But you didn't respond to the bomb he left on your lap?"

I rolled my eyes. "It wasn't a bomb."

"Honey, we were all there with you through the whole thing. You expected him to come home for months, and it destroyed you when he didn't. I told you to talk to him when he called you and at least let him know."

"And what good would that have done? He didn't want me or need me, and he's doing wonderful now, *without* me," I spat out, the anger boiling in my gut with every word.

"He didn't leave you for anyone else. Didn't cheat, didn't string you along—"

"And in a lot of ways that's worse!" I cupped my forehead, trying to get a handle on the swirl of emotions in my restless stomach. "He left because I wasn't enough for him."

She rested her elbows on the table and leaned closer. "And you never let yourself be angry at him for it because he was so shattered when his mother died. And now, he's the Dom we all remember. The same charismatic, good-looking bastard, who is seeking you out again," she pointed a finger at me, "whether or not you realize that."

"I realize it," I allowed. "He volunteered to be the point person for construction on the restaurant, so we'll see each other even more." My head fell back as I sucked in a breath. "I'm only here for the summer. He can seek all he wants."

"We're going to his restaurant tonight."

My head whipped to hers. "No, we're not."

"Yes, we are. I love a good cover band. And when he lingers around you like he did just now, you're going to find the lady balls to tell him how pissed you still are at him and how hard it was for you after he left. That is the only way this project has a chance of being the least bit bearable for you." She let out a long breath, a sad smile pulling at her lips. "Maybe even tell him about—"

"*No.*" My jaw clenched as my sister reared back. "I can admit how angry I am, but he doesn't need to know that." I straightened in my seat, vehemently shaking my head. "That won't help anything."

"All right," she conceded. "I'll save that argument for another day. Come on." She slapped my hand. "Fuck the wine coolers. I'll get some vodka and cranberry juice and you can drink up some courage."

11

DOMINIC

"Dominic, do you mind if I take my break now? Tommy said he'd watch my tables for the next few minutes." Jordan's face twisted in a grimace as she leaned on the bar. They'd been at each other's throats not a week ago, but once again, Tommy folded like a deck of cards when Jordan batted her eyes in quest of his forgiveness.

If I was a betting man, I'd wager she wanted an early break to go outside and scream at her boyfriend like she'd been doing all week. I'd also hazard a guess she was leaning on Tommy again while this douche she was dating gave her daily trouble, but it was none of my business. I did hope poor Tommy would stop pining over a woman who gave him nothing but grief.

"Go on," I told her, nodding outside. Her shoulders drooped in relief before she rushed outside, already digging her cell out of her pants pocket. I guessed when it came to love, we were all a little stupid. I'd been reminded recently of just how much of an idiot I was.

The woman I wanted was back in my life but couldn't bear to even look me in the eye. Since I'd seen her on the boardwalk today, a torturous reel of our memories had played on repeat in my head, old events now feeling new and raw.

I scanned the busy July fourth crowd. Since Memorial Day, we'd been non-stop, and I was nothing but thankful. Now to figure out how to bring the crowds to the new space. I was excited to run the new restaurant and have a place I could almost call mine, even though I ran The Beach Pub with Joe and he valued my opinion on most decisions he made.

At some point, during the past four years, Ocean Cove had gone from a place I'd escaped to, to my home.

My eyes landed on a familiar form. She was one of two women who occupied a table in the back corner, and my pulse jolted with recognition as I peered closer.

Thea was here. She wasn't scouting the place this time or here because she had to meet with us on business. The selfish asshole in me wanted to believe she was here for me.

I came over to her table, trepidation and hope pumping through me as I got closer.

"Good evening, ladies." Thea and Moira swiveled their heads in my direction. "Glad to see you could make it." I flashed them a wide grin, but Thea only nodded as she focused on swirling the liquid around in her glass.

"We're glad we made it, too," Moira said with a snicker. "We almost didn't get in. You guys have a big line."

"This band usually draws a good crowd. I bet I could even get them to play a little Backstreet Boys for you." I lifted a brow at Thea, but she didn't look up. "Anyway, the next time you come here, and there's a line, tell the hostess to come get me, or any one of us. You shouldn't have to wait."

"Shouldn't, but I seem to anyway, right?" Thea raised her wine glass at me and took a pull, glaring at me over the rim. The way she snapped at me caught me off guard. Even towards the end when things had been so tense between us, I'd been the broody asshole always lashing out.

I noticed her sister nodding to the back patio with her chin. Moira was always about as subtle as a heart attack.

"Can you talk for a few minutes?" Thea glanced over my shoulder. "I know it's busy but—"

"Of course. The patio is a little crowded, but come with me to the office where we can actually hear each other speak."

Thea rose from her seat, and I stepped behind her, drop- to the small of her back as I led her into the

stomach in a knot as I shut

hand through

r the air in case
we ended much, but now
that we *are* going to be dealing ther all summer,
there are a few things you should know."

She sucked in a long breath and let out a slow gust of air. My breath stilled when she leveled her eyes, narrowed to angry slits, at me.

"You broke me, Dominic."

My heart dropped into my stomach as I fell back on the edge of the desk. When I opened my mouth to voice some kind of reply, I had nothing. For once in my life, no words came out.

I knew I'd hurt her, but the thought of breaking her drained the air from my lungs.

"Do you have any idea how it feels to have the person you love suffer right before your eyes and there isn't a damn thing you can do about it?" Her voice cracked before she swallowed. "For a whole year, instead of leaning on me, you pushed me further and further away until I had no place in your life. But I hung on because all I wanted to do was help you. And keep you. And I felt awful for being so selfish when you were going through something so terrible."

"Thea, I ..."

She shot me a glare and shook her head. I nodded, letting her continue.

"As stupid as it was, I waited for you to come back. For months. I guess, in the back of my mind, I'd always expected you to come to me and say you needed me after all." Her shoulders jerked with a sad chuckle. "You said you couldn't be with me anymore, yet, I didn't quite believe you." She leaned her elbows on her knees and clasped her hands under her chin.

I scrubbed a shaky hand down my face, overcome by the realization of all the damage I'd done.

"I was in a terrible place at the time. I was too fucked up to realize what I was doing."

"You said that, but you aren't now, are you?" She leaned forward. "You're fine. Big smiles, jokes, I would have given *anything* for you to let me in. To see you like this. But I wasn't what you needed, or wanted." She lifted a shoulder, dropping her gaze back to the floor.

I'd never understood the way my leaving had affected her. I'd broken her. I'd broken us. And it was too late to try to put the pieces back together.

She pushed off the couch and marched up to me, her eyes shining as a small smile played on her lips.

"I *am* glad you're okay and that you're happy. I can be a grown up and manage this restaurant opening with you. But, I thought you needed to know. Or, at least, *I* needed to tell you." A heavy sigh fell from her lips.

On instinct, my hand cupped her cheek. She raised her head, her eyes clenching shut as she stiffened under my touch.

"I am so, so sorry, Thea. You can't even begin to know how much."

I pressed a kiss to her forehead and rested my chin on the top of her head. I expected her to push me away, but we stayed there a long minute, a surprisingly comfortable silence washing over us.

I swiped a tear escaping down her cheek with my thumb. "My mother would be so pissed at me right now. She would have kicked my ass back then if she'd known what I was doing."

"She knew," Thea whispered, lifting her head with a smile tugging at her lips. "She knew we were...struggling before she passed away. I went to see her when she was in hospice." Her gaze dropped to the floor. "I brought her those *pignoli* cookies she liked and kept asking what she needed, but she yelled at me to sit and tell her what was wrong."

"Sounds like Mom."

More flashbacks raced through my brain. The two of them ganging up on me all the time, all of us laughing at my mother's table on Sundays when I'd relentlessly tease them both. Life had been good before it had all gone to shit.

"When she dragged it out of me, she told me not to be upset because you just needed time to deal with things your own way, but you'd come around." She swallowed before she continued. "Because you loved me."

The ache in my chest made it difficult to breathe. What Thea and I'd had only came around once in a lifetime, and I'd thrown it away.

"She loved you," I croaked out, my eyes clouding up. "Thank you for going to see her."

"You don't have to thank me." She crossed her arms and

shook her head. "I loved her, too. I hated letting both of you go." Her watery smile almost made me lose it.

"I hate that I let *you* go. I wish I could make you see just how much." I swallowed, the urge to bring her back into my arms almost palpable.

"I better get back to Moira. She was anxious to order, and you know how she gets when she hasn't eaten."

Thea's hazel eyes were red and glossy. She bit her full red lip, but I could still see it quiver. I wanted her back so badly it pulsed in my fingertips, but now it seemed too cruel to try.

My eyes drank her in where she stood. So gorgeous, inside and out. No woman ever compared to her in my eyes or ever would.

Neither of us said a word as she opened the door and left.

Seeing her every day would be the torture I'd earned, and living without her was the punishment I deserved.

12

THEA

I WOKE up Monday morning anxious, but free of the dread that had plagued me since I'd been assigned to the Halston Hotel. I was ready to get this job done: finalize the estimates and get this place up and running. Weeding through the paperwork on my desk, I cringed at how unfocused I'd been for the past few days, but as of today, my head was officially out of the clouds.

Would working with Dominic be easy? I was sure it would still be awkward at times, but a weight had been lifted from letting go of most of the exhausting pretense.

"Good morning."

My head whipped toward Dominic's voice. He stood in the doorway of my office with dark jeans and a tight black T-shirt. His beard was cropped, and a tiny smile curved his lips. Now that I could look him in the eye, I had to figure out how to ignore his mouth.

"Good morning." I returned his smile and motioned to the seat across my desk. "You're just in time."

"I brought coffee for you." Dominic placed a plastic cup on my desk, a shy grin pulling at his lips. "I didn't know if it would stay hot from the pub so I picked up iced. You never drank hot coffee anyway, but maybe..." He trailed off before his head fell back on a sigh. My heart squeezed a bit at how flustered he was over simply bringing me coffee.

"I still mostly drink iced. Even when it's below zero outside." I tapped the straw on the desk to open the wrapper. After stabbing the top of the cup with the straw, I took a sip and tasted the cream and sugar.

"Thank you. This is perfect." His shoulders relaxed as he leaned back in the chair. We still knew each other, but we didn't. We were strangers who shared memories.

"I told Joe I'd be here for most of the morning—not sure how long you wanted to meet." He took a sip of his own coffee and crossed his legs.

"Not too long, today." I handed him the estimate folder. "I'm guessing you'd want to keep the decor the same as Ocean Cove, so I scoped out wood shiplap and the same type of bar stools. Not sure how specific you want to get or if you'd like to change up anything. It's your space, so you can feel free to fill it however you'd like. If you want to bring in your own contractors for some of the work, you can, but I'd need to get them approved."

He nodded as he skimmed through the folder. "I like the idea of keeping it mostly the same. It doesn't matter if the same crew does the renovations or not. Besides, I'm not sure if some of them are still around anyway." He snickered. "Joe and I bartered from everyone in the area to get everything done at the beginning."

"Bartered?" I asked.

"He had money saved, but he, well *we*, I guess, basically gutted out the whole space and rebuilt it. It was weird coming from New York to that small town we'll-all-pitch-in type of mentality. One of our neighbors, at the time, was a retired contractor and did the walls for free. So we'd really have nothing to compare the price to." He shrugged.

"That's pretty amazing that you had that kind of help."

He nodded. "It's a big reason why I felt so at home here, and why I guess Joe wanted to move out here in the first place. Not that I don't miss the old neighborhood, but you'll find even around here, small towns show up for each other." His smile faded before his eyes grew. "I'm sorry if I sounded like an asshole just now."

I narrowed my eyes. "Why would you say that? It's great that you both found community out here, why would that make you sound like an asshole?"

He raked his hand through his hair. That one stray curl draped over his brow and distracted me more than his mouth.

"I guess, after we talked, it feels mean to talk about coming out here." He grimaced at me. "I'm sorry."

I shook my head. "Please don't be sorry. I don't want you to walk on eggshells around me all summer. We...we got it all out there and it's okay."

I didn't say *fine*, because it still stung, but he was trying, and so would I.

"Like I told you, I *am* happy you found what you were looking for out here. And knowing you, you probably know everyone between Ocean Cove and Pentier Beach by their first names," I couldn't help my eye roll, "so that can help all of us."

His mouth twisted into a smirk as he dangled the coffee cup at his side. "Still getting on my case for that?"

"For what?"

"You don't remember giving me grief in Florida for talking to *everyone* we saw."

"And you said it was to make up for how antisocial I was. Which I *wasn't*." I slurped my coffee and glowered at him over my straw. "Do you want me to get estimates on setting up a stage area so you can sing for your fans?"

He chuckled as his smile became wistful. "I haven't sang since that weekend."

"Even with the live bands that come to The Beach Pub? I figured that you wouldn't be able to help yourself." I laughed, but the smile evaporated from his lips.

"The last time I sang was to you."

The air between us became thin as our eyes locked. I didn't know what to do with that, or what to say. We sat in a loaded, heavy silence until Dominic shifted in his seat and cleared his throat.

"Is it okay if I give Joe a quick call? I forgot the name of the flooring company that we used. I know they're still around and could probably give you a better price than this."

"Oh, sure." I stammered a bit before pointing into the hallway. "There's an extra office next to this one or you could go outside but there's a lot of drilling going on in the front. I guess you'd rather be able to hear Joe when you speak." A nervous laugh bubbled up from my chest, and he flashed me a shy grin.

"Thanks. I'll be right back."

I dropped my head into my hands with a groan. It was hard to stop looking back on a life that didn't exist anymore.

13

THEA

"Hey Thea, can you do me a favor?"

Violet rushed into my office and plopped in the chair across from my desk.

"Sure. Everything okay?" I took in her defeated slump and stifled a laugh.

"I need to have a quick meeting with the housekeeping union, and I told Caterina she could come in to talk about the marketing position." She rubbed at her temples and shot me a pleading glance. "Would you mind meeting with her? You know the details of the job since you had to get her cost per hour approved. It would be a *huge* help. The owners are asking when we're going to start promoting, so I was hoping she could help us soon. But I've put off this union meeting so many times."

"Of course, is she here now?"

"In the hallway," she said with a wince, and we both laughed.

"Good thing I said yes, then. Go talk to the union, I've got this."

Her shoulders drooped in relief. "Thank you. You've truly been a godsend."

"It's no problem." I smiled as I spotted Caterina's head in my office doorway after Violet rushed off.

"Everything is happening all at once for Violet right now." I stood to greet Caterina. "Please don't take offense or think she doesn't want to offer you this position. It's just a little crazy around here."

Her smile was warm when she shook her head. "It's no problem. Dominic said that this place is taking shape quickly. No offense taken, I promise." She cast a glance at the vacated chair in front of my desk and tapped her chin. "How would you feel about a lunch meeting? I had a busy morning with my other freelance job, and between that and getting Ava settled at her babysitter, I didn't eat. I can talk business much better with food in my stomach."

"Honestly, that would be perfect. There's not much around here, I was thinking of sneaking to the boardwalk in Ocean Cove to grab a sandwich from Finley's." I shrugged. "We could do that."

"For one of those chocolate chip cookies, I'll even drive us." She jerked her chin to the hallway. "Let's go."

Since I'd started this assignment a couple of weeks ago, I'd spent my downtime by myself, and the solitude was beginning to make me itchy. Caterina reminded me so much of my friends at home, and our easy chatter, as we stepped into her car, eased my loneliness.

"Do you have other projects that you're working on, or is this the only one?" she asked as she kept her eyes on the road.

"If an old project changes scope, and they request additional funding, or if there's something to troubleshoot, I'll get involved. But mostly it's just one at a time."

Caterina took us through a couple of backroads to the boardwalk as I stared out the window.

"Ocean Cove is a nice little town. Big change from Queens," I said softly, more to myself than Caterina.

"Big change from Brooklyn. I never thought I'd ever leave the city, but ..." she trailed off as we pulled into a spot. "Sometimes, life surprises you."

It certainly does.

"I still visit my family, and have a few agencies I freelance with, so I'll travel to Manhattan for a day if I need to be at a meeting, but mostly I work from home. I do miss traipsing around midtown where my old office was."

"Our main office is in midtown, too. Ocean Cove seems like a great place to settle in and raise a family." I scanned the boardwalk as we made our way to Finley's. I didn't lose Dominic to another woman, but I was developing a resentment towards a town for stealing him away, even though he'd left me long before he'd arrived.

"We can split one." Caterina dropped a wax paper covered cookie in the middle of our table after we grabbed lunch from the front counter. "My husband always says the way to kidnap me is to lure me into a bakery van."

I laughed as I peeled open my wrap. "I have a huge sweet tooth, too. Why I've made reluctant friends with the elliptical at my gym. Here, I've been running on the beach before work."

"Hmm," she noted through a mouthful of her own sandwich. "Maybe I should join you. Although, I'm not sure how a jogging stroller would work out on the sand. Joe and Dominic can't take her in the early mornings when it's this busy."

My stomach had a sudden drop I couldn't explain, or maybe didn't want to consciously acknowledge.

"They both watch her?"

Caterina nodded as she sipped her iced tea. "Dominic is Ava's godfather, and he's great with her. She's crazy about him, too. I think Joe gets a little jealous when she reaches for Dominic first." Her smile faded as she leaned forward. "Is it weird if I bring up Dominic?"

"No," I answered honestly. It was a touch painful picturing Dominic taking care of a baby, maybe, but that wasn't something I could easily explain. "We've learned how to be friends while I'm here. It's fine."

"How long were you and Dominic together? If you don't mind me asking. Joe said you all went to high school together." She crossed her arms and rested her elbows onto the table.

"We were together for a little less than two years. We went to the same high school, but I was a year younger, and we didn't run in the same circles."

"Ah, I see. I'm a little older than you guys. My friends tease me about being a cougar because Joe is only thirty-two." Her mouth turned down in an exaggerated frown. "I was hoping you'd give me some intel on what they were like."

I smiled around my glass as I took a sip.

"Most of my friends crushed hard on Joe."

"I could see that." She nodded with a snicker. "I crushed on him pretty hard when I first met him, too." A wide smile stretched her lips. "I picture him as this understated and aloof hunk full of swagger. Am I right?"

"Mostly." We shared a laugh. "Joe was always nice, though. He didn't let the swagger go to his head."

She leaned in closer. "So, if your friends crushed on Joe, did you crush on Dominic?"

My cheeks heated a little. "Maybe." A smile danced across my lips remembering how he'd hardly known who I was, but my skin would prickle with goosebumps when I passed him in the hallways. He was always in the midst of a large group of friends, a constant center of attention.

Even back then, he'd had me.

"He was as you'd expect. Making everyone laugh and being a general pain in the ass."

"Why does that sound like you're talking about me?"

I turned to find Dominic behind me, as if he'd appeared out of thin air.

He nodded toward my wrap. "Came back for more croutons?"

We'd been meeting on an almost daily basis going over estimates and timelines and, to my surprise, we shed the tension between us enough to be friends, or at least friendly. The lines still blurred from time to time, the bursts of familiarity between us still messing with my head, but bringing up old times wasn't always so painful. At times, it was even nice. Sometimes, too nice.

He wore a tank top and sweat shorts, the tattoo on his bicep in full view. We weren't together and hadn't been for a long time, but, unfortunately for me, he'd always affect me somehow. The view of all that bronze skin over toned muscle affected me a whole lot.

My gaze caught his after my eyes lingered on the ink on his arm. I spotted his mother's name surrounded by angel wings.

"Think she'd like it or be pissed at me?" he asked, crinkling his nose at me while tilting his chin down toward his arm.

His hopeful smile drained a little air from my lungs.

"I think she'd give you a dirty look when she first saw it but then would check to make sure her name was spelled correctly." The light in his eyes as his smile grew triggered a lump in the back of my throat. "She'd love it," I croaked out.

Caterina cleared her throat, breaking the trance we'd fallen into.

"Thea was just spilling a little tea about you guys in high school."

His shoulders shook with a chuckle. "There isn't much to tell. Sorry if she's disappointing you."

"So wait, if you weren't friends in high school, how did you guys end up..." She motioned back and forth between us with her finger.

I slipped a glance toward Dominic, both of us wearing the same smirk. The question should have triggered tension between us, but even in the darkest times, this was one of the few memories of us that still made me smile.

"One night, my friends and I ended up in the same bar in Manhattan as Joe and Dominic and all of their friends." I inhaled, heat creeping up my cheeks as my skin prickled under Dominic's stare. "Dominic came up to my table and asked if I was hurt."

Caterina's brow furrowed. "If you were hurt?"

"From when I fell out of heaven. Because I looked too beautiful to not be an angel."

She fell back in her seat. "Stop it. You really said that?"

He replied with a silent, slow nod, his lips twitching.

She gaped at Dominic before she looked back over at me. "What did you say?"

"I asked him if he hit his head." I peered back at Dominic, his eyes still on me as his lips lifted into a half smile. "He didn't realize at first that he made a total ass of himself in front of Thea Kelly from high school, who used to live just a few blocks away in the same neighborhood."

The memory of the look of recognition dawning on his face was still priceless. I thought at the time the realization would have made him retreat, but he never wavered.

"Dominic, I'm embarrassed *for* you." Caterina slowly shook her head as he laughed. "Did that really work on women before that?"

"I never said it before that night. And for your information, it *did* work, in the best way." He stuffed his hands into his pockets, his dark eyes boring into mine. "And I meant it." I spied the same regret that seeped into my bones but for different reasons.

He asked me to have a drink with him after that and we talked for hours. He took me home at four o'clock in the morning and asked me out to dinner that night. From that point on, for the next year, we were never apart for more than a day or two. It was a huge contrast to our second year together, when all I did was reach out to him and all he did was shut me out.

If someone had told me we'd end like we did, or end at all, I never would have believed it for a single second. We'd shared a simple but powerful love before it became strained and complicated.

"Anyway," Dominic scratched the back of his head as he inched away from our table. "I better get going. I told the crew I'd help with the walls today."

"Already? Wow, I can't wait to see how it looks." I forced a wide smile, thankful for the change in subject.

"Me too. Did you both drive here? I can take you back if you want."

"No. I mean," I cupped my forehead, flustered at the thought of riding in Dominic's passenger seat like old times. "Caterina and I came here for a meeting and got a little sidetracked. But when I'm back, I'll head down there and take a peek."

"Awesome. Well, I'll let you guys get to back to business. I saw you through the window when I was walking by and just wanted to stop and say hi." His sheepish grin made me take pause.

"For a busy guy, you spend a lot of time on the boardwalk."

He laughed at my lifted brow. "When I can make it here. The long walk clears my head. See you later."

He turned to leave, my eyes following him until the chime from the bell on top of the door signaled his exit.

"So, here it is." I didn't address Caterina's sad eyes as I lifted the folder from my purse. "I think Violet went through most of this with you. The contract has the hourly rate agreed on, and there are some tax forms to fill out."

"Thanks," she told me before taking it from my hands. "Do you need me to sign all of this now, or can I look it over and drop it off?"

"You can look it over and bring it by this week. If you have any questions, I'll give you my cell. Violet is a little tough to get a hold of these days, but I can reach out to her if there's anything I can't answer."

"Sounds good. I'd actually love if we could do this again soon." She tilted her head to the side. "This was fun. My friends are still in Brooklyn, and talking to you makes me much less homesick."

"I was thinking the exact same thing on the drive here. That would be great." I exhaled and splayed my hands on the table. "I could use a friend right now," I whispered.

"I know," she said, reaching across the table to give my hand a pat. "If you need someone to talk to, I promise I'm a vault. The guys wouldn't know anything."

"It's hard," I admitted, surprised at how easily my confession slipped out. "But I'm trying."

"I know," she said, nodding slowly. "He is, too. He looked

so sad before, I can't even tease him about that lame pickup line he used on you when I see him later."

That dopey line had been the beginning of something beautiful until it became a sad story with an ending I still couldn't understand.

14

DOMINIC

FIVE YEARS AGO

"So this is it, you can get rid of me for a little while," I teased as I pulled up in front of Thea's building, not realizing how short the ride back from the airport was. Seemed like it took forever to drive there Friday night, but on Tuesday afternoon, the drive home seemed all too quick.

"I know! What a relief," Thea heaved an exaggerated sigh before opening the passenger door and climbing out of my car. "You're draining as hell." She bit back a smile.

I knew separating after the past three days was going to suck, but I was actually itching to leave and head to my mother's house. I needed to propose soon, before I lost my damn mind, but I wanted to give Thea my grandmother's ring. Before she'd passed away, my grandmother made me promise I'd use it when I met the right girl, and since I'd been a kid at the time, I brushed it off and told her sure. All I'd thought of since stepping off the plane was asking my mother for that purple velvet box.

Maybe I could come back and do it tonight. Planning something elaborate where I hid the ring in something didn't seem right for us. I wanted to do better than just running back to her apartment and begging her to marry me, but I knew I couldn't wait. I wanted a life with Thea, and I wanted it now. And I had a great feeling she wanted the same thing.

"You don't have to carry my bag in," she said over her shoulder as she unlocked the door to her first-floor apartment. "I know you said you have places to go."

I spotted a little frown when she pushed the door open and tossed her keys in the glass bowl by the door. I set her bag down and grabbed her hand.

"I need to stop at my mom's for something, but I'll be right back here, tonight."

I pressed her body flush to mine, my hands drifting down her back. "You know how I hate sleeping alone." I nuzzled her neck, dropping kisses along her jaw until I covered her mouth with mine. She moaned into my mouth as the kiss heated up quicker than I'd anticipated, my anxious mind momentarily distracted by the glide of Thea's tongue.

I forced my lips away from hers, trying to catch my breath and bring down the bulge in my jeans. A weekend away had turned us into a couple of sex fiends, which was great, but I had other important things to do today.

"See you later," she whispered, pecking my lips before I turned to leave. A wide, dopey smile stretched my lips as I headed down her outside steps.

I jumped into my car, blasting the radio on the way and singing along like a moron. The sun was shining, the sky was clear and blue, and I was so high on life and the beautiful woman I was going to ask to marry me.

The second I closed my mother's front door behind me, something felt off. I still had a key, and I'd texted her when we'd landed to tell her I'd be stopping by, but I found her huddled in a whisper with Steve after I came into the kitchen as if they hadn't heard me come in. Their door had two loud locks and closed with a rattling slam no matter how much I eased it shut, so for them to not even lift their heads up when I arrived made the tiny hairs on the back of my neck stand at attention.

"What's going on? No greeting for your baby boy?" I joked and met my mother's tentative gaze. My heart accelerated along with my breathing as I rushed closer.

"What's wrong? Tell me. Now."

Steve dropped a hand to my shoulder and motioned to the kitchen table with his chin.

"Have a seat, Dom."

I shook my head as I looked back and forth between them.

"No, I'll stand. Just tell me."

"Honey, please," Mom whispered and cupped my cheek. "Just have a seat. Don't panic, it's all right."

I let a little air out of my lungs and fell into one of the wooden chairs.

"First of all, tell me why you rushed over. I didn't think you'd be able to leave Thea so fast." She placed her hand over mine and squeezed, a big smile lifting her cheeks but not making it to her eyes.

"I...um..." I stammered, no longer feeling even an ounce of the elation I'd flown over here with. "I wanted Nonna's ring. Thea's the one, and I want to ask her to marry me as soon as I can."

Mom gaped at me, her glossy eyes lighting up. "I knew it! Oh honey, I'm so happy for you," she croaked out, her voice heavy with tears, but I wasn't sure if they were from joy or sadness. My eyes darted to Steve, and he had the same morbid smile, like when something great happens in the midst of something awful.

"Can the two of you spill it before I have a heart attack?"

Mom took my hand in both of hers.

"I got a chest X-ray last week for that cough I can't seem to shake. The doctor saw a mass on the bottom of one of my lungs and wasn't sure if I had walking pneumonia so he sent me for a cat-scan on Thursday."

The second she said 'mass', my heart free-fell into my stomach.

"Why didn't you say anything?"

"Because I know how you are, kiddo. Look at you," she chuckled, rubbing the top of my wrist. "It's not pneumonia, it's lung cancer, but only stage two."

"Only?" I scoffed. The word 'only' didn't belong anywhere near cancer. "You quit smoking years ago. I don't get it."

"She did," Steve said, rubbing her shoulder as she kept hold of my hand. "But it doesn't undo all the damage. We made an appointment with the oncologist for this Friday—"

"I'm going with you, and this is the last time you keep anything about this from me, got it?"

I shot up from the chair and trudged over to the sink, clutching the edge as my head drooped. My mother had cancer. The more times it rattled around my head, the more unbelievable it sounded. The thought of losing her chilled me to the bone, and I couldn't move.

"Oh baby," her voice was muffled as she leaned into my back. "Please don't be upset with us. Why would we ruin your vacation for no reason?" She grabbed my shoulders and turned me around. "And your news was the best gift I could have gotten today. Thea loves you, and the two of you are going to be so happy. And let her mother know I already decided my dress will be blue for the wedding, so she needs to pick something else." She quirked an eyebrow at me, and a smile crept across my lips.

I wrapped my arms around her and dropped my head into

the crook of her shoulder, holding on as tightly as I could, as if that would stop her from getting sicker, or worse. Not many guys thought of their mother as their best friend, but she was everything to me. She had to beat this because I couldn't consider an alternative.

"Give me a minute." She kissed my cheek and then left the kitchen.

"Congratulations," Steve stood from the table and slapped my back. It took me a minute to figure out why he was congratulating me. After learning my mother had cancer, I'd forgotten everything else.

"Thanks," I muttered. "Listen, I mean it. I'm going with you on Friday and to any other appointment she has. We leave no stone unturned. There are a ton of options out there, and we don't take any no's for an answer from anyone if it's something that can help."

"Of course," he said, shutting his eyes as he nodded. They'd known all this time while I'd been living it up in the Keys with Thea without a clue. While they'd been right, knowing then and knowing now didn't make much of a difference, I still felt like the worst son on the planet. Instead of bringing her all those stupid exotic teas to help her throat, I should have pushed her to go to the doctor sooner.

"Here it is," Mom sang as she came over to me and planted the box into my hand. "Take it to a jeweler and have it cleaned before you give it to her. All the carvings on the band catch a bit of dust and the diamond is a bit dull."

She opened the box, and my grandmother's ring shone back at me. It had a nice-sized diamond and an old-time, intricate band surrounding it. I remembered the story she always told about the village in Italy my grandfather bought the ring from.

I smiled thinking of slipping it on Thea's finger, but when

I spotted a tear snake down my mother's face, anything that wasn't about my mother being sick faded into the background.

Even the woman I wanted to marry.

I stuffed the ring into my pocket and told them both good-bye, heading to my car with a broken spirit and heavy legs. My head fell back before I started the engine as I wished it was still a half an hour ago and everything seemed too good to be true. That's because it was.

Still unable to drive away, I grabbed my phone and dialed Thea, needing to unload this before the bile in the back of my throat came up and did it for me.

Thea's gasp on the other end made me feel ten times worse.

"I'm so sorry, babe. Linda is tough. She's going to be fine. I know it. I'll be over in a little while."

My thumb drifted over the fuzzy box in my hand. If things happened like I'd thought they would, like they were supposed to, I would have been headed to the florist to buy the biggest bouquet of flowers I could find, and dropped to my knees to ask Thea to spend her life with me the second she opened her front door. I would've had the ring cleaned after because there would have been no way I could've waited.

Now, asking her to marry me on the same day I found out my mother was sick seemed all kinds of wrong. The guilt over having a good time while my mother was making oncologist appointments gnawed at my gut and wouldn't let me sit still.

Until my mother was better, everything else had to go on hold.

"I'm sorry, sweetheart, but I need to be alone right now. I'm not good company, anyway. I'll come by tomorrow."

"Whatever you need, babe. Let me know if you change your mind, no matter what time it is. I can sneak into your bed at all hours of the night if you need me."

The side of my mouth ticked up for a moment. I didn't want to push her away, but I didn't know how to be around anyone right now. I knew I'd be running worst case scenarios in my head all night long alternating with being pissed at myself for being so damn distracted to not realize what was going on.

"I love you." I hung up before she could say it back, not able to handle anymore guilt about anything today.

It was amazing how life, as you knew it, could derail with a single conversation.

15

DOMINIC

PRESENT

THE WOOD WALLS were the only thing I'd call close to complete, but that one addition made all the difference. Gazing around the still mostly empty area picturing what it would look like when it was all done, and knowing it would be mine to manage when it was complete, made my skin prickle with goosebumps.

It'd been a long time since I'd had news this good, and despite how long she'd been gone my first instinct after any rush of excitement was still to call my mother. A smile snuck across my lips as I imagined her bringing her friends all the way out here for a day just to brag about how well I was doing.

"Not bad! I can't believe you guys did this in a couple days!"

I was so into my own thoughts, the sound of Thea's voice made me jump. She smiled at me from the doorway when I turned to face her, the gorgeous sight of her at that moment was a sucker punch in the stomach. She was the last piece of good news I'd brought to my mother, and mom would have hated the fact that because I couldn't handle her death we hadn't stayed together.

"Getting there." I made my way over to her and leaned against the wall.

Thea moved next to me, taking the same stance. Another strong urge that never went away was the urge to touch her. I put my arm behind me as I leaned back to trap it against the wall, the need to snake it around Thea's waist and pull her to me so strong I couldn't trust myself to resist.

"Do you know what this reminds me of?"

I shook my head as I searched her gaze.

"Remember when we decided to redo the floor in your mom's kitchen for her anniversary? And we insisted we could pick everything out and do it ourselves."

My head fell back with a thud before I barked out a laugh.

"We thought it would be *so* easy." I shut my eyes as Thea's carefree laughter chafed my sore and battered heart. "And it would have been if *someone* hadn't made me go back to the supply store so many times because she couldn't decide on the right shade of blue."

I fought a smile when her mouth fell open.

"I could decide, *you* wouldn't listen. That was the whole issue. Linda wanted a blue tiled floor, and what you picked out was purple."

"It was a purplish kind of blue." I tilted my hand back and forth. "Little of both. You were just closed minded and stubborn." I shook my head with an exaggerated sigh.

"And they couldn't use the kitchen for two weeks because we scraped up the old floor before we could decide. She wanted to *kill* us."

The both of us burst out laughing. Thea's arms wrapped around her torso as she chased her breath. I couldn't remember the last time I laughed so hard I gasped, but I was fairly certain that it was probably with her.

"Then, to add insult to injury, when we took her and

Steve to the diner at the last minute to make up for it, you told her they made the best lasagna. First time I ever saw my mother drop her fork in horror. When I saw her the next day she made me promise to have you over for dinner more often so you didn't mistake that for real food ever again."

She clenched her eyes shut and groaned.

"Yes, that's when she offered to teach me how to make meatballs on Saturday afternoons." Her smile faded as she stared off into the distance. "I think I almost became good at it."

"You did," my voice softened, strained from the flood of emotion triggered from the memory of them both side by side in front of my mother's counter. "She said she was proud."

"She told me that too, but I wasn't sure if she was just trying to encourage me. It was fun. Linda was the best."

"That she was."

I pushed off the wall and let my arms fall to my sides. Even remembering the good times with my mother before she got sick still knocked the wind out of me.

Thea slid her palm over mine and entwined our fingers. I raised my head to hers, and her warm smile brought me peace. I lifted her hand to my lips and pressed a kiss to the top of her wrist. Her grip tightened around my fingers, but she didn't pull away. If I would have found a way to accept her comfort all those years ago, maybe she'd have my ring, and I'd still have her.

I brought our joined hands to my forehead and exhaled a long gust of air. Since we'd reconnected, I'd apologized so many times for pushing her away. In those heavy but poignant moments of silence, my skin both relaxing and coming alive as it brushed against hers, it was as if I finally found the right way to say sorry.

"Arguing with you was always fun." Thea's voice was

thick with unshed tears as she cracked a joke. "It made me feel alive."

I lifted my head, still holding onto her hand.

"*You* made me feel alive."

Her grin faded as she bit her quivering lip.

"Thea! There you are." A familiar male voice echoed against the bare walls. "The woman in the front office said you might be down here. Sorry I'm late, still up for lunch?"

As he came closer, I recognized who he was. Adam was a close friend of Thea's, at times a little too close. It wasn't Thea I didn't trust, but I'd noticed little things that she didn't.

I never wanted to come across as an alpha asshole who didn't want her to have male friends, but I'd known his feelings for her had always been a little more than friendly.

"Hey." Thea slid her hand away from mine and padded over to where he stood, greeting him with a quick hug. "Sure, just let me get my purse from my office. You remember Dominic, right?"

"Sure. Hey, Dominic." His smile was tight as he squeezed my hand a little too hard.

"I'll meet you back here." Her gaze shot back to me before quickly averting.

Talk about bad timing.

"How have you been?" Adam shoved his hands into the pockets of his khaki shorts.

"Good. Busy." I smiled, trying, once again, to be nice for Thea's sake. All our pleasantries were forced—even back then. "What brings you to the shore?"

"My family has a rental near Wildwood, so I thought I'd stop by to see Thea on my way over there. I found a nice seafood spot not too far from here. You know how she gets around a pile of shrimp." He chuckled, and I forced the most natural smile I could muster.

"I remember." I nodded, a sour taste in my mouth thinking of him as a constant in her life after I'd left. I had no right to feel that way, but being in his presence made us pick up the same pissing contest when it came to Thea. "I took her to City Island in the Bronx all the time for a seafood fix."

His smirk twisted into a scowl. "When we were engaged, I'd offer to take her there, but she'd refuse. I guess that explains why she never wanted to go." He laughed without humor but full of intent.

Engaged. Adam was who she'd been engaged to? Rage ran hot in my veins, but I forced myself to reel it in, because what right did I have to be angry? I'd left her, so she could marry him or any other jerk who crossed her path, and I had no say or right to slam any of them into my new, shiny wooden walls.

But, fuck if I didn't want to.

"Something you'd like to say?" I stepped toward him.

"Nope." The slow shake of his head coiled around my already frayed nerves. "I saw the way the two of you were when I walked in."

"Well, if you're not engaged anymore, I don't think that's any of your business—"

I trailed off when he stepped closer, almost chest to chest with his defiant eyes thinned to slits.

"That you're probably stringing her along again and hurting her?"

His nostrils flared as the rest of his features hardened.

"I won't hurt her again. You have my word."

He opened his mouth to speak but stopped as the click of Thea's heels came closer. The vacant space amplified all the sounds in and around it.

"I'm ready to go. Everything okay?" Her brow furrowed as she glanced between us.

"Fine. Just catching up. Let's go." He held out his arm and

I fought a wave of nausea when she slid her hand inside the crook of his elbow.

"Will you be here when I get back?" she asked, and I could almost hear Adam's teeth grinding.

"No, I'm heading out now, but I'll be back tomorrow. Enjoy your lunch." I nodded goodbye and headed out and into the parking lot without looking back.

After I got into my truck, I stilled before turning on the engine. Adam's dig cut so deep because he was right. No matter what still lingered between us, I'd hurt her enough. I wasn't worthy of taking anything more from her than I already had.

16

THEA

"WHEN ARE YOU HEADING BACK HOME?" Adam asked after our drinks came.

I was never one to drink at lunch during a workday, but Violet wouldn't mind as long as I didn't return tipsy. And after whatever that was with Dominic and me earlier, I needed something to calm the conflicting emotions flooding my system.

"My boss said she'd like me here until the opening, so probably late September. I actually don't mind. The area is nice." I poked the fruit in my glass of white sangria with my thin straw.

"Are you sure? You look about a thousand miles away."

My eyes flickered to Adam. His scrutinizing stare wasn't helping my general discomfort.

"I'm fine. Just a lot of work to be done, a lot of daily reports and whatever. Sorry if I seem distracted to you." I smiled, but he didn't return it.

Adam and I should have stayed friends. I went against my better judgment thinking a relationship with him would help me move forward. But it hadn't been right to use him like that, even if I hadn't done it consciously at the time.

I wanted to stay friends, but Adam always wanted more. Once we'd crossed the line, it hadn't been as easy for him to go back.

"Are you sure Dominic isn't the one distracting you?" He took a long pull from his beer glass while glaring at me with a raised brow.

"It was a little weird at first, I won't lie, but we've gotten more comfortable with each other. And, I had no other choice." I laughed and took another sip.

"I'm sure," he said slowly, his eyes still holding mine. I hoped he hadn't caught Dominic holding my hand, but judging by the sour slant of his mouth, no such luck.

I leaned back in my chair, considering the irony of it all. Adam and I could've been married by now. Maybe staying in his life at a friendly distance was cruel. I'd never wanted to hurt him, but that seemed to be exactly what I kept doing by simply being in his presence.

"Things will always be a little tense and complicated between us, I suppose. But he's happy here, and I'm glad."

The waitress laid two plates piled high with shrimp and stuffed clams. After all these weeks of being on the shore, this was the first time I was able to indulge in seafood. Because of the tension now pulsing between us, it was hard to hold on to my appetite.

"When I walked in, it didn't seem so complicated. It seemed like I was interrupting something."

I dropped my fork and reared back in my seat.

"Adam, I don't know what you think you saw—"

"It's his fault," he spat out.

I jerked back and squinted at him. "What's his fault?"

He huffed out a laugh and crossed his arms.

"I knew we rushed into getting engaged, but I figured if you had a little time away, maybe you'd clear your head and we could get back to how we used to be. But, since your time away is with Dominic, no such luck."

He scooted closer to the table, angrily slicing into an innocent piece of shrimp and not sparing me a glance. Despite the childish way he was acting out, I understood him. I was all too familiar with waiting for someone who wasn't coming back, even when it appeared to be a lost cause.

"Adam, breaking up with you and not getting back together had nothing to do with spending time with Dominic this summer."

He didn't look up, but I continued.

"We were always better off as friends, and I think deep down, you know that. Maybe I'm being mean by staying in your life if I've hurt you this much."

He stilled, picking his head up and peering at me with wide, glassy eyes.

"You don't have it in you to be mean. I don't want you to not be in my life. We started as friends, and that's what we should be. I can deal with...the rest of it, I promise." His sad smile killed me. If only I loved him that way, being with Adam would have been perfect. If only I could pick who I wanted to give my heart to. That choice was out of my hands and seemed pretty damn irrevocable.

"I am worried about you, though. Aside from my own personal issues with you and Dominic, I don't want to see you get hurt again."

"I'm a big girl," I teased. "I'll be fine. Can I just enjoy my lunch and my friend's company the rest of the afternoon?"

He laughed, his smile genuine, this time, and a couple of inches wider. "Of course. And if for any reason, it's...not fine,

I am still your friend above all else. You don't have to shut me out if you need me."

"Thank you. But it won't come to that."

I returned to my plate after my lie.

The distance I'd originally put between Dominic and me shrank little by little with each day. I was becoming attached, and it was dangerous. Plus, his life was here, but mine was still back in Queens.

Starting up anything between us wasn't a good idea for lots of reasons.

You made me feel alive.

Holding Dominic's hand was like waking up after a long sleep and jolting awake. When it was good between us, it was *so* good. We'd fit in every way, and our life together was wonderful, until it wasn't.

"Are you coming back down to the shore at all this summer?" I asked Adam as he pulled up in front of the hotel.

"Maybe. If not I'll see you when you get back." He studied me for a moment, his blue eyes lingering on my lips before he leaned over to kiss my cheek. "I'm glad I got to see you for a little while, anyway." His smile didn't make it to his eyes, and guilt jabbed at my stomach.

"I'm sorry, Adam." I pressed my lips to his cheek and rested my head against his temple.

"Me too, Thea. Take care of yourself out here, okay?"

I nodded and climbed out of his passenger seat, the loneliness hitting me so hard it seeped into my bones.

I realized not being able to settle for second best might mean ending up with nothing at all.

17

THEA

AFTER I ARRIVED BACK at the hotel, most of the construction crew had gone home for the day. The masochist in me wound up back at the restaurant space, overcome with Dominic's presence and his absence. I still didn't know how to be with him or without him.

The anger and hurt I'd come out here with was still right below the surface, but I couldn't see it so clearly anymore.

"Hey, there you are!"

I jumped when Violet grabbed my arm.

"Why don't you take an early day? It's Friday. And it's gorgeous out, go have some fun." She nudged my shoulder. "I've seen enough permits and paperwork to last me until next week. I'm running away, and you should, too."

"If you insist," I smiled and nodded goodbye before she charged out the door.

If I went back to my rental, I'd wallow to the point of madness. I pulled out my phone and took a chance on a reprieve.

Thea: *Hey! It's Thea. Are you free tonight?*

Caterina: *Depends on what you call free. I'm home with Ava, but you're more than welcome to come by. How does pizza and wine on my deck sound?*

We exchanged cell numbers after we agreed to meet up again for lunch, but this was the first time I'd ever texted her.

Thea: *Like heaven. Let me stop at the rental to change, and I'll be there at 7 if that's okay. Text me your address.*

Caterina: *Sounds great. See you soon!*

Caterina was close with Dominic, but I trusted her to keep whatever spilled out of me tonight between us. The relief already washed over me at the notion of having somewhere to go and someone to speak to. I was only a little over a month in, but it was turning out to be a long and grueling summer.

I pulled up in front of Caterina's house, grabbing the wine and cake I'd picked up at a small supermarket along the way. I had to stop myself from sprinting up her walkway and up her front steps.

I loved a night of TV binging and a good book as much as anyone, but being left alone with only my thoughts to keep me company, especially lately, was becoming my undoing. Until I rushed to meet Caterina, I didn't realize how much the solitude was getting to me.

"Glad you made it!" She said after she opened the door with Ava resting on her hip. "Come on in."

I followed her and stood to the side as she shut the door. Her house was deceptively large on the inside, Ava's portable crib was set up in front of the TV, and all her toys were aligned neatly in the corner.

"Your house is beautiful," I told her as I handed her the brown bag. "I've never seen toys arranged so neatly before."

"Thanks. I'm sure as she gets more mobile, they'll be all over the place." She carried the bag to the kitchen, bouncing Ava in her arms.

"Pizza is already here. And this little lady is just about to hit the hay, right missy?" She lifted the baby and kissed her chubby cheek. I couldn't help the smile creeping across my face. Ava's mouth split in a toothless sleepy grin before her head plopped onto her mother's shoulder, drawing out a laugh from both of us.

"Such a silly girl," Caterina cooed. "Say goodnight to Thea."

I smoothed a golden-brown lock of hair behind her ear, her heavy blue eyes blinking a couple of times before I was rewarded with a sweet baby gurgle.

"Sweet dreams, cutie."

Ava's cupid bow lips curved into a smirk reminiscent of her father. In fact, the more I looked at Ava, the more she resembled a tiny version of Joe.

"Looks just like her daddy, right?" Caterina whispered. "Plates and glasses are already set up outside. She's exhausted, so I should be right out."

Their grass-covered yard was huge, and when Ava started walking she'd have a ball running back and forth. I leaned on the railing, shutting my eyes as the warm breeze wafted over me.

This could've been me in a year or two. I couldn't deny the touch of envy being in Joe and Caterina's perfect house brought on, but I'd never pictured this kind of life with Adam, even though that was the path we were supposed to be on.

When I did dream about it, it wasn't with Adam and had

been a distant fantasy at the time, but I still mourned the loss of it.

"I never saw anyone so entranced by our little trees before." Caterina chuckled behind me. "And my apologies for sending you out here without a cork screw." She held one up in her hand. "Feel free to dig into the pizza box while I pour."

"Sounds like a plan." I slid into a wicker seat at the glass patio table, placing a slice on each plate as I waited for her to sit down.

"I'm glad you decided to come by." She settled next to me and raised her glass. "To new friendships and sleeping babies."

"I'll drink to that." Our glasses clinked, and we both took a sip, mine a bit longer than hers.

"I heard the walls are almost done. That's quick, we only signed the lease what, three weeks ago?" She took a bite, holding my gaze.

I nodded. "All the contractors have a timeline, which they probably won't meet exactly, but we're on track, so far. My boss is pleased."

"Is something wrong with the space? I only ask because when I mentioned the walls your face fell."

I put down the pizza and rested my elbows onto the table, folding my hands under my chin.

"Nothing is wrong with the space. Dominic has been a huge help keeping everything on schedule and on budget." I sucked in a deep breath. "I'm also finding it harder and harder to stay away from him, and it's actually making me a little crazy. But you don't need to hear about that."

"Hey, remember what I said? Vault. I honestly don't know much about you guys, at all. Only that you broke up after his mother died, and he came out here to help Joe." She leaned back in the chair. "And since you arrived, he's extremely preoccupied. I'm guessing it wasn't an amiable split?"

"That's the thing." I frayed the edge of my paper napkin. "He just wanted to be alone. It wasn't as if there was someone else or we stopped loving each other. There were arguments but no screaming matches. How could I yell at a man who was losing his mother?"

Caterina didn't react, only listened. The great thing about unloading to her was that she hadn't known us as a couple and hadn't witnessed how I'd crashed and burned when he'd left. If I told Sue or any of my other friends, about my softening feelings toward Dominic, she'd list out every detail of how he'd left me until they were re-ingrained in my head.

"You still had feelings. It's okay to be upset with him for hurting you—no matter what state of mind he was in. Joe told me he took her death pretty badly, and when he reached out to you when he felt better, you wouldn't answer."

"And I should have, but I couldn't..." I rubbed at my temples, the memory of the stab I felt across my sore abdomen each time Dominic's name appeared on my phone screen. I'd wanted to answer his call every time, but my entire body had frozen.

"I don't know if I would have answered, either. I'm also a stubborn Italian girl. Grudges are the song of my people."

It felt good to laugh. "We Irish girls are about the same. It was more hurt than a grudge. He was everything to me." I felt silly saying *was*, since everything I was still feeling mapped back to Dominic. "And until I found out he wasn't coming back, I hadn't accepted us as over. I thought if I kept my distance now, it would help but—"

"Dominic has a magnetic kind of charm." She chuckled. "He's hard to ignore and endears himself pretty easily, but there was always something about him that seemed off-limits."

Her brow furrowed as she leaned in closer. "He's more open with Joe, but even he says Dominic isn't as open as he seems."

Even before his mother passed away, there was a vulnerable, serious part of Dominic that he liked to mask with jokes, but his eyes always gave him away. I still caught a glimpse of it when we'd talk about old times, or this morning when I'd taken his hand without realizing it, my yearning to comfort him never having subsided. His troubled soul called out to me like it always had.

"You're both right. I always felt the weird need to protect him, and when I tried to take care of him before his mother died, I pushed him away."

Her eyebrows lifted. "He pushed himself away from what it sounds like. It's obvious how the regret is weighing on him. Do you ever catch how he looks at you? Or realize how you look at him?"

"I do," I whispered. Time still stood still when we were in the same room, but I didn't know what to do about it.

"I had lunch with my ex-fiancé, today. And all I could think was how easy life would have been if I loved him. An aunt used to tell me the secret to a happy life was finding a husband who loved you a lot more than you loved him."

I turned to Caterina's amused grin. "I can't see that as a happy life at all. Falling in love with Joe was inconvenient as hell at the time, but I can't picture life without him." Caterina's eyes danced whenever Joe's name came up. "Joe and I fell fast, like two weeks fast. I came here on vacation and..." She trailed off with a shrug.

"He became your souvenir." I raised a brow over my wine glass.

"Something like that." She giggled as she refilled our glasses. "It didn't stand to reason, but nothing without him made sense after that. I'd had relationships out of necessity that looked good on paper, but I didn't come alive until I met Joe. That story makes me sad for your aunt." She grimaced as she picked up her pizza for another bite.

I nodded with a laugh. "She'd tell me how I'd have the power, and he couldn't make me crazy. A man you were in love with could only bring you trouble, she said. And quite honestly," I took a large bite of pizza and washed it down with another mouthful of Pinot Grigio, "she's right. The entire time I was with Adam, I didn't worry about a thing. It was easy, if a bit boring. My heart was never in any kind of danger."

"But you couldn't go through with it?" she asked, a wry grin curving her lips.

I shook my head. "I couldn't do that to him. He deserved a woman who loved him so much he made her crazy. I didn't have it in me."

"Because you loved someone else."

I cocked my head from side to side.

"Hey, you can tell me as much or as little as you want."

"I don't think I'd ever stop loving Dominic, not completely. But loving someone doesn't mean you belong with them." I swirled my wine around the glass.

"Are you saying that to me, or saying it to yourself? Either way, you don't sound very convinced."

My eyes darted from Caterina's raised brow.

"It's funny when you think about it. Of all the projects that you could have been assigned to, it was in this sleepy part of New Jersey, back in Dominic's path." She sighed and shook her head.

"Oh, it's funny all right. In fact, the first thing I said when I found out was 'you've got to be kidding me'."

We shared a laugh before Ava made a funny noise on the baby monitor.

"Excuse me one second."

I nodded before Caterina jogged inside.

It was kind of comical. Fate was either nudging me or laughing at me.

But no matter how strong the pull to Dominic still was, I knew there would be no way I'd survive losing him a second time.

Maybe I was letting fear guide too many of my actions, but if I was going to make it through the summer in one piece, it was the only way.

18

DOMINIC

"Do you really feel comfortable with this?" Joe asked me, his arms crossed and brows raised.

"Yes," I reassured him for what seemed like the hundredth time. "Danny and Aiden have worked for us the past three years, and helped at the festival each time. And it's not like we'll be far. We'll be walking around and can stop by to check on them. You can have the same trust in them as you do in me when I always manage it."

I dropped a hand on his shoulder. "Sometimes letting go of control is a good thing. This is why we're the same age and I look so much younger than you, dude."

We turned toward Caterina's snicker behind us.

"Come on, baby. Dom is right." She came up behind Joe and wrapped her arms around his waist. "About giving up control, not looking older. I'm still the cougar with the sexy, younger husband."

He craned his head to give her a close-mouthed but with just enough intention to make everyone around them queasy kiss.

"Ugh," a gagging sound rose from my throat. "Can I have

a second cup of coffee before the two of you turn my stomach?"

I was nothing but happy for them, but fighting the jealousy over not having any of that in my own life from the one person I wanted it with, grated on me, more often than not lately, and made me a cranky jerk.

Ava lay in her carriage next to them, ignoring all of us as her brows pulled together focusing on the stuffed animal in her hands. I leaned down to pluck her out of the seat.

As usual, when I lifted her up, her smile for me was wide as she kicked against my chest. She tried to grab hold of my head in a hug but her toy kept bashing me in the face.

"Tell Daddy that you want to go on the cool rides and eat ice cream instead of being chained to a tent."

"She's *not* going on those rides." Caterina vehemently shook her head. "My baby isn't going on anything that was assembled overnight."

"They're both kind of a drag," I told Ava in a loud whisper. "That's why you're so lucky to have me." I lifted her up high above my head, her loud squeal echoing throughout the pub.

As I bounced Ava in my arms, losing myself in her adoring blue eyes, I sensed Caterina's dopey stare.

"What?"

"You're a natural with her."

She tucked a piece of Ava's hair behind her ear where she was now nestled on my shoulder.

"I'm her godfather. And someone has to save her from the fun police she has as parents."

Caterina climbed onto a bar stool and regarded me with wary eyes.

"I hope you don't mind, but I asked Thea to join us tonight."

"Oh," I stilled for a moment. Friday afternoon had me all kinds of confused. I had no idea where we left things, especially since I'd bolted out of the hotel before I could see her leave with her ex-fiancé or whatever the hell Adam was.

I had zero right to be jealous, but after stealing a glimpse of who we used to be, and watching her go off with someone else right after, I was a green-eyed, unreasonable, selfish asshole.

"That sounded like a loaded 'oh'." Her nose crinkled at me. "Something I should know?"

I shook my head. "Nope. The more the merrier." I caught Caterina's glare in my periphery but kept my attention on Ava.

"I think she's getting antsy from all this time being out here alone. When she came over on Friday—"

"Came over?" I asked as my head whipped around. "Are you guys hanging out now, or something?"

"Would it bother you if we did?" She quirked a brow and crossed her arms. "Thea and I have a lot in common, including close friends that live three hours away. I would think you'd be happy if she had friends out here."

"I am. I mean it's fine." My eyes darted around the room, and even my goddaughter regarded me with a puzzled stare. I blew out a long breath, once again feeling like a jerk for the dumb way I was reacting.

"Yes," I conceded. "I'm glad she's got a friend out here, and I'm actually happy she's coming along. Thea would love the festival, the both of you will probably be stuck to the shrimp stand for most of the night."

She laughed. "Good. She seemed to perk up a little when I asked her to join us."

"Perk up? Was she upset? It wasn't Adam, was it?"

She squinted at me. "The friend she went to lunch with?"

"So, she mentioned him?" I grumbled. "I knew it."

Caterina rolled her eyes. "Whatever we talk about is none of your business."

Joe chuckled as he scooped Ava out of my arms.

"But I bet Caterina could ask about you when she sees her in English class."

A growl of frustration rubbed at the back of my throat.

"Funny," I said as Joe cracked up, rubbing his daughter's back as her head rested on his shoulder.

"So, she was engaged to Adam? Interesting."

"Just a friend, Adam," I spat out. "Yes."

"Why are you so pissed? They aren't engaged anymore, and even if they were, you can't really get mad, you know."

"Yes, I know," I answered and stalked away from the bar.

I couldn't get mad, but I was all the time.

At myself.

I weaved my way through the bustle of customers, losing myself in the din of the crowd. I'd fought against a restlessness since Thea and I had been interrupted. I replayed that five minutes over and over again in my brain, wondering what I would have done next. Would I have kissed her? Hell, I'd wanted to, and maybe she would have let me.

The time when I could kiss and touch her whenever I wanted seemed so long ago it was almost as if it never happened.

I was about to help one of the new waiters with a heavy tray when my phone buzzed in my pocket.

Thea: *Caterina asked me to come out with all of you tonight, but I won't go if it makes you feel weird.*
Dominic: *Why would it make me feel weird? I've seen you almost every day for a month.*

Dominic: *Does it make YOU feel weird?*
Thea: *Honestly, yes and no.*

I forgot my job and leaned against the wall, her words slicing something inside of me. This was the first time she'd texted me for a reason not involving paint chips or the hourly rates of contractors, but it wasn't what I'd call a friendly reason.

We used to go everywhere together, and although we'd bicker at times there was never anyone else I wanted to be with—until I didn't want to be with anyone.

Dominic: *I was happy when I heard you were coming. Whatever you decide, don't not go because you think I don't want you there.*
Thea: *I'll go. I heard there's a shrimp stand.*

A smile tugged at my lips.

Dominic: *Figured as much. You were worried about seeing me, I bet you won't even realize I'm there.*
Thea: *That would be pretty impossible.*

Scraps of Thea were a double-edged sword. They kept me going, but were painful reminders of the treasure I'd had before I fucked it all up.

"SEE, I TOLD YOU. FINE." I jutted my chin toward The Beach Pub's tent at the festival after Joe came over to look. Danny and Aiden had a big crowd but had it all under control. I enjoyed running the tent but it was time Joe and I both delegated, especially since we were expanding. This summer we were busy but finally able to breathe.

I willed my eyes away from where Thea stood with Caterina and Ava, but it was no use. In only a simple tank top and denim shorts, Thea was stunning. I loved when she'd wear shorts in the summer. She'd be embarrassed because her legs were always so pale, but they were long and curvy, and the nerve endings in my palm already tingled with the urge to glide up and down her thigh. Her hair was down and wavy like she'd always worn it during the summer. She looked like my Thea, but she wasn't.

"If we can pry my husband away from the tent, we could all go explore a little."

Thea smirked as Caterina shot Joe a scowl.

"He could stay." I shrugged. "I'm taking a walk. I hear sausage and peppers calling my name."

"Your first sandwich of like three, right?" Thea cocked her head at me, her smile easy and beautiful. If she was going to look like that and throw memories at me, I was only human and would crack in no time.

"No, have to watch my figure." I rubbed my stomach. "And there's too much here to overindulge on one thing. Keep that in mind when we get to the shrimp."

She laughed and came closer. "What else is here, besides ice cream and a ton of fried food."

"Other stuff, too. Want to take a walk with me? They'll catch up."

She looked back at Joe and Caterina, rocking Ava back and forth as she wailed. Caterina waved a hand at us to keep walking. The baby had been unusually cranky since they'd arrived.

Thea cast me a tentative glance before she nodded. "Sure."

I offered her my arm. "It's crowded, so I don't lose you."

If only I'd held onto her when I should have.

She peered up at me, eyes wide, before a bashful smile lifted her lips.

"Safety first, right?" She slid her arm into mine, the spark from her touch sending a current up my arm.

"Right," I agreed, my voice low and husky as my dark eyes met her hazel ones with the same longing. I broke our gaze and led her down the beach, the warmth of her hand triggering the same jolt across my skin. I'd take whatever time she gave me as a gift, not a tease for all I wanted but would never have again.

19

THEA

I TRAILED Dominic as he led me from tent to tent, speaking to every vendor as if he'd known them for years. He was always so social, sometimes to the point of grating on my nerves, and small-town life suited him perfectly. We'd leave one tent, and he'd whisper some gossip he'd just heard about them into my ear. I didn't miss how engrained he was in his business and the customers he'd gotten to know over the years.

Something else that didn't go unnoticed was how he introduced me. "This is Thea." Not my friend, Thea or my ex-girlfriend, Thea. It was amusing to watch people look between us as they drew their own conclusions.

For two people who'd spent most of the past month skating around each other, touching was easy tonight. I linked my arm with his for most of the time as we made our way down the beach, and if he spotted something he wanted me to see, he'd grab my hand and pull me over. We were having fun like the old days, and for once, I let myself enjoy it without pondering the meaning behind it all.

"You've got to be kidding me." Dominic said, shaking his

head as we came to the last tent in the row. An older woman with a veil and a long flowy dress sat hovered over a large bowl.

"Is she a fortune teller?" I whispered, not realizing my cheek was resting on Dominic's shoulder. This close, his woodsy and familiar scent flooded my senses.

"She's a dry cleaner," he whispered to me as he snaked his arm around my waist and drew me closer.

"You know Eliza the Oracle?" I chuckled, despite the rush of heat at the feel of Dominic's body against mine.

"Her name is Betsy, and she's always claiming she can talk to the spirits." He rolled his eyes. "I guess they let her finally pay the entrance fee, and she's trying to cash in on it with some gullible tourists."

I giggled, dropping my head to his chest without realizing it. I breathed him in for a moment before lifting my head. His blinding smile stole my breath, but I feared it was robbing me of my senses, too. His grin faded a bit when I took a tiny step back.

"Would you like to know your future?" Betsy cocked her head to the side as she beckoned us with her finger.

"Come on," I told Dominic. "It could be fun."

He squinted at me and shook his head. "I could think of better places to throw twenty bucks away."

"I heard that, Dominic," Eliza or Betsy admonished with a scowl.

"Oh right, you're psychic." He held up his hands. "My apologies."

I swatted his chest, a laugh slipping out. I hadn't had any alcohol, but I was drunk from all the laughing and smiling.

He glanced over my shoulder and waved.

"Aiden is calling me over, let me see what's going on. If

they messed up, and Joe was right, I'll never hear the damn end of it." He pointed at Eliza. "If you want to waste your money on a reading while I'm gone, feel free. Ask for the lottery numbers for tomorrow night, I'll give my father a call and let him know."

He elbowed my side before he jogged away. My eyes stayed glued to Dominic as he made his way down the row of tents. I remembered all the lonely nights I'd yearned for just this.

All I'd wanted was one more day with my beautiful, chatterbox boyfriend, not the broken man who only found the relief he'd searched for by leaving me. I was high from walking up and down memory lane tonight, and I didn't doubt I'd feel the crushing low the second I arrived back at the rental. I had the Dominic I loved back, but he wasn't mine to love anymore.

I sat in front of Eliza and dropped a twenty onto her table. She smiled and scooped it up before motioning for me to sit closer.

"Now, let's see." She hovered over the water bowl with an intense stare.

"Are those tea leaves?" I asked, trying to decipher the black floating objects.

"Yes, when they gather together I can see things. Lovers, right?" She squinted at me, tapping her nail on the side of the bowl. "You and Dominic?"

"Not anymore. I mean no." When she cocked a brow, I was embarrassed by my flustered reply.

"Are you sure that's the truth? I'm sensing a lot of energy in the present."

We had a ton of evident energy and history between us, tea leaves weren't needed to see it.

"Epic love is once in a lifetime. You define each other, but you're resisting."

"Define?" I asked, not liking the turn this was taking. Whether she was reading the bowl or how Dominic and I reacted to each other, she was hitting too close to home.

"You react off of each other. Even apart, each action is caused by a reaction to the other. And it looks like you're joining again, but a secret holds you back."

I froze, my back rigid against the chair. What she was saying wasn't anything carrying much depth or difficult to figure out. Plenty of lovers fed off of each other and had secrets. I always thought supposed psychics made money from throwing out the most common plights, eventually hitting a vulnerable target who would empty their wallets wanting to know more, but this was the first time I'd ever understood the inclination.

"Years and distance lie between you, but when all is revealed, it will either put you back together or tear you apart for good."

"Thank you for your time. I'll keep that in mind." I rose from the seat and charged away from the tent as fast as my legs could take me until I reached where Dominic stood.

I had no interest in exploring the two nails she hit on the head.

"Hey," he wrapped his hand around my bicep. "Did she spook you?" A smirk twisted his lips.

"It's fine. Like you said, bullshit, right? Let's go catch up with Joe and Caterina." I crossed my arms and didn't look back to Dominic's steps behind me.

"They left, the baby wasn't feeling well. I think she's teething Caterina said. I told them I'd give you a ride back, but would you mind if we took this all back to the pub first? We're dismantling in like an hour."

"Sure," was all I could say.

A slow grin split his mouth. "I'm glad you came tonight."

Caterina had invited me here, and I shouldn't have gone off so long with Dominic. She was right about how endearing he was.

To me, he was the goddamn pied piper, and it was pissing me off.

20

DOMINIC

"I THINK that's all of it," I told Thea after we loaded the last tray into our industrial refrigerator.

"It seemed to go well, did you tell Joe 'I told you so', yet?" She wrapped her arms around her torso and raised a brow.

The longer the night went on, the harder it was to stop touching her. For the first time since she'd come here, we were just us. Nothing from the past or complications of our present were in the air tonight.

Fighting the urge to kiss her the past few hours exhausted me. I loved hearing her laugh, feeling her settle into my side without tensing up or pulling away, although at one little moment the small step she took away from me didn't go unnoticed.

"No, I'll wait until the morning when we're both fully awake and he can appreciate it." Her shoulders shook with a laugh as she rubbed the tops of her arms.

"Are you cold? Come upstairs, I'll give you a shirt to wear home." We made our way out of the kitchen and left the restaurant. After I locked the door behind me, Thea regarded me with a caution I hadn't seen from her in the past few hours.

"I don't want you to go to any trouble." She waved a hand at me. "My place is a short drive away, I can manage until then."

"Thea, you're never any trouble. Come on, you can see my inherited digs."

I unlocked the door next to the restaurant that led up to my apartment.

"Inherited?" Her eyes narrowed as a chuckle escaped her.

"This was Joe's apartment," I told her, nodding to my front window. "Then Joe and Caterina's until they had Ava. There's only one bedroom so they outgrew the place. Moving in made sense, and makes early opening days a hell of a lot easier, although, maybe I should be looking for something more in the middle now."

I jerked my chin to the staircase. "After you."

She took a reluctant step forward. I shut the door behind me and placed my hand on the small of her back. She climbed the stairs, my eyes fixating on her curvy ass filling out those tiny shorts to perfection, as it always did.

Things might have felt different tonight, but in the end, they weren't. I needed to view tonight as a gift, a nice glimpse of the best time of my life and nothing more.

"This is a lot neater than your apartment in Queens," she teased as she scanned the living room.

"I'm not here as much to mess it up," I quipped, a nervous chuckle falling from my lips.

After spending so much time thinking about her here, I didn't want her to go. Once she did, I knew she'd never be here again. We'd be business only, which I'd mostly accepted, but I wanted more—if only for now.

"I'll give you the five-cent tour." I motioned to my kitchen table. "That's the kitchen, obviously. My bedroom is behind the living room. It's good for a guy who lives alone, but you can see why a family of three would feel a little cramped."

"I can. It's nice." She arched a brow. "Your mom would be happy you made your bed."

"Yeah? She got on me all the time at my old apartment for that. I'd purposely leave it and make it after she left, which she probably figured out." I lifted a shoulder in an innocent shrug.

"Always a ball breaker. Even with your own mother." She shook her head, still running her palms up and down her arms.

"Let me get you that shirt," I said before rushing over to my closet.

I'd dated here and there, but I never wanted more than a few nights with the same woman. I always found a flaw that I used as an excuse to never call her again.

I'd always want more of Thea, but I'd kept us both waiting too long.

"Here you go." I brought her my Yankee hoodie and held it open for her to slip her arms in the sleeves.

"You still have this?" She gaped at me before shrugging it on. Her back was to my front, but I spied her hard swallow. I put my hands on her shoulders and stilled as a heavy silence fell over us.

"I do, it's been washed so much it's the softest shirt I own. You can keep it until tomorrow."

Her eyes filled with something I couldn't decipher. Did she want me to back away or come closer?

"Do you have a bottle of water? My mouth is a little dry." The quick rise and fall of her chest gave away her rapid breathing, matching my own.

"Of course, give me a second."

My own mouth parched, I grabbed two bottles of water and came back to where she was waiting on my couch. Before she noticed I was there, I caught her dip her nose under the neckline and inhale.

I sat next to her and handed her the bottle. Thea seemed so lost in her own thoughts she jumped when she noticed me standing there. I missed the days when she'd steal my clothes because they smelled like me. We had so many amazing memories, but the happiness we shared had only brought pain when I glanced back at it from where we were now.

"Thank you," she whispered before grabbing the water from my hand, taking a long sip without looking at me.

"I had the best time tonight," I told her, sliding my hand across my couch cushion to find hers. My clammy palm slid against hers and I laced our fingers together. "With you. I've missed you so much. I know you probably don't believe that."

I was surprised when she nodded. "I do. I know you..." she trailed off, taking in a quick breath. "You didn't mean to hurt me. No harm in remembering the old days, right? I had fun with you, too." She squeezed my hand and pulled back. I wrapped my fingers around her wrist, unable to let her go.

"The old days," I repeated, inching closer to her on the couch. "What about now?"

Her shoulders slumped before her chin dropped to her chest. "Now, we can't go back. We're different people." Her tired eyes met mine. "We live in different places and want very different things out of life."

"I still want *you*," I blurted out.

Her eyes widened as she fell back on my couch.

"Like...like I told you," she stammered, raking her fingers through her hair. "We were a long time ago—"

"No, I think we're right now." I cupped her cheek and ran my thumb along her jaw. Her eyes fluttered in a mix of pleasure and pain. "We're more now than you want to admit, Thea." My thumb grazed along her bottom lip, and a sigh rolled through her.

"I miss kissing you so much. Your lips aren't mine to taste anymore, but I remember them, sweetheart. I've done nothing but remember for four years."

Thea's eyes clenched shut when my lips found her forehead. All the plans I had for us, some I never even shared with her, came back to me in a rush with her so close to me.

"I remember, too. You're a difficult man to forget."

She smiled at me, but I didn't miss the quivering of her chin. I framed her face with my hands and kissed her jaw. When I heard a tiny whimper escape, I peppered more light kisses down her chin.

"Good," I whispered, my lips so close to hers they almost brushed. Thea's hand slid to the back of my neck, her fingers drifting up to slice through my hair. I groaned when her nails scraped along my scalp.

Hope was something I ignored because it never did me any good, but as Thea's glassy eyes zeroed in on me, I was bursting with it.

I tilted my head, tracing her lips with the tip of my finger but not closing the distance. She needed to meet me halfway. Once she did, no matter how much guilt I carried for ruining us, I'd fight for her like I should have from the beginning. And I wouldn't stop until she was back where she belonged —with me.

She fisted the collar of my T-shirt, and, finally, gave in, attacking my mouth with a hunger and a desperation that obliterated the last bit of self-control I was clinging on to. We rolled back and forth on my couch, grabbing and pulling at each other in a mess of whimpers and sighs. A growl rose from deep in my throat when she slipped her hand under my T-

Shirt, the graze of her soft fingertips down my torso setting me on fire.

"You taste the same," I murmured against her lips before I dipped my head to nip at the sensitive spot in the crook of her shoulder. I smiled against her skin when she jerked in my arms.

"You still talk too much."

Our lips came together again, our kiss a frantic battle for control as if we were taking all we could before the other disappeared.

My hands drifted down her chest, the slow whir of the zipper on my sweatshirt mingling with all the desperate panting. I swallowed a moan when I cupped her breast over her tank top, dipping my finger along the inside of the lacy cup of her bra. Her back arched with a whimper, pushing her deeper into my greedy hands. I skated my thumb around her hard nipple, wanting to take it between my teeth and bite it more than I wanted air, but I held myself back, letting her take the lead.

Thea backed away from me and peeled off my sweatshirt, followed by her tank top. She regarded me with heated, vulnerable eyes before she leaned in to kiss me again. I took her face in my hands and kissed her slowly, or as slowly as I was able to. A half-naked Thea in my arms had been nothing but a dream to me all these years. Now, she was with me, and every part of my body wanted every part of hers.

She moaned into my mouth as she dragged me closer. I responded with my own desperate growl and lifted her onto my lap. I inched down both of her bra straps until she spilled out of the cups, holding her gaze before I started a trail of kisses down her throat.

"So many freckles, I can still connect the dots," I told her, running my tongue back and forth over the new trail along her tan lines. I moaned around a nipple, my cock jerking in my pants when the rigid peak pebbled against my tongue. I kissed across her chest and took her other nipple between my teeth. I was starving for her, and the hunger was about to make my brain short circuit.

Her head fell back with a groan as she rubbed against me. I was hard and throbbing but still forced myself to go at a slow pace.

My hand drifted down her stomach before I dipped my finger into the waistband of her shorts, stopping before I popped the button open.

"Can I touch you, sweetheart?"

Her eyes clenched shut as she nodded. I slid my hand inside her shorts, muttering a curse when I found the wet silk between her legs, I pushed the material aside and stroked her, her breathing more shallow as I picked up the pace.

"There's my girl. I still make you feel good?" My tongue was jealous of my fingers, remembering how sweet she tasted when she'd come in my mouth.

She grabbed my head and kissed me so hard our teeth scraped, her quivering body rocking against my hand.

"So good, Dominic. It was always so good," she said against my lips, her voice soft and shaky.

I fisted a handful of her hair as I deepened the kiss even more, licking inside her mouth with long, desperate strokes, praying the taste I was lucky enough to get tonight wasn't the end.

I slid two fingers inside her and pumped them in and out while my thumb circled her clit. She'd always loved it this way, and when she let out a loud scream and bucked her hips harder against my hand, I knew she was close.

"Please, Thea." My voice dipped to a guttural, husky rasp as I begged. I begged for her not to leave, to spend the night in my bed and let me show her how much I loved her, how much I'd *always* love her, begged for another chance.

Her legs went rigid as she almost slid off my lap, clenching around my fingers before she groaned into my shoulder.

"Hold on, baby," I told her, unable to move as my cock pulsed inside my boxers.

My head fell back as she melted into me, her arms easing against her sides like limp noodles.

"And you said we couldn't go back," I chided, still chasing my breath as I cinched my arms around her. "You just made me come in my pants like a sixteen-year-old."

I laughed as she shook her head against my chest.

"Stay with me, tonight," I whispered then cringed when she stiffened in my arms.

"I can't. I'm sorry I lost myself like that. I need to go." She climbed off my lap and stood.

I popped off my couch, grabbing her arm and pulling her to me.

"Hey, talk to me," I crooned, cupping her neck. "Neither of us planned this, obviously," I ran my thumb back and forth along her jaw, "but maybe we can finally get back—"

"No, we can't...I can't do this again." Her voice trembled, thick with unshed tears.

When I was able to pull her guard down just a little, I rushed in and pushed too far. *Fuck.*

"Can you give me a ride home?"

"Sure." I stopped pressing when her jaw quivered. "Just let me clean up." I nodded toward my bathroom. "I'll only be a minute."

I ran into my bedroom to change into sweats.

Maybe fighting for us was wrong.

Maybe I'd put her through enough and I should just leave her alone.

Maybe I was a selfish asshole because I loved her too much to do that now.

We left my apartment and rode to her rental in silence. I parked in her driveway and walked around to the passenger side to open her door.

"Since when do you do that?" She peered up at me, a hint of a smile dancing across her lips so faint, if I'd blinked I would have missed it.

"Add it to the miles long list of all I should have done when it came to you." I held out my hand, and she stared at it for a couple of beats before she took it and climbed out of my truck.

"Walking me to the door isn't necessary, but thank you."

We trudged to her front porch, the both of us looking everywhere but at each other until we got to her door.

"I know I screwed up."

She shook her head before turning back to me.

"You didn't. I was right there with you, and—"

"That's not what I mean. Not tonight. Then. I wish that I could go back, undo the worst mistake of my whole life."

She sank her teeth into her bottom lip before lifting her cloudy gaze to mine.

"Dominic—"

She trailed off when I leaned in to kiss her cheek, my lips lingering before I pulled away.

"Thank you for tonight," I whispered in her ear before I headed back to my car, hoping against hope it wasn't all we'd get.

21

THEA

"I TOLD YOU, MOM," I said to the Bluetooth speaker in my car, "I'm fine. It's like a vacation."

She didn't reply right away. I could almost hear her brows lifting in disbelief.

"You're by yourself, not even coming home on weekends, and seeing Dominic every day. I almost believed you until you threw in 'vacation'."

Being the youngest in the family, I was still babied to the point of asphyxiation. Like my sister and Sue, my parents were there for everything I went through with Dominic, and all that happened after he left. These worried calls came at least three times per week since I'd arrived.

"It's a long drive to make every weekend. I'll try for next weekend if I can take Monday off. Happy?" I pulled into the Halston Hotel parking lot. Thankfully, the drive was only ten minutes, so I didn't have to argue with her for more than a round or two.

"I'll be happy when you're happy, Thea. You worry me."

I leaned back on the headrest and shut my eyes. I worried me, too but wouldn't admit it to her.

"Listen, I'm here. I mean it, I'm fine."

"Okay, just take care of yourself. You know you always get sick during the summer, and there's no one to take care of you."

A smile pulled at my lips as I shook my head.

"I live alone at home, too."

"Yes, but I'm at least close enough to see you. Remember that one summer you had bronchitis so bad it almost turned into pneumonia?"

Thanks to bad allergies and asthma, I could look forward to at least one rotten sinus infection each summer, although it had only become that awful the one time.

"I remember. And I do have a friend out here, now, so I'm not *all* alone, I promise."

I said goodbye and ended the call, inhaling a deep breath before I shut off the engine. After a full day to process what happened between Dominic and me on Saturday night, I had no idea what to do with it or about it.

A night of sharing sweet memories had led us to lose total control on his couch. I'd told myself that the attraction I felt for Dominic was residual, left over from all the time we were together. The minute his lips were back on mine, it ignited a hunger that robbed me of every sense I had. The only thing I cared about was more: more of his hands, more of his lips. The aftermath hadn't dawned on me until after, when he asked me to stay, and it frightened me how much I wanted to say yes.

I stepped inside the hotel, as I'd done every day for weeks, on shaky legs. Heading right to my office, I plopped in my seat and let my head fall into my hands, almost laughing. I swore to be professional, amiable, and not let my past with Dominic get in the way of my job.

Yet, every time I shut my eyes, Saturday night replayed in my head. Dominic's hard body against mine, the heat in his hooded eyes when he said he remembered me. It was a huge contrast to how it used to be right before we'd split. Our kisses were hollow, his heart and mind too far away to ignite much passion.

This was how it used to be, only better. How had I walked away from that?

I had no clue, so I ran. But unfortunately, until this hotel was almost up and running, I couldn't go very far.

"Hey," Caterina appeared in my doorway. "I was going to call you yesterday, but we had a rough rest of the weekend with a screaming baby."

"I didn't expect to see you here so early. I meant to call you yesterday." I stood with a grimace. "I'm sorry I went off with Dominic for so long. That wasn't right since you're the one who invited me."

She waved me off. "Ava's gums didn't make us very good company." She chuckled and shook her head. "And it looked like you were having a great time. I was glad."

"Is she better now?" I avoided Caterina's comment. I'd had a good time during, and after, but I wasn't to the point of processing what had happened to talk about it.

"She is. And I have an early morning planning meeting with the general manager. But after, if you have time, maybe we could have some coffee and discuss that little dodge just now."

I chuckled at her tapping foot.

"Coffee, yes." I exhaled some of the tension in my shoulders. "The second part is a conversation over alcohol."

She laughed, nodding her head. "Okay, I won't press. Would it be okay if I took a look at the space?"

"Sure, I'll walk with you."

We headed over, and I noticed figures behind the frosted glass of the door. When I knocked and opened it, I found

Dominic and a woman I'd never seen before. They were laughing in mid-conversation, her head falling onto his shoulder before they turned around.

"Good morning, ladies." Dominic's smile was so easy, and sexy, I wanted to punch him in the stomach. He looked free of all the turmoil plaguing me since we parted ways the other night, and was standing too close to the beautiful redhead.

But, we weren't together, so there really wasn't a *too close*, or, at least, there shouldn't have been.

"Sorry to interrupt, but Caterina wanted to check out the space while she was here." I forced a tight smile. "I hope you don't mind."

"No, of course not." His brows knit together. "This is Jill. She's a hotel manager in town and offered to come check out the space to see if she had any suggestions. Early was the only time we could both come in. Jill, this is Thea," he said, his eyes searching mine for a moment before he turned back to Jill. "She works for the investors here."

"Nice to meet you, Thea." She flashed a grin, showing off her perfect white teeth and full red lips, which only agitated me more. I needed to step away from all things Dominic before it made me even crazier.

"Same." I forced my lips into the widest smile I could muster. "No need to explain." I dropped a hand on Caterina's arm. "I have lots of paperwork to go through this morning. Come find me after your meeting."

I stalked back to my office and shut the door. Running my hands through my hair, I dropped my head and groaned into the wood of my desk. Finding Dominic talking to another woman shouldn't have triggered any kind of jealousy. There was no need for the surge of anger when she dropped her head onto his shoulder, laughing carefree with him like I was just a couple of nights ago.

I was reacting and behaving like a child. And I was disgusted, not only by my petty behavior just now, but also not having the guts to acknowledge what had happened between Dominic and me, or what had been *happening* between us. My sanity was hanging on by a fraying thread and was just about to snap.

I was finally able to lose myself in budgets when a knock at my door made me jump.

"Come in!" I replied without looking up.

"Is something wrong?"

I stilled, clenching my eyes shut before I lifted my head to Dominic's voice.

"Nothing," I clipped. "I'm busy, so is there something you need?"

Dominic chuckled to himself and shut the door behind him.

"You weren't jealous or anything, were you?" I wanted to slap the snide grin right off of his face. "Jill is just a friend of ours."

"No. Why would I care? I told you there was no need to explain," I rambled, trying to appear occupied with whatever I could grab from my desk.

The smirk faded from his face. "I would have called you yesterday, and I should have." He fell into the seat in front of my desk. "I let you have some space because you seemed a little freaked out."

"I'm not freaked out," I denied, my voice squeaking and not convincing to even my own ears.

"Not even a little?" He squinted at me.

"No, not even a little." I tried to relax my tight chest with a deep breath. "It's not a big deal—"

"Really?" His brow crinkled before he crossed his legs and leaned back. "Well, it was a pretty big deal to *me*." His eyes raked down my body. "You're gorgeous when you're flustered." His voice had dropped to a husky rasp, and it ran right through me, stopping at the ache between my legs.

"I'm not flustered," I denied, pretending to look at the spreadsheet on my screen but not really seeing any of the numbers.

"You are." His lips curled into a wicked grin in my periphery. "Your cheeks get all flushed and you bite your bottom lip so hard, I'm surprised you don't draw blood."

He stood and cupped my chin, pressing his thumb down until my mouth opened, my teeth releasing my raw bottom lip.

"Dominic," I whispered. "We can't. Not here."

"Not *here*?" He lifted a brow as he leaned closer.

I blinked away the image of Dominic spreading me on top of my desk to finish what we started. He needed to go. *Now.*

"Not here. Not anywhere. Not again." I crossed my arms and fell back in my chair. "I'm...I'm not ready for this. I can't do anything other than casual right now."

I grabbed a random folder on the desk and sifted through it, trying to escape Dominic's dark eyes full of lust.

Casual? Where the hell did that come from?

"All right." He shifted to leave, and I let out a breath of relief until he came back around my desk. "And listen," he whispered before his hand cupped the back of my neck, "I don't want to tell you how to do your job or anything, but you may be able to read the numbers better if it's right side up." He nodded his chin toward the upside-down folder in my hands.

I dropped the folder on the desk, narrowing my eyes at his chuckle before he stepped out the door.

After finally regaining enough focus to work, my phone buzzed across my desk.

Dominic: *Just so you know, I can do casual if that's what you want.*

Thea: *Right.*

Dominic: *I actually haven't thought about you at all today.*

Thea: *Okay.*

Dominic: *I'm serious. I didn't give a second thought to how amazing you felt in my arms. Didn't think about your lips, or about your perfect ass in those goddamn shorts. And I absolutely did not think of your beautiful body quivering in my lap when you came. Not even once.*

I wanted to be annoyed. Bothered. But I was annoyed over how *not* annoyed or bothered I was.

I'd fooled myself thinking that I wouldn't fall right back in love with him if I let myself forgive him. But falling back meant there was a time I hadn't been in love with Dominic. And even I couldn't entertain that nonsense in my head.

Dominic: *And I never wanted to grab the back of your neck in your office and kiss you until your knees gave out. Nothing is sexier than when you slump against me all flushed and hot. Not that the image of it is burned into my brain or anything.*

Thea: *That all sounds very casual.*

Dominic: *See? And I'm not thinking of excuses to come back to see you today.*

Dominic: *I need to come back around 4. We can talk about my visions for seating.*

Thea: *There are no tables or chairs yet, and they're wiring for electric today.*

Dominic: *So? Are the chairs supposed to glow or have shocks? Even so, we can still plan. See you later.*

Thea: *Do I have a choice?*

Dominic: *Always a choice. But I think maybe you're not thinking about me, too. Just a hunch.*

22

THEA

"I'm so sorry," I told Caterina, trying to keep from hacking in her ear, but the horrid tickle in my throat got the best of me.

"Stop it. Don't be silly. We can hang out another night. You sound awful."

It was as if my mother had some kind of voodoo. She mentioned the word sick, and my sinuses clogged by the end of the day and I woke up with chills and a deep cough. I really hoped that I wouldn't get sick out here but no such luck.

"I feel awful, but it passes in a couple of days. Usually. The worst of it, anyway." My head fell back on the arm of my couch. The room spun because I'd raised my head too suddenly.

"Do you need anything?"

"I found a small pharmacy close by, and they'll deliver my prescriptions this afternoon. I wish I had some soup. I stocked up on everything here but that."

"I could help with that. My husband makes a kick ass chicken soup. What else would you like?"

I smiled, despite the death I felt like. Caterina was good people.

"A roll would be amazing, but do you guys deliver out here? I know it's not very far, but it's a different town."

"I sleep with the owner. I'll hook you up. Until then try to get some rest."

I chuckled as we ended the call and cuddled up in the blanket I'd found in one of the closets over me. Caterina was great, but not having any friends or family around when you were sick sucked. The loneliness hit me hard and zapped the little energy I had left.

The pharmacy knocking on my door woke me up from a dead sleep. When I rose from the couch, I wasn't even sure what time it was.

After trudging into the kitchen in search of something quick to eat so I could swallow the first antibiotic pill, I swore I heard a second knock. My bell didn't work, and I'd never followed up with the rental manager to get it fixed since I had no visitors anyway. On the walk back to the door, it registered how sadly pathetic that was.

I prayed it was the soup Caterina promised me, but when I opened the door, I found Dominic with two huge shopping bags.

"What are you doing here?" I managed to say. My voice had surpassed that sexy rasp I'd had at first and was now a frog-like croak.

Dominic laughed and shook his head. "I heard you were sick and wanted soup. Can I come in?" He nodded behind me with his chin.

"Yes. Sorry. I'm a little fuzzy." I opened the door and stepped aside to let him in. Another shiver ran through me and I zipped my sweatshirt higher, cringing when I realized I was still wearing Dominic's shirt.

"I'll make sure to wash this before I give it back to you," I said after I followed him into the kitchen. "It's the heaviest thing I have right now, and the chills come and go."

I folded my arms around my torso, leaving out how even with my weak sense of smell at the moment, the remnants of his scent inside the collar brought me a little comfort.

The side of his mouth lifted in a lopsided grin. "Keep it. I'm glad it's making you feel better." He stopped and looked me over with a sigh. He, of course, looked gorgeous like always with every inky black hair in place. Although I hadn't glanced at the mirror in a few hours, I was sure I looked two steps away from death.

"I know, I'm a sight for sore eyes." I ran a hand through my tangled hair.

"No." He shook his head and sauntered over to me. "You're always beautiful, even during your summer sinus infections from hell."

He rubbed my back, and now, I had a chill for a different reason. But instead of stiffening at the contact, warmth ran through me from his touch.

"I can take you to the doctor in town after you eat."

I shook my head, woozy from the rapid movement. "I get these often enough that my regular doctor called in antibiotics. I was just about to take one. I'll be better in a couple of days."

"How's the cough? Judging by the frog in your throat, I'd say pretty bad."

I had to laugh at the concern in his crinkled brow.

"It's there, but I can manage. I would love some soup now," I told him, wincing as the words scratched at my raw throat. "Which bag is it?" I asked as I sifted through the bundles on the counter.

"I'll get it. Go sit." He grabbed my forearms and walked me to the table in the kitchen.

"What's in all the bags?" I fell into one of the chairs and rubbed my clammy forehead.

"I have a quart of soup, and I brought you shrimp and pasta for later if you're up for it. And some cookies from Finley's. I stopped there on my way over."

My heart squeezed as I watched him bustle around the kitchen. He was being so sweet and considerate, my heavy eyes almost teared up. I was still wishing for my own apartment now that I was sick, but having him here soothed the lonely ache.

"That's really nice of you. Aren't you guys busy today? Doesn't Joe need you?"

He came over and set the container of soup down in front of me, and even grabbed the bottle of antibiotics and a bottle of water.

"We have a good enough staff now that we both don't need to be there at all times. A couple of summers ago, Joe was off with Caterina for God knows how long. He said he'd make it up to me one day, and I figured why not start now." His smile faded as he studied me. "I didn't like the idea of you sick and alone. Did you know the bell doesn't work?"

I couldn't help smiling as I nodded. "Yes, but I don't have any visitors, so I thought it was silly to make a big deal out of it." My eyes fluttered when I slurped the first delicious spoonful of soup.

"Your friends haven't been by all summer? I'm surprised." He sat down on the chair next to me.

"Most of them are married with kids now. We keep trying to figure out a date they can come out, but it's hard." I grabbed one of the huge pills from the bottle and chased it down with some water.

"I'm surprised Adam hasn't been over more often to visit."

I eyed Dominic as I kept drinking. Adam had never been his favorite person, but he'd faked it enough for my sake.

"No. He only came out because his family happened to be here and I was on the way. Any reason why you're asking?" I squinted at Dominic as I tried to breathe some air through the nostril that was still clear for the time being.

He leaned back in the chair, studying me as I ate. "I remember him...hovering around. During the short time we spoke, he made sure to mention that you two were engaged."

I dropped the spoon into my soup, causing it to splash on my sleeve. Or Dominic's sleeve as the case was.

"He told you that?" I rubbed at my throbbing temple. "*Used* to be engaged. We should have stayed friends, but I had an easier time going back to that than he has. So, I think that was the last lunch we'll have for a while. And this is too deep of a conversation for my heavy head." I reached for the roll and tore off a piece before I dipped it into the soup.

"I'm sorry." He scrubbed a hand down his face. "I...I always hoped you were happy, even if it wasn't with me." He crossed his arms and leveled his sad, dark eyes at me.

It was on the tip of my tongue to say I was happy enough, but nothing compared to how happy I'd been when things had been good between us.

That clouded my head even more than my infected sinuses.

I ate the rest of my soup in silence, Dominic and I just sitting together, but not together. It all still seemed so natural, even while I was doing my best to avoid him.

He needed to go, and I needed another nap.

"Did you sleep all day?" Dominic leaned forward, more concern pinching his brow.

"Mostly. On and off since I can't really breathe." I sniffled in a vain attempt to get any air through my nose.

"Your bathroom is upstairs?" he asked before pushing off the chair.

I nodded, causing the room to spin a little too fast. "Right at the top of the stairs."

Dominic padded up the stairs, and I heard the squeak of a faucet in the distance. Before I knew it, he was standing over me again.

"I made the shower hot for now, so you can breathe in some steam before you step in." He held out his hand. "Come on, you'll feel better."

"You turned on the shower?" I took his hand, my fuzzy brain taking a few minutes to catch up. The fog and the fatigue at the beginning were always the worst.

"Yes, and when you come out, maybe you'll feel up to eating something else." His mouth tilted in a crooked smile. Blaming my lack of resistance on sickness, I let him lead me up the stairs and to the bathroom door. The steam was already billowing out of the shower and fogging up the mirror.

"Are you leaving?" My voice was sandpaper.

"Well," his lips curled into a wry grin, "I figured you'd want to shower alone, but I'm happy to come in with you if you need help."

I tilted my heavy head to the side, stifling a laugh at the mirth in his eyes.

"I meant do you have to go back?"

He shook his head slowly and leaned against the banister.

"If you want me to stay, there's nowhere else for me to be."

Air expelled from my tight chest. I didn't want him to go, and for this one time, I wouldn't deny it.

"Thank you for this." I nodded to the bathroom. "It would be nice to decongest." My gaze stumbled back to his. "I won't be long."

"Take your time." Our eyes locked for a few long minutes before he shifted toward the stairs.

I stepped into the bathroom, inhaling a big gulp of steam before I stripped and climbed into the shower. I'd spent all day bundled up to ward off the chill, and it was finally gone thanks to the stream of hot water pouring over my body, and the warmth I wanted to ignore spreading inside my chest.

23

DOMINIC

I SHOULD'VE LET Thea come to me. She wasn't ready to talk about what had happened between us, and I did intend to give her the space and time she needed to figure it all out.

But when it came to her, I wasn't very good at space or time.

I believed that she was back in my life for a reason, like the universe was giving me the chance to make it right and get my girl back.

When I'd overheard Caterina ask one of our delivery drivers to make a stop in Pentier Beach, my nosy ass had gotten in between them to ask who it was for. When Caterina said it was soup for Thea, I'd figured out that she was sick. Every summer she came down with these awful infections, one was so bad I had to take her to the emergency room because she couldn't breathe.

I told our driver I'd take it from there and packed two more bags of food for her, yelling to Joe before I left that I'd be out for the rest of the day. He didn't fight me, only nodded with a laugh. He probably thought I was pathetic, and I had no problems owning that when it came to Thea. But either way, I wasn't allowing her to be sick alone.

I planned on lingering at least until I made sure she ate something of substance and didn't have a high fever. When she'd asked me if I was leaving, I knew that meant she wanted me to stay. So, I wasn't going anywhere.

When she opened up the door in my shirt, I'd had to stifle a smile. My chest might've puffed out a little, too. I took any and all scraps of hope where she was concerned.

I wanted to prove to her that I could be the man she'd always deserved, the one who loved her so much that she still haunted his damn dreams. Not the lost soul drowning so deep in grief that he'd checked out of his own life and had lost the best thing that ever happened to him.

"Hey."

I turned toward Thea's raspy voice. Her eyes were a little brighter as one side of her mouth curled up.

"The shower helped. I'm still wiped as hell but not quite as miserable." She trudged over to where I was sitting on the couch and plopped down, tucking her legs under her.

"Of course it did. I'm always right."

She rolled her eyes but the corners of her mouth twitched. "And humble."

She sniffled and reached for a tissue on the end table before turning back to me. "Thank you." She stared at the floor. "For all of this. I've been sick alone before, but at least my mother or one of my friends was around if I needed something. I'm a little isolated out here."

"As long as I'm here, you aren't isolated." I dropped a hand to her pajama covered knee. "You just have to let me in." I gave her a light squeeze and expected her to tense up and close off, but a smile played across her lips instead.

"I know that." She coughed into her tissue. "You may not

think so, but I let you in a lot more than I'd intended to when I came here. You make it almost impossible not to."

I closed the tiny space between us and stretched my arm across the couch cushion behind her. "Lovably annoying is what you used to tell me, right?" My lips found the side of her temple. Her shoulders jerked with a chuckle before she leaned into me.

"And some things never change." She lifted her head, and instead of uncertainty or pain, I glimpsed a little sparkle in her golden eyes.

Her eyes fluttered when I threaded my fingers through the damp and wavy strands of her hair.

"Do you feel up for eating a little more?"

She crinkled her red nose. "Some tea and a cookie would be amazing." She leaned forward to stand, but I pulled her by the arm to sit back down.

"I'm here to serve you. Rest, and I'll be right back."

I rummaged through her cabinets and managed to find a kettle and a tea bag. When I came back into the living room, she was curled up against the arm of the couch.

I nudged her awake. "Drink some tea and then you can go back to sleep."

She regarded me through hooded eyes and slowly sat up.

"I should have told you where the honey was in the cabinet."

I gingerly placed the hot mug into her hands. "I brought you some. We have local honey delivered. It tastes better, and it helps with allergies."

"Thought of everything. I always loved that about you." She smiled around the rim of the mug.

"What's that?"

"You were lovably annoying, yes, but," she snickered and looked away for a moment, "but you were the most thoughtful person I ever knew." Her smile turned sad before she took another tentative sip. "You have a big, beautiful heart." She reached out and dragged a finger down the left side of my chest. "That's what I've missed the most."

I grabbed her hand and kissed across her knuckles. She didn't have to miss my heart because she'd always had it. Even when I'd fucked up and lost her, it was hers for the rest of my life, whether she could accept it or not.

But that was too heavy of a confession for today.

She took three bites of the cookie before she set it back down on the plate.

"I think I need to lay down."

She slowly pushed off the couch, and I followed, thinking this was going to be my cue to leave.

"Would you mind," her eyes clenched shut. "Would you mind laying with me for a little bit? I know I'm not exactly fun but," she trailed off.

"I told you. I have nowhere else to be but here with you." I grabbed her hand again, entwining our fingers. "Do you want me to put one leg on the floor to make it like we're *not* really in bed together?"

She swatted my chest after I waggled my eyebrows.

I followed her upstairs, her hand still in mine, and a wave of guilt snuck up on me. She was vulnerable, and I couldn't shake the feeling that I was taking advantage. She was so open, almost affectionate, but I was fairly certain once she felt better, the walls would go right back up.

She plucked the remote from the edge of the nightstand and turned on the TV before handing it to me.

"You can watch whatever you want. I'll be out in a few minutes, anyway." She didn't meet my eyes before crawling on top of the bed and settling on her side.

"You can't blame sickness for that." A smile pulled at my

lips as I kicked off my sneakers. "You never lasted past opening credits on any movie we rented." I fell onto the bed and started searching channels. "Netflix and chill with us was Netflix and snooze."

She huffed out a laugh followed by a coughing fit. I sat up to pat her back until she settled down.

"Do you need your inhaler?"

"I'm fine," she whispered and cupped my cheek. "Wasn't always snooze, though." Her sleepy smirk gutted me.

"No," I tucked a lock of hair behind her ear. "No, it wasn't."

Her chest rose and fell with a heavy sigh before her breathing slowed. I shifted slightly away when her arm snaked around my waist and pulled me back. I wasn't sure if she was asleep when her head drooped into the crook of my shoulder, but I gently lifted my arm and drew her into my side.

It still felt like stealing, but I rested my chin on top of her head and my heavy eyes closed, joy mixing with despair over a dream of Thea that was already too good to wake up from.

24

THEA

I woke up to a sheen of sweat draped over most of my body, my pajamas sticking to every inch of me when I stretched out my arms and legs.

Relief flooded through me, since this usually meant the worst of the stupid infection was over, but then my sleepy eyes fell on the arm around my waist.

Dominic was fast asleep on top of the sheets, his grip on me still tight as I tried to slip from his hold. That seemed to be our theme this summer.

Instead of getting up, I rested my head on his shoulder, brushing the matted hair off of his forehead with the tip of my finger. Whatever he used to slick it back had worn off as his hair stuck up every which way around his head. The top button of his polo shirt was open, offering a teasing glimpse of the dusting of hair on his chest.

The urge to cuddle into him and press my lips to that tiny spot right before I reached inside his shirt and skimmed my fingertips down his torso, as I'd done countless times, almost overpowered me as I still didn't have the energy to fight it.

Rather than lament my lapse in judgment and ignoring

the knee jerk reaction to push him away again, I didn't regret a damn thing. I nestled into his side and breathed him in, thankfully with somewhat clearer nostrils, enjoying it without worrying about what it all meant.

A growly moan vibrated against my cheek.

"It's not very polite to ogle someone as they sleep." His arm tightened around my waist before he kissed the top of my head.

I didn't attempt a feeble denial, only smiled when his eyes opened and met mine.

"Good morning, beautiful."

My teeth sank into my bottom lip, the too familiar greeting both slicing me open and causing my heart to swell.

"Good morning to you, too. Thank you for staying and for, for everything."

He rubbed his eyes with the heel of his other hand.

"No need to thank me, I'm happy to be here. You look a lot better, how are you feeling?" His fingers threaded through my still-damp tangles.

"Much better. Antibiotics usually work fast."

And the sweet, tender loving care my stubborn self was able to accept for a change.

We laid together for a moment, not saying anything or acknowledging how we were in the same bed, almost draped over each other like the lovers we used to be. I didn't want to get up and stop the blissful game of pretend.

"I'd offer you some breakfast, but I guess you have to get to work. I'm sorry if I made you late."

He shook his head. "You didn't make me late. And living right upstairs means I can get ready in no time."

I nodded and rolled off of him to sit up on the bed.

Craning my head over my shoulder, I watched as he slipped on his sneakers and stuffed his phone into his pocket.

A strange wave of separation anxiety washed over me, and I didn't want him to leave. My head still ached a bit, and my throat was still scratchy, but my sudden attachment hadn't come from being sick and needy.

The attachment to Dominic was anything but sudden. I always needed more, and usually hated myself for it.

Running a hand through my tangles in vain as he'd already seen me at my worst, I followed him down the stairs. Yet, the way he looked at me when he'd opened his eyes hadn't been disgust. It was pure love, the same love I'd been running from for weeks.

It was that he didn't love me enough. Not enough to stay, not enough to be there when I needed him the most, although I shouldn't have held that against him. He didn't know what happened or why I'd needed him. But years of resentment still left a bitter taste all the same.

On the nights I fell deep into my hole of self-torture, I wondered if that had never happened, would I have accepted his calls? Would we have had a long-distance type of relationship, or would I have been the wimp I always was when it came to Dominic and moved out here for him.

I probably would have accepted him any way I could have had him. Now, I could have him for real, but my bruised ego kept stepping in front of my battered heart in a futile effort to prevent any more damage.

"We have a live band tonight, so it's going to be a little crazy. Hopefully." The side of his mouth curved up. "But if you need anything at all, text me."

"Thank you. Now, that I feel somewhat normal I'm going to work on the deck for a while." I nodded toward the small wooden deck behind the screen door.

"This is a pretty nice rental for the summer." He swept his gaze around the room.

"It belongs to my company. They invested in homes out here, too. I just happened to be lucky this one was available. My boss told me to think of it as a gift." I shrugged, remembering when I'd found out all the details, this house and this project had seemed more like a punishment.

"I'd say so." He leaned in and brushed his lips over my cheek. "Get some rest. I brought you some muffins, too. They may be a little hard but you can slip them into the toaster oven."

"Thank you," I told him, again. There was a lot I had to say, but those two words were the only ones that were able to slip out.

He squeezed my hand before he made his way out the door.

Sucking in a deep breath that was still followed by the rumble of a cough, I searched through the bags and found four blueberry muffins. He really did think of everything.

I cut one in half, scolding myself for being so weepy over muffins, and after shoving it into the toaster, sat down at the kitchen table to log on to my laptop to work for the day. My boss was familiar with how often I came down with sinus infections and usually was the first one to throw me out of the office. When I'd told her I was sick, she insisted I work from the rental for the next couple of days before I went back to the hotel.

My work emails were light, and I found myself bothered by the silence, the only sound in the room was me chewing on the crispy part of the toasted muffin. Eying my phone, I scooped it up and called Sue.

"Good morning." My stomach dropped at her gravelly greeting followed by a yawn.

"I'm so sorry, I thought you'd be up."

"Oh honey, I have been. We've been playing the make

Jared stay in his own bed game and losing. We finally stopped walking him back to his room at two this morning but he woke up right on time at six-thirty. I really need to escape to you for a weekend."

"Come anytime you want. I'm free, all the time," I sang the last part in my still hoarse voice.

It sometimes felt as if my feet were stuck in some kind of mud. My friends were all moving along with husbands and babies, and here I was. I could have moved along too, but that would have been settling. It was the one decision I never doubted, even if I was still left in limbo.

"I hear the Kathleen Turner sinus rasp. Another infection?"

"Of course. Every summer without fail."

"But you're all by yourself out there. I wish you would have told me. I could have snuck out for a day or two. I know how bad they can get."

"This one wasn't so terrible, and I'm not that alone out here. I made friends with Joe's wife."

"Oh good, I'm glad you weren't sick by yourself."

"I wasn't." I cringed before I confessed the reason for my call. "Dominic came over yesterday."

"Dominic? Your Dominic? Well, your old Dominic? The Dominic you told me was only a business associate this summer?"

"Yes, that Dominic. We hung out a little last week," I reluctantly admitted, leaving out coming on his hand at his apartment and retreating like a coward.

"What are you telling me, Thea? You caught feelings for him again? How long was he there yesterday?"

"He just left. Nothing happened." This time. "He brought over food and stayed because he heard I was sick. Then we both drifted off watching TV."

I was met with nothing but silence and had to glance at my phone screen to make sure the call hadn't dropped.

"I'm still unsure of the reasons for this call, babe. Are you looking for permission to start something up with him again? It's no one's business but yours if you do. I support you either way."

I smiled when she shushed her husband and son in the background.

"I'm scared. You say caught feelings as if I never lost them. I've been making myself walk away from him since I got here, but..."

My head fell against the table, the frustration and fear hitting me hard and all at once.

"I can't tell you what to do. Your sister and other friends may have a different opinion, but I say do what makes you happy. There's moving on from the past, and there's running from it. I think you know which one you've been doing. If you have another chance, can you live with yourself if you don't see it through?"

"I don't know." I winced at the pain behind my eyes when I clenched them shut. I wasn't sure if congestion or unshed tears were the cause.

"Yes, you do. Get some rest, and I'll call you later."

We hung up, and I popped off the chair, with what energy I had to pop with, and dug out a teabag from the drawer, my eyes landing on the bottle of local honey Dominic brought me. I filled the kettle and leaned back on the counter.

Before I lost my nerve, I grabbed my phone again.

Thea: *What if I said I wanted more than casual with you?*

I expected a long wait for a reply since he was heading

home to get ready for work, but I almost jumped out of my skin at the immediate buzzing behind me.

Dominic: *What if you said it, or are you saying it? Because my answer will depend on if you're really saying it, or may possibly say it in the uncertain future.*
Thea: *You're a pain in the ass, did I ever tell you that?*
Dominic: *Many times. Okay, fine. I'll pretend you ARE saying it.*

Three dots started then stopped, my heart skipping a beat each time I anticipated his reply.

Dominic: *I would love nothing more than to have another chance with you. A real chance. Be with me, Thea. I promise I won't fuck it up, this time. You belong with me, and I belong with you. It's how it always should have been, and we finally can make it right.*

My hands froze around my phone. It was the answer I was expecting, and the answer I wanted, but I didn't know if I had the guts to accept it.

Dominic: *But I won't push you. Just know if you really did say that you wanted more than casual, or that you wanted me back, I'm yours. All fucking yours.*

25

DOMINIC

Joe and I stood to the side as Dave trained a couple of new waitresses. He was doing a good enough job as a manager to allow him a little more responsibility, and allow Joe and me to have some kind of life this summer. Well, Joe anyway. I was working on mine.

"Good thing we have a new space opening soon. Doesn't look like I'm too needed around here anymore," I joked, nodding in Dave's direction.

"As long as this place is open, you're needed. More like what am I going to do without you? Getting my balls broken has become such a huge part of my day." He shook his head before heaving a dramatic sigh. "Not sure I'll be able to function."

"Don't worry, my friend, I can always work that into my schedule. It's as important to me as it is to you." I slapped him on the back. "I'll be back later, I just want to run over there to check on a few things."

Joe stuffed his hands into his pockets, stepping back as he squinted at me.

"Didn't you just check yesterday? What's going on today?

Other than Thea going back to work?" I raised a brow before his shoulders shook with a chuckle.

"Did Caterina tell you that? I miss the days when you both were too interested in pawing each other in public to notice anything going on around you."

"Now look who likes to dodge. I only know because Caterina said she was having lunch with Thea today since she was back at the hotel. I expected you to head right back there, especially after blowing us all off to take care of her the other day." His head tilted as he raised a brow.

"Does this story have a point? I have things to do."

He laughed and dropped a hand to my shoulder. "I'm rooting for you guys. We both are. It wouldn't be any fun if I didn't give you shit about it."

A smile snuck across my lips as I shook my head.

"I guess I have that coming. See you later."

I waved to Dave and the new staff before heading out the door.

I meant what I'd said, I wouldn't push Thea. It had taken a lot for her to reach out to me after I'd left the other morning, but I still needed her to make the next move. Even though I couldn't stop making that easy for her, I wouldn't be in her face about it.

I pulled into a spot in the front, nodding hellos to all the construction workers I'd gotten to know over the past few weeks. That had been my old profession before I'd left for Ocean Cove, and being in the thick of all the drilling and sawing almost made me a little nostalgic.

When I opened the door to the restaurant, a thrill ran through me at how it was all taking shape. There was still a lot to be done, but I had a good feeling. That was different: having good feelings and being so damn optimistic. I tried to manage my growing expectations, but no matter how I tried to manage them down to a lower, more likely outcome, sleeping next to Thea had blown them all out of the water.

"Are you ever at the pub anymore? Joe must get lonely."

I turned toward Thea's voice, then fought the widening of my eyes. She was not only better, she was gorgeous. Her eyes were bright, and the color was back in her cheeks. Her hair spilled down her back in waves and the simple black dress she wore did a lot of not so simple things to me below the waist.

"He's fine. He probably likes the break." Her smile grew as I came closer. "You look..." My needy rasp made me cringe. "Better. Much better."

"I feel a lot better. I got two breakfasts out of those muffins, so again, thank you."

"You're very welcome."

There was something about her today that I hadn't seen, at least not since she'd been here. An ease in her smile, a less rigid stance. The way she was inching closer without looking like she'd jerk back at any second.

"I guess you're working late tonight since it's a Friday."

I shrugged and leaned against the wall. "Most likely. Usually, in the summers, the night of the week doesn't really matter."

"I figured as much." An audible sigh fell from her lips. "I should get back, I have a lot of paperwork to catch up on today."

I grabbed her arm when she shifted to leave. "Is there a reason you mentioned it?"

Her shoulders tensed before she raised her gaze to mine. "I thought if you weren't working late you'd want to maybe get something to eat, but it's not a big deal."

"Oh, but I think it is. Are you asking me out, Thea?"

I caught a huff before she turned her head.

"I asked if you wanted to eat with me. And I didn't even

ask. I said I was thinking of asking if you weren't working late, which you said you were." Her eyes shut before she rubbed at her temple and shook her head.

All that ease faded, but this tension I liked. She was flustered and so damn adorable I couldn't take it.

"There are ways around that. Joe still owes me days of covering for him all alone." I pulled her toward me, spying the corners of her mouth twitching despite the scowl in her eyes. "So, if you want to go on a date with me, all you have to do is be direct." She gasped when I brushed the hair off her shoulder and drifted my hand down her back.

"You're loving this, aren't you?" She narrowed her eyes and groaned.

I lifted my shoulder in an innocent shrug. "Maybe a little. Or a whole hell of a lot." I framed her face in my hands. "Ask me," I whispered so close to her lips they almost brushed against mine.

When Thea gave me an inch, it was impossible not to try for a mile.

She rolled her eyes but couldn't hide the flash of heat. Getting to her had always been my favorite pastime. After we shed some of the hurt that lingered between us, I felt us growing into who we used to be. If only I could get her to take that last jump.

"Are you free for dinner tonight?" She said each word slowly, and the urge to devour that mouth almost made me stumble.

"I'll be at your rental at eight. Wear the red dress you wore for the budget meeting last week."

She flinched back. "That's a little formal."

"I have plans for us." I pulled her flush to my body. She stiffened in surprise for a moment, but leaned into me after.

She cocked her head to the side, an exasperated breath falling from her lips.

"Already?"

"Always."

"Seriously?" She pursed her lips and shook her head.

"I told you," I cupped her cheek and ran my thumb along her jaw. "All you had to do was say the word."

I pressed a long, light kiss to her lips, loving it when a whimper slipped out of her.

"I'm all yours. Go back to your paperwork."

She glared with a tiny smile playing across her lips. A blush stained her cheeks before she turned to leave.

Maybe I was pushing a little bit now, but being this close to having the love of my life back *in* my life, there was no way I could stop.

26

THEA

AFTER I SLIPPED into my red dress, I looked myself over in the bedroom mirror for a long minute. The skin under my nose and around my eyes had thankfully healed from how chafed it had become when I was sick. I gazed into my smoky eyes before touching up my crimson lips, the deep red almost matching my dress perfectly.

What the hell was I doing?

I'd sworn to myself I wouldn't get too close to Dominic, and here I was meeting him for dinner. More than dinner: a date.

A date *I'd* asked him for.

Twirling the ends of my hair so they would fall the right way on my shoulders, the one thing that surprised me the most was that I wasn't filled with panic or self-doubt. Don't get me wrong, it was still there, along with the blinding fear of closing the protective distance I'd put between us.

When I thought of Dominic and me now, all I felt was tired. Putting up so many walls and denying my feelings exhausted me. I craved him the same way I always had. And if I didn't, at least, pursue what was still between us, I'd regret it.

I already had plenty of regrets to keep me up at night, and I owed it to myself to try to avoid one more.

Even if we crashed and burned a second time, at least, I'd know—and not spend the next fifty years of my life wondering, just like the last four years I'd second guessed myself for not returning his calls.

At seven-fifty-eight, I grabbed my purse and locked the door behind me. It was silly to bounce off the walls inside when I could enjoy having a front porch for once. Looking eager was a moot point, and I was too jumpy to care.

Before I sat down on the bench outside, I noticed Dominic's truck pull up. I guessed we had jumpy in common although I doubted he'd show it at all tonight.

I came down the stairs at the same time he shut the engine off and climbed out.

"You're early," I told him, not able to stop my smile as he made his way toward me.

The cocky grin faded from his lips when his eyes met mine. "Thea, you're...wow." His eyes raked over me, heat singeing my skin along the path of his gaze.

"Thank you," I whispered, my cheeks flushing hot. "You aren't so bad, either."

Dominic wore a black button-down shirt and black pants. My eyes fell to the top open button and the tease of his collarbone. A collarbone usually isn't considered an erogenous zone on most men, but on him, it was my kryptonite. I could still taste the sweet saltiness of his skin as I ran my tongue back and forth, loving the growl that always vibrated against my lips.

"Are you all right?" Dominic asked with a chuckle, breaking me out of my fantasy. "Do button-down shirts still do it for you?"

He laughed at my scowl. No one read me better than Dominic.

"I'm fine. Curious where we're going since you had to be all secretive about it."

I stifled a smile when he opened the passenger side door for me.

"I'm not secretive, I'm spontaneous. Go with the flow, sweetheart."

He cocked a brow, and the way he leaned against the door, his crooked grin and the light dancing in his dark eyes, it simply wasn't fair.

He snaked an arm around my waist before I climbed into the cab.

"I've been waiting for this all day long. Well, if I'm honest," a bashful smile drifted across his mouth, "I've been waiting for years." His hand slid to the back of my neck, triggering all the tiny hairs to stand straight up.

"That's a long time to be waiting for dinner." I attempted a joke to deflect the weight of his stare.

"I've been waiting for *you*."

I had so much to say, but the words caught in my throat.

It didn't matter where we were going, because despite my efforts at resistance, I'd follow him anywhere.

We both relaxed a bit on the drive, the both of us stealing glances at each other like a couple of lovesick teenagers. At thirty-one, my heart pounded harder for Dominic than any silly boy I crushed on, and more than any other man I'd ever known.

"You didn't have to go to all this trouble. Dinner was relative, I could have eaten anywhere," I told Dominic as we pulled into the parking lot of what appeared to be a fancy hall on lush grounds next to the water.

"We could have." He nodded as he put the truck into

park. "You keep saying it's not a big deal, but it is." Dominic's mouth flattened to a hard line. "I have a lot to make up for with you. Maybe it's a silly place to start, but it's still a start, right?"

He slid his palm against mine and squeezed. Dominic could always charm me into anything, at least, that's what I told myself on the drive here. But when he was like this, so vulnerable with his open heart on his sleeve, there wasn't a damn thing I could do to resist.

We were seated at a table on the patio overlooking the water. The restaurant was packed, and judging by the way Dominic greeted so many people on the way to our table, I'd bet he'd pulled some strings since I'd seen him this morning.

"This is nice," I admitted. "I haven't really been to many restaurants around here other than the seafood place near the hotel."

"I wanted better than that for us tonight." A frown dipped the sides of his mouth.

I set down my menu and glared at Dominic. "This place isn't meant to like, one up Adam is it? Because that would be ridiculous." I raised my brow until he lifted his head.

"I don't know what you're talking about."

I leaned back in my chair and folded my arms. He lifted his shoulder in a shrug.

"Do you want to know why I broke things off with Adam?" I scooted my chair closer to the table and rested my elbows on the edge.

"Do I like thinking of his ring on your finger to begin with? Fuck, no." He barked out a humorless laugh before he finally brought his eyes back to mine. "But, I have no right to be angry at that, and it's none of my business."

"You're very right on both counts. You don't, and it's not." I tilted my head. "But I think whatever exchange you and

Adam had the day he came to the hotel is gnawing at you a little bit. So if we're going to move past it, I need you to listen."

He squared his shoulders as if he were bracing himself.

"A couple of weeks after we were engaged, Sue thought it would be fun if we went to a bridal salon to try on dresses, although I couldn't fathom even thinking about a date at that point. We picked out a few, and I came out to one of those big three way mirrors to give her a thrill and leave, but I didn't expect to *like* the dress so much."

My own eyes dropped to the table as the flood of emotions came back, how it only took less than a second for a silly way to pass an afternoon to knock the wind out of me and become all too real.

"Even Sue got a little choked up, which, if you remember, is pretty rare for her." I chuckled and shook my head before meeting Dominic's eyes again. He said nothing as he waited to see where I was going with this story.

"I totally saw myself getting married in that dress. It was the fairy tale every little girl wants coming true. But when I pictured walking down the aisle, Adam wasn't who I saw waiting for me at the altar."

His eyes widened a moment as he sat stoic. A silent Dominic was rare enough to be unnerving.

"That's when I realized what I was doing. I needed to move on from you, but I didn't know how. Adam was safe. Although I wouldn't give you the satisfaction of being right, I knew how he'd always felt about me, and I thought if I went through the motions..." I cringed before I trailed off, the shame still jabbing me right in the chest at what I'd done, even if I hadn't intended to do it.

"I thought that if I went through the motions, maybe I'd feel something. But that's not how it works. You can't train yourself to fall in love, and you can't learn how to feel something. You just do, whether you want to or not."

I squinted at Dominic and spotted a sad smile pulling at the corners of his mouth.

"We broke up that night, because I was so disgusted with myself. I couldn't lead him on another minute longer." I reared back in my chair, the memory and confession draining a little air from my lungs. "If you're thinking there's still some imaginary competition, or that you have to impress me somehow to prove something, you don't. You never did."

He reached across the table to grab my hand, lacing his fingers in between mine before he raised our joined hands to his mouth. His warm lips lingered on my skin as he shut his eyes. Now, I slumped in my chair for a different reason.

"So, stop being ridiculous," I whispered as he kept hold of my hand.

"Stop trying to seduce me."

I glared at his quirked brow.

"Seduce you?"

He cocked his head to the side. "The nice words, the dress—"

"You asked me to wear this dress," I said, sighing in exasperation but fighting my smile. "Told me, actually."

"And you complied." He dipped his finger into the collar of his shirt and smoothed it back and forth. "I see you staring at this, too. Temptress."

I burst out laughing and dropped my head into my hands.

In my periphery, Dominic rose from his seat then crouched in front of me, peeling my fingers away from my face.

"I promise, that's the last time I'll act like a jealous asshole. Well, at least, about him."

I chuckled at his pursed lips. "Good." My hand drifted

down his shirt, my fingertips tracing his collar before I could help myself.

"Touch it, you know you want to," he teased, his voice low and husky.

I leaned forward, giving his collar a little pull to reveal my favorite spot. I inhaled the familiar scent of his spicy cologne before I peppered kisses across his skin, smiling when his chest fell with an audible, deep sigh.

He cupped the back of my neck and shook his head.

"Any minute now, my alarm is going to wake me up, and this is going to be another damn dream." His grip tightened as he searched my gaze.

"You dream about me?"

"All the *fucking* time. Even before you came out here. I may have left, but," he leaned his forehead against mine, "I never let you go."

I roped my arms around his neck and shut my eyes. I'd never let him go, either.

He kissed the corner of my mouth and backed away with a tiny shake of his head when I leaned in for more.

"Once I start kissing you tonight, I won't be able to stop." His thumb drifted across my bottom lip. "Then we won't be able to come back here ever again."

"Now, who's a tease?"

He laughed, beaming as he rose from the floor and sat back down. My cheeks already ached from the huge smile stretching across my lips.

Dominic had always been the one. It was a fact I hated at times but could never deny. No matter what happened tonight or after, I couldn't run from it anymore.

27

DOMINIC

"You DON'T WANT to rename the restaurant in the hotel?" Thea asked, as I focused on her lips, the red lips that teased me all damn night.

With every sip she took from her wine glass or each glide of her fork passed her lips, I craved that mouth on mine so badly I could almost taste it. Anticipation was poking holes in my patience, but I'd waited a long time for this chance. I'd deal with trying to cover the growing bulge in my pants.

"Believe it or not, I'm actually the one that came up with the name, 'The Beach Pub'." I swirled the wine in my glass in an effort to distract myself. But no matter what I did, I couldn't tear my eyes away from the gorgeous woman sitting across from me.

Thea raised an impressed eyebrow. "I didn't know that, but I can believe it. It's a simple but very cool play on words, like the beach clubs back in the city. I feel like Joe would be the type to complicate it."

"You think?" I huffed out a laugh. "He spent weeks trying to think up a name, and they got more ridiculous by the day. A couple of months before we opened, a local newspaper came by and wanted to do a story on the place, so we had to call it something. When the reporter asked him what the name of the business was, I chimed in behind him."

"Did he get mad? Joe is kind of a control freak like that. I remember how when we'd all go out, everything had to be so precise and not mess with his order of things." She chuckled, the swells of her breasts pushing against the neckline of her dress as she leaned forward and robbed me of my train of thought.

"All he said was, 'that could work.' I think the poor bastard had exhausted himself, and he knew it. We got started on a logo and a sign, and never really discussed it afterward."

"Keeping the name equity could work to your advantage, for sure. You must be excited about running it all." She crossed her arms and deepened the slope of her cleavage. The tip of my tongue tingled to start a trail right there and not stop until I'd tasted her all over.

I cleared my throat and blinked away the fantasy, dizzy from the blood flow ping ponging back and forth from my brain to my cock.

"I've never thought of myself as Joe's sidekick, although that seems to be my reputation. He never made me feel like a second in command either, I was always a partner. But, it's nice to have something where I'm seen as the guy in charge, not Robin to Joe's Batman."

Thea shook her head. "I did always see you guys as Batman and Robin, but the other way around. Joe had all the crazy dreams but *you* were the one who made sense of it all. I remember Joe would suggest if he ran whatever restaurant or bar we were at he'd do this or that, but you'd know the right way of whatever he was thinking better than he did." A slow smile crept across her lips. "I think you'll be great."

Joe and I were like brothers and looked out for each other,

but there were only two people who believed in me yet didn't take any of my shit.

I'd lost one and was trying to get the other back.

"Thanks, I actually think I will, too. Finally, those business classes I took in college will pay off. I wish you could stay to see it." A sour pang settled in my gut. I'd gotten so used to her being here, I kept forgetting she didn't *live* here. The new restaurant would open, and she'd head back to Queens right after.

I'd been so focused on getting her back, I hadn't thought of what we'd do after she left.

"I'll see it. Queens isn't so far away. I could come back sometimes."

"Only sometimes? What if the next assignment sends you far away?" Now, that I let myself think about her leaving, the more I hated it.

"I stay local for the most part, but I'm not sure if I want to keep doing this. Like I said," she shrugged, "this is as nice as a project could get. But I'd like to come home to my actual home at the end of a day. Have something to show for my life other than a plethora of hotel rewards points." She shrugged. "I'll figure it out when I get back."

"What would you want to do instead?"

And how can I keep you here?

"I was thinking about applying for a few hotels, or seeing if there were any permanent positions in my company as a relationship manager at one. I'm getting too used to sitting on my deck at the rental, so I was considering moving outside of the city. I've been looking around in Westchester County and New Jersey, but I'll wait to see what my options are in the fall."

"Ocean Cove has a lot of hotels. And you seem to get

along with Violet really well, maybe you can get something there."

She reached across the table and ran her nails back and forth along my forearm. "Maybe we can take things one dinner at a time, okay?"

I nodded as my breathing evened out. I recalled how she used to scratch her nails along my arm every night in bed until I'd calmed down enough to fall asleep.

My eyes fell to the table as I nodded.

"I tend to get ahead of myself, especially when it comes to you. I don't like thinking of letting you go when I just barely got you back." My words were hoarse, the thickness in my throat making it hard to swallow.

"I'm here now," she whispered. "Let's just focus on tonight, and we'll figure out the rest." She squeezed my arm when I attempted to pull away.

Every second I spent with Thea, the more I realized how lost I'd been without her. I couldn't let my panic at not being able to keep her push us toward something we weren't ready for.

So, I'd wait, and find a way to hold in the crazy even though I was so nuts about her I could barely see straight. I wouldn't blow it and lose what I was sure was my last chance.

I didn't realize how much time went by until I noticed some of the lights inside the dining room flick off.

"I'll just leave this here." The waitress smiled and dropped the check on the table.

"Are they closing now?" Thea asked as she scanned the almost empty dining room.

I glanced at my watch and laughed when I read the time. "They close in about thirty minutes. The check is a nice way of saying get out."

"We've been here that long?" Thea peeked at her own watch. "At least it's not four a.m. yet."

I remembered not wanting to take her home that first night either. I kept finding things to talk about so I wouldn't have to.

"Keep your money. Tonight is on me."

"I did suggest dinner, so it's only right I go half with you."

"By suggest you mean asked me out, and it's all good. I'll still put out later if you want me to." I winked and reached into my back pocket for my wallet.

She stilled, a wave of lust flashing in her eyes before she leveled them on me.

I slipped a few bills into the tray with the check and stood.

"Ready?" I asked, extending my hand. My chest swelled when she took it without hesitation.

"Thank you for dinner. It was nice," she said as we strolled through the parking lot.

"It was," I agreed before unlocking the doors to my truck. I opened the passenger side for her to climb in.

Instead, she dropped her head against my chest.

"I missed you," she whispered so low it was almost inaudible.

I kissed the top of her head and wrapped my arms around her.

"You wouldn't believe how much I missed you."

Would she ever believe it? There was still so much between us, but had I hurt her too much to ever really get what we used to have back?

She nuzzled into my neck with a tiny moan, her quick breaths fanning hot against my skin.

"Look at me, Thea."

When she raised her head, her eyes were dark and pained.

I framed her face and drifted my thumb over her lips. If this was our second chance, I wasn't wasting any more time.

I pressed my lips to hers, my hands shaking from holding back. She leaned into the kiss and sucked on my bottom lip. A growl erupted from my throat as I fisted my hand into her hair. I pulled back and flicked the seam of her lips with my tongue. They parted on a whimper, and the rest of my control snapped. I crashed my mouth into hers as she fell back against the side of my truck.

I licked deeper into her mouth, devouring all I could and starving for more.

All those times I could kiss her whenever I'd wanted, all those times I'd been inside her, and the rest of the world faded away—I wanted that back. I wanted *her* back, and there was nothing I wouldn't do to make that happen.

She grabbed at my collar, undoing the next button before inching open-mouthed kisses over my collarbone and across the top of my chest. I clutched the back of her head and groaned, my cock so hard it was ready to burst through my zipper. There had never been this kind of passion with anyone else, and I knew there never would be.

"*Fuck*, Thea," I growled when her lips strayed lower. Sliding my hand down her leg, I felt for the hem of her dress and skimmed my fingertips over back of her bare thigh, hooking her leg across my hip.

"Tell me what you want," I rasped as I ground my erection against her core. The parking lot was empty, but I wouldn't have cared one bit if it wasn't. Thea met every thrust of my hips as her hands slid under my shirt, the scrape of her nails setting my skin on fire.

"Take me home," she begged in a breathless whisper. She'd told me the same thing on my couch after we'd both lost ourselves in each other and she hadn't known how to handle it. That was a frightened and confused plea. Her flushed cheeks and hooded eyes made the words a very different request.

"If you're asking for another sleepover at your rental, I'm all in, sweetheart. I just need you to be sure," I panted, my heart racing too fast for any air to get into my lungs.

"I..." She swallowed, gasping for air like I was. "I want to go home with you. I want to be in your bed and drown in you, tonight."

I wasn't going to last five minutes when she was in my bed, but I had all night. *We* had all night. Later, I'd figure out how we'd make all night forever. Here and now was all that mattered.

I brought my mouth back to hers but kissed her slowly this time, savoring the sweet taste of her soft lips and the warmth of her body against mine.

"I'm officially seduced," I murmured against her lips, smiling at her giggle. "Get in, and let's go."

28

THEA

"For a small town, there are a lot of traffic lights," I murmured against Dominic's lips after we came to a stop.

"I never realized it, either." His hand inched higher up the inside of my thigh at every red light. His husky chuckle vibrated against my neck as his lips grazed the sensitive skin behind my ear. "All I want is to get you home, but I'm enjoying the hell out of the ride."

He cupped my chin and took my mouth in a raw, frenzied kiss that burned my already swollen lips.

The blare of a horn behind us broke us apart.

My head fell onto Dominic's shoulder as it shook with his laughter.

"We're here," he whispered into my hair.

I lifted my head to his wide grin.

"Hopefully, no one saw us groping each other on the way here." I scrubbed a hand down my face.

"Honey, this is a small town, gossip is rampant. In fact," he said before he shut off the engine and leaned over the console. "I can't wait for the first jackass to come into the pub tomorrow and ask who was in my car." His lips drifted along my jaw before nipping down my neck.

"What will you say?" My legs fell open as his hand glided all the way up my thigh, and found the blinding ache at my core.

"I'll say," he began before slipping a finger into my panties and taking a slow swipe across my wet, swollen flesh. "I'll say that I was taking my girl home with me. And it was the greatest night of my whole damn life."

I roped my arms around his neck while our lips came back together in a bruising kiss. His head fell back against the head rest as I climbed on his lap. I'd only had the one glass of wine, but my head buzzed as all my inhibitions and reservations dissipated into the ether.

"Baby," Dominic panted before he grabbed my face and pulled back. "I have a whole bed for us. You on top of me like this is heaven, but there's not enough room to do everything I want to do to you."

"I can't wait to be in your bed." My hands drifted up his arms and framed his face. I'd been worried about leaving myself too vulnerable and losing myself in Dominic tonight, but a visceral need overtook any coherent thought in my head. Too fast and too close weren't dangers, they were good things now. Amazing things.

I wanted to roll around in the sheets that smelled like him, claim him as mine, if not with my words, with my body. My tongue darted across my bottom lip, still tasting his soft skin from when I dragged kisses across his chest. My hands shook not from fear, but from almost crippling anticipation.

His eyes widened as his fingers dug into my hips.

"I'm not sure if blowing in my pants is a good thing or a bad thing, but if you keep moving like that and looking at me like you want to eat me alive, I won't have very long to think about it." He grabbed my head and leaned his forehead against mine. "I want you in my bed too, so fucking much." He tapped my leg and kissed the tip of my nose.

I jutted my lip out in a pretend pout and climbed out of the cab after he opened the driver's side door. When we got to the entrance of his apartment, he pulled me in front of him, his hand dropping to the small of my back. As soon as we shut the outside door behind us, his lips were on my neck. I popped the rest of the buttons of his shirt open as we made a sloppy ascent up the stairs. Dominic's lips stayed on mine as he hastily unlocked the door and pulled us both inside.

He threw his keys and they landed with a loud clank somewhere on the floor before he shut the door behind us. I laughed against his lips as he backed me toward his bedroom, so damn sexy with his shirt half off his arms and his hooded dark eyes full of delicious intent.

"You have too many clothes on, Gallo." I pulled at his shirt with one hand while my other fumbled with his belt buckle.

He spun me around, and pulled me flush to his body, my back to his front.

"Do you know why I asked you to wear this dress?" He weaved his fingers into my hair and lifted it off my neck, brushing it to the side. Warm lips grazed the nape of my neck before the pull of the zipper mingled with our labored breathing.

"Told me, you mean," I breathed out, so turned on my voice creaked.

"Right," he mumbled against my skin as his lips dragged along my bare exposed back. "Because all I could think about was this."

A loud mewl escaped me as his lips lingered on the sensitive slope of my lower back. I reached back to slide my now open dress down my arms when he playfully swatted my hand away.

"Not yet, sweetheart."

I turned to where Dominic was crouched on the floor behind me.

"Not yet?"

"Nope," he said, turning me around again and drifting his hand up the inside of my damp thigh. "There's one thing I want to do first, and it's hotter if the dress is still on." He wrapped his hand around my ankle, his sexy brow quirked up. "Hotter with the heels, too."

He dipped his head to lick a path up to the apex of my thighs. My clit had its own heartbeat and pounded harder the closer his mouth came to where I needed him.

"Holy shit, Dominic. Stop torturing me."

I grumbled when his laugh vibrated against my leg.

"Would I do that?" He shot me a crooked smile as his thumbs hooked into my panties, dragging them down until they pooled at my feet.

"A job worth doing is worth doing right." He hooked my leg over his shoulder and buried his head between my legs.

I cried out, not caring if The Beach Pub crowd downstairs heard me as Dominic licked his way around my pussy as if he were reacquainting himself with an old friend. He still knew where I needed tiny kisses and where to bite and suck, the both of us moaning at the same time when he hit all my favorite spots. My fingers speared into his hair, my hips bucking against his mouth before I fell back onto the edge of his bed. My hand was still wrapped around a fistful of Dominic's hair as my elbow anchored onto the mattress for balance.

His gaze slid up to mine as he stood, a wicked smile curving his wet lips. My back fell against the bed as he grabbed my other leg and rested both of my ankles on his shoulders.

"I'd never let you fall," he whispered, lifting my hips towards his mouth and diving back in between my legs. He kissed me deep and long, killing me with every swipe of his tongue. I wiped the beads of sweat from my forehead and chuckled to myself a moment. Moving on from him, from this, was never possible, and I'd been a jackass for even fooling myself with an attempt.

"Is that good, sweetheart?" He peered up at me before he licked along his bottom lip, his eyes fluttering as if I were the best thing he'd ever tasted.

"Too good." I panted out. "It was always too damn good—"

My orgasm rippled in my lower spine and ricocheted down my legs, the lower half of my body shuddering against his mattress.

"Think anyone heard me?" I asked, my voice hoarse from screaming Dominic's name.

He stood, peeling his shirt off with a shrug. "Downstairs or back in Queens? Either way, I'd say, yes, pretty sure they, and everyone in between, heard you."

I shoved his shoulder as he settled himself on top of me, my eyes falling on the tattoo spanning from his shoulder down to his bicep. It was a reminder of our time apart, and what had broken us apart. The tribute to his mother memorialized a deep scar for us both. I shut my eyes, a reflex to throw the errant thought out of my head.

If I was doing this, if *we* were doing this, I'd have to make amends with all the ghosts of our past and eventually come clean about one that only I carried.

"Hey, where'd you go?" he crooned, cupping my cheek.

"Right here, babe," I whispered, grabbing his wrist. "Nowhere else for me to be."

"Hearing you call me babe is everything. Every *fucking* thing. Time to take this off." A grin split his mouth before he came back to my lips. He inched my dress down from where it hung off my elbows. I lifted my hips, smiling when he dropped kisses on my knee before he slipped it off and threw it onto the floor, a swoosh filling the silence when it landed on the carpet.

"These, too." I looped my finger into the waistband of his pants and yanked him closer. He opened his belt buckle and popped open the button. I slid my hand inside and wrapped it around his length. He was still perfect. Smooth and long, velvet steel against my palm. His shoulders slumped with a tortured groan as I stroked him up and down, making circles with the sticky drops at the crown.

I let go when he slid his pants over his hips, his cock bouncing against his stomach when he stood to kick them off. My God, he was still so beautiful. Slightly more muscular than I remembered, especially across his chest and down his stomach, the dusting of hair over his strong torso making my fingers itch to sift through it as I kissed him everywhere.

"There you go again." His hungry, dark eyes met mine. "Looking at me like that."

"Like how?" I sat up, skimming my hands up his bare thighs. "Like I want to eat you alive?" I bent down to take him in my mouth and whimpered around his cock. I'd missed this so much. He never let me do it for very long, but I reveled in how he'd turn to a puddle of incoherent mush the deeper I'd take him to the back of my throat.

"Please, baby," his tortured voice was low and husky. "As good as your sweet mouth is, I need to come inside you." He pulled my head back, his cock falling out of my mouth with a wet pop.

I licked my lips and reached back to unhook my bra, flinging it along with the rest of our clothes.

"You better hurry up, then," I teased and scooted up on the bed.

He climbed back on top of me, kissing me as if it was the first and last time. His hands cupped my breasts before he dipped his head down to suck on a nipple, moaning and biting before he kissed across my chest and took the other one in his mouth.

"Hold on one second," he panted, reaching over me to feel around his nightstand drawer.

"Thank God," he exhaled in relief when he showed me the foil packet, ripping off the edge and sliding the rubber down his length. I stilled again for only a second, the memory of our last time and the events that had followed too bitter-sweet to think about.

He didn't seem to notice before he slid into me, his body falling into mine as he moved slowly, inch by inch until he was fully seated inside.

"Thea," he groaned as he moved faster. I raised my hips off of the bed to get him deeper. Dominic was making love to me, but I wanted him to fuck me. Fuck away all the bad memories and the doubts, create a place where only we existed. Where we craved each other like a drug and only made sense together. Fuck away all the time we'd spent apart, and all the nights I'd felt so lost without him in my life it was as if I hadn't belonged anywhere.

His arms snaked around me as he pulled me closer, both of us eerily silent other than our heavy breaths and the creak of his bed.

When Dominic plowed into me, his eyes hooded and

wild, it was as if he'd heard my wish and made it his mission to grant it. My legs went rigid as my body shook from the inside out, a second orgasm hitting me hard. He grunted my name as he spilled into me, collapsing into the crook of my neck as his breathing slowed.

"I love you." He lifted his head, threading his fingers through my tangled and damp hair and weaving around a fistful. His body was limp against mine, but need and desperation radiated off of him in waves. "I love you so much." He swallowed before his forehead fell against mine, his eyes clenching shut. "Tell me we can go back, Thea." His voice faded into a whisper as it cracked. "That we can have it all back. I'd give anything—"

I cut him off with a kiss. I loved him more than anything, too, and there was nothing I wanted more than to be back here with him, not lose each other ever again and look forward to a future.

He didn't say anything else as he lay next to me and wrapped his arms around me from behind. I scraped my nails up and down his arm, my soul sighing as we melted together on his bed.

This was home, I just needed to figure out a way to stay.

29

DOMINIC

My eyes popped open, without fail, every morning at six a.m. This was the first time the alarm beat me to it, blaring in my ear from underneath my pillow.

Keeping my arm around Thea's naked waist, I reached with my other hand to shut it off. She groaned in my arms and stirred before leaning into me again, her breathing slow and peaceful.

I ran my lips over her shoulder and buried my face into the back of her neck. While I loved waking up with her in my arms, I didn't know what to expect. It felt like we'd turned a corner, but last night was more than I'd hoped for and most definitely more than I'd expected. The years that passed since the last time Thea was in my bed had broken us both, but when it came to how we felt about each other, that had never faded.

For a ton of reasons, it was as if I'd been asleep since I'd come out here. Once I'd stopped grieving enough to function, I went about my life taking things at face value and not expecting much. The woman sleeping next to me was all I'd ever wanted, and now that I almost had her back, had *us* back,

I was afraid to move an inch or say a word, terrified she'd wake up and rush for the door.

"Five more minutes," she mumbled into the pillow. "I know you have to go to work." She rolled over and nuzzled into my neck, planting a kiss on my throat before her mouth opened in a wide yawn. I pulled her closer, my chest deflating with a bit of relief. She wasn't fully awake yet, but she wasn't trying to escape the minute she woke up. I was all about the little victories.

The way back to each other was a marathon—not a race—no matter how much I wanted to sprint toward the finish line.

"Do I look like I'm going anywhere?" I drifted my hand along her hip, chuckling to myself when she purred against me like a sexy little kitten. Thea had always been passionate and brave, it was what I loved the most about her. She never held back affection or love. She gave me all she had without limits or apology.

She'd told me she wanted to drown in me last night, but I'd been the one pulled under, and I never wanted to come up for air.

"I already told Joe I'd be in around ten. So you could go back to sleep, if you want." I traced the sweet spot behind her ear with the tip of my tongue until I drew a moan out of her. Her nails dug into my back when I grazed my teeth across her shoulder. "Or I could crawl under these sheets and wake you up the right way."

I cupped her breast and drifted my thumb over her nipple. Her head fell back with a loud whimper, and I burst out laughing.

"I love when you're loud." Our mouths fused together in a sloppy kiss, all the passion between us igniting again so easily. She pushed against my chest and straddled my hips, showing me how soaked and ready she was for me already.

I'd lost count sometime after one o'clock of all the orgasms we'd passed back and forth. Thea was still my little freckled tiger.

She didn't say it back, but I knew she still loved me as fiercely as she always had.

I just had to prove to her that I loved her even more.

"Ride me, sweetheart," I rasped, reaching into my nightstand drawer and palming what felt like my last condom. "I want to start my day inside you."

Her eyes glazed over before she ripped the foil edge and rolled the condom on, drifting her palm up and down my cock before guiding me in. Raising my hips off the bed until I was all the way inside, I was hypnotized by the slow roll of her gorgeous body as she took me deep, inching me in and out of her until I let out a moan at the sweetest torture. We were sleepy and slow, but my heart pounded for more.

"That's my girl," I growled when she moved faster, rubbing her quivering hands across my chest and dragging her nails down my stomach. I sat up, grabbed the nape of her neck and brought her mouth to mine.

"So beautiful when she comes." I reached between us and traced lazy circles around her clit that made her eyes roll back in her head as she rode me harder and faster.

When her mouth fell open as she clenched around me, I crashed my lips into hers to muffle the screams. She mewled into my mouth over and over until her body softened and her breathing slowed. Having her close, so pliable in my arms and holding on to me as if I was her lifeline, it was almost too much. I flipped us over, plowing into her until her body went rigid under me. I shook all over, spilling inside her with a guttural moan.

My head fell onto her chest as I snaked my arms under her, gasping to catch my breath. She wrapped her arms around my neck and kissed the top of my head. This was heaven on earth, and I didn't want either of us to let go.

"Well, I'm up now." I flashed her a hazy smile.

Thea covered her eyes as her shoulders shook with a chuckle.

"I guess I am, too."

I dropped a kiss on her forehead and dragged my lips over her eyelids and down her cheeks until I came back to her mouth. Now, that I was able to kiss her again, I couldn't stop.

"Stay right here," I said, tapping her nose before I shot off the bed to get rid of the condom.

When I came back to my bedroom, Thea's hands covered her face as she lounged on the bed. My stomach was queasy, afraid that all we did last night, and just now, finally sank in, and her possible panic tripped mine.

I sat on the edge of the bed and cupped her cheek. "What's going on in that brain of yours?"

She shifted to lie on her side, folding her hands under her head.

"I was a little selfish in asking to come back here last night without a way home."

I reared back, squinting before I shook my head.

"Why would you think I minded taking you home? Again, Joe still owes me, so you're not making me late or bothering me in any way. I'll get you some breakfast and take you back to the rental, if that's what you want." Her eyes closed as I sifted my fingers through her hair. "Right now, I'd like the sexy blonde to stay in my bed."

She sighed and shook her head. "You should have seen it when I first had it done. My sister didn't even recognize me. I wanted to look ... different."

She shrugged and gathered the covers around her as she sat up.

"Different?" I didn't like the way her eyes darted from mine.

"I'd look in the mirror and see us. I thought a hair cut would help me forget, or at least separate from it a bit. I know it sounds weird." She shifted on the bed with a nervous laugh. "Sue begged me not to chop it off like I wanted because I'd regret it, so I bleached the hell out of it, instead." She took a tangled lock between her fingers. "Shocked everyone, but I didn't totally hate it. I let it grow out a little so I looked different but still like me."

My stomach clenched as I bit back a cringe. Even with all the progress we'd made, I wondered if I'd ever repair all the ways I'd hurt her.

"What made you grow a beard?"

"Laziness," I admitted, running my hand along the bristles on my chin. "When I first came out here, I was lucky if I showered. We'd work on the restaurant all day and I'd just come home and pass out. I'd gotten used to it for so long, I found trimming it was just easier than shaving all the damn time."

Maybe I'd wanted to be different too, since I saw no clear path back to my old self and my old life, but admitting that to her was just plain cruel. I wanted to heal the old wounds, not douse them with salt.

"Works for you." Her brows jumped. "I sort of like it."

"I sort of figured that," my voice was husky as I moved closer until the back of her head fell against my headboard. "You seemed to appreciate it when my mouth was between your legs. Like the scratch on your thighs, baby?"

She laughed and scratched her nails along my jaw. "Yeah, I do."

"Maybe we can both be different but better. Like Dominic and Thea 2.0."

Her eyes narrowed as she squirmed back on the bed.

"Did you really just say 2.0? We're not a Terminator movie, babe."

"I know." I grabbed her hand and grazed her knuckles with my lips. "I want more time with you. Now that we're not skating around each other."

"I want that, too. But, small, slow steps. Although, this was a leap and a half." She cupped her forehead and massaged her temples. I searched her gaze, praying I wouldn't find regret looking back at me. "I was never good at resisting you. Even when I was trying to stay away from you, I wasn't." Her mouth turned down in a frown.

"Good." I smiled at her thinned eyes.

"For you, maybe. Can you take me back before the restaurant opens? I really don't want to do the walk of shame in front of Joe and Caterina in my dress from last night."

"They take almost daily walks of shame out of Joe's office. Those two are nothing to be concerned about." I cupped her chin. "But I'll take you back if that's what you really want. I have to work today, but I thought tonight, maybe if you were free or something?"

She inched closer, the corners of her mouth twitching.

"If you're asking me out, be direct."

"Direct?" I tapped my chin with my finger. "All right. Can I come over after work with some dinner for us to eat on that sick deck I spotted in the back of your rental, and can I make you come on one of the patio chairs?"

A blush crept up her cheeks as she covered her eyes. "Oh my God, stop."

She lifted her arm to push against my chest, but I pinned her down and tickled her sides.

"Yes," she gasped between breathless giggles before her

eyes went dark. "Bring me dinner, and we'll figure the rest out."

"Your wish is my command, my lady." When I leaned in to kiss her she laid her palm over my mouth.

"Since we're both up, before we get sidetracked again, I'm starving. Busy night, you know?"

I couldn't help the stupid smile cracking my cheeks.

"I do know. I don't have much here, but it's our early morning downstairs. I can get you breakfast and take you back. And," I ran my finger along her jaw. "I'll talk to Joe about a day off tomorrow. And I could stay, and not have to rush back. That is, if you want me to."

"I always want you to, which has always been my problem." She kissed my cheek. "Let me find my clothes and I'll get dressed. I think I have flats in my bag so hanging out in my dress for a while shouldn't be terrible."

I moved back to let her get up, my eyes following her as she scooped her clothes off my floor.

My chest pinched at what she said. She still didn't trust me completely, but again I was working on that.

Last night may've been a leap, but I still had miles to go.

30

DOMINIC

"So you guys are," Joe motioned from me to where Thea sat with Caterina and Ava on the patio near the beach with his finger, "together now?"

When we came downstairs, the pub was already open since Joe had wanted to train a couple of new waiters in the early morning. Caterina, I guessed, wanted more time with Joe before she took Ava to the beach like she usually did on Saturdays. They were more attached than Siamese twins. How perfect they were together often highlighted how lonely —and miserable—I was.

Now, I was attached to a woman of my own, although she wasn't mine in the official sense—yet.

"Yes, and no," I said, my eyes drifting to where Thea sat laughing with Caterina. "We're not, not together."

"Are you speaking in code or something?" Joe snickered as he lined the glasses up behind the bar.

"I meant I'm not rushing her, but she's not running from me anymore," I answered Joe while I kept my eyes on the wait staff as they set up.

My issue was getting her to stay.

"Her, too?" I heard Tommy ask Ben, one of the newer waiters who started last week. Ben did an all right job serving tables from what I could tell, but was so full of himself he barely fit his head in the door.

"Yep. These tourist towns are all the same. Women go on vacation with their friends, looking for a hook-up with a guy with a decent set of abs and without a receding hairline. All I have to do is crack a smile, and they jump in my lap."

My eyes rolled as I glanced back at Joe. Ben was your typical All-American college douchebag with a hard-on for women in their thirties. He hit on Caterina his first day here, before knowing who she was, and had been on Joe's shit list ever since. She'd laughed in Ben's face, but Joe wouldn't stop giving him a hard time. My opinion was that we were too busy to worry if the waiters were dicks or not. We just needed them to be reasonably polite to customers, keep the orders straight and not to drop anything on the way to the tables.

"Like that one outside." He pointed his thumb over his shoulder—in Thea's direction. "No one wears a dress like that to eat breakfast here. I love the ones who bounce from one hook up to another. You don't need to worry about drama or weird attachments after. Older women are the *best*. You need one to forget the Jordan bullshit you put yourself through, man."

While I appreciated his effort to help Tommy, suggesting my girl as a way to do it didn't sit very right with me. Joe and I leaned against the bar, waiting to hear what ridiculous crap would come out of his mouth next.

"Did he mean Thea?" Joe mouthed to me.

When I nodded slowly, he cracked up and shook his head.

"I'm serious," he pressed when Tommy tried to ignore him. "Watch, I'll go outside, and in five minutes I'll have a date for tonight, or my lunch break."

When Joe straightened and opened his mouth to say something, I held my hand up to stop him. Maybe I was a dick too, for looking a little too forward to his reaction when he realized how far he lodged his foot into his mouth.

When he turned to go outside, Thea was already back in the restaurant and heading back over to us with Caterina wheeling Ava behind her. Ben rushed over to approach her, chatting her up for a minute before leaning in to mumble something I couldn't quite hear. I bit back a smile when her eyes widened and she shook her head.

"Thanks for the offer, but I'm with someone, and he's the jealous type." She backed away and met my gaze with a half-smile tilting her lips.

"I don't care." Ben shrugged. "I won't tell him if you won't."

Caterina gaped at Joe and me, Joe covering his mouth with his fist to hide his smile. I leaned back on the bar and crossed my arms. It wasn't her refusal that made my chest swell since she would have shot him down whether or not I was in the picture, but she said she was *with* someone.

I had another straw to go along with all the others I'd grasped at this summer.

"He's right behind you, if you'd like to ask." She motioned to me with her chin.

Ben turned around, speechless and pale. This was the most amusement I'd had during the breakfast rush in a long time.

Thea made her way around Ben and wrapped her arm around my waist.

"Caterina is going to drive me back. We're going to take Ava to that little beach by the hotel. You don't have to be disturbed after all." She drifted her hand over the collar of my polo. As many times as I made fun of Joe for not so nonchalantly dragging Caterina to his office, I was *this* close to whisking Thea back to my apartment and not giving a single fuck who was watching.

"You don't disturb me, sweetheart." I pulled her in for a kiss. No tongue but hard enough to make the message loud and clear. "See you tonight."

She nodded with a tiny smile. "See you tonight."

"Make sure you cover up," I told her as my hands drifted up and down her arms. "I don't want you to get burned."

"I will, promise." She kissed my cheek. "How long are you going to make him suffer?"

"Only a few more minutes." I shrugged. "You have to make your own fun around here." I pecked her lips, searching her gaze for a long minute before she turned to join Caterina.

"Hey...look...um...if I knew," Ben stammered as he came closer. As comical as it still was, I decided to put him out of his misery.

"If you knew what? If you knew that she only hooks up with *me,* then you wouldn't have been talking all that shit about her in front of me?"

His eyes widened at my raised brow.

"A word of advice, women don't like to be conquests, no matter how decent your abs are."

I left to check on the busboys toward the front, peering over at Thea as she made her way out. A sexy grin stretched across her lips before she followed Caterina out the door.

Warmth exploded in my chest as a smile drifted across my lips.

Maybe we were more together than I thought.

31

THEA

Ava babbled to me while I bounced her in my arms. She was an adorable, feisty little thing. Her brows furrowed as she rambled on, already with so much to say.

"Her big mouth comes from my side of the family." Caterina laughed as she packed up the rest of their things into a huge beach bag. "Thanks for letting us come by. I'm used to the Ocean Cove crowds, so it was nice to spread out and relax."

"Well, with the hotel opening, there may be a bigger crowd next year, hopefully." I crinkled my nose at Ava, and my heart melted when she reached out to touch my cheek.

It had taken a while until the sight of a baby no longer gutted me, but I came around. Holding babies wasn't something I'd normally offer to do, but when Caterina handed her to me so she could gather their belongings, I didn't have the time to refuse or explain. Playing with Ava for the afternoon had been an unexpected joy. But it still reminded me of a time I wanted to forget, even though I knew I'd never be able to.

She scooped Ava out of my arms and buckled her in her stroller.

"Now you have plenty of time to get ready for your hot date tonight."

She glanced up with her eyebrows raised.

"I don't know if I'd call it a hot date. Dominic is coming by with some food, that's all."

"Shrugging it off doesn't work if you smile that big." She laughed, shaking her head as she stuffed everything under the carriage seat.

"Is it possible to be so happy you want to burst out of your skin and terrified at the same time?" I sighed, scooping the hair off my sweaty neck and twisting it into a bun on the top of my head.

Caterina looked me over with a sad smile before she unlocked the wheel in the back of the stroller. Ava's eyes were already growing heavy from digging in the sand all afternoon.

"Both of you light up whenever you're together." She dropped her hand on my arm while she wheeled Ava up the ramp leading us away from the beach. "I know you guys have a complicated past, but in the present, anyone can see the love is still all there."

"It's there," I allowed as I trudged along next to the stroller. "It's *always* been there."

But it wasn't enough then, and as much as I wanted to believe it was now, I couldn't shake the fear that it wasn't.

"I'm trying to understand the sudden long face of someone who went to breakfast in her dress from last night." She quirked a brow as we began the walk back to my house. I usually drove the short distance back and forth to the hotel but Caterina felt like walking, and I welcomed the opportunity to burn off all my nervous energy.

I couldn't help but laugh. "I told Dominic I didn't want to do the walk of shame in front of you guys, but he said you do it all the time out of Joe's office."

"Of course, he did. And for your information, we don't do it *all* the time." She rolled her eyes as we made our way down the street. "As much as he loves to give us a hard time, he's done so much for us."

"Like what?"

"He was always pushing Joe out the door, covering for him so we could spend time together when we first met. When I thanked him at our wedding, he said seeing us happy was thanks enough." She pulled Ava up my driveway and parked the stroller next to her car. "Because when you meet the one, you shouldn't blow it."

My nose burned for a moment, but I managed to bite the inside of my cheek hard enough to will away any threatening tears.

I nodded, taking the bags from the stroller and loading them into the trunk as Caterina settled her sleeping daughter in her car seat.

"And when I met you, and saw you both together, I realized why he'd said that. It kills him that he lost you back then."

It killed me, too.

"He told me he loved me last night, and I couldn't say it back. Not because I don't. I love him so damn much. But," I rested my elbow on top of Caterina's car and rubbed my eyes, "he scares me."

"He scares you because you love him too much?"

I shut my eyes and nodded. "You have no idea."

"Can I offer you my two cents?" she asked after shutting the car door.

"After I've unloaded more to you about what's going on with Dominic and me than to my family or any of my friends, please do."

She chuckled and squeezed my shoulder. "It's not quite

the same thing, as Joe and I don't have the same troubled history. When we tried to do long distance, and it became too hard, I ran because I didn't want to get hurt. I always felt too much for him, and I was scared, too. But my life without Joe," she glanced at her baby in the back seat, "wasn't a life."

I nodded, sucking in a deep breath and easing it out slowly. For the past four years, there was always a Dominic-shaped piece missing from my soul.

"Try to give it a shot, just for tonight."

She pulled me into a hug before climbing into her car and driving away.

I made my way inside, dropping my keys and setting my purse on the kitchen counter. When I dug through my bag to charge my phone, figuring it was dead since I purposely put it away for the afternoon, unread message alerts were still on the screen.

> **Dominic:** *Just checking to make sure you aren't sunburned. In case we do end up like we did last night, I don't want you sore. Or at least not sore like that ;)*

A loud laugh fell from my lips. We made do in Florida with my terrible burn, but we'd been a lot more athletic last night than in years past. It would suck to have limitations if we did end up in my bed tonight—which was the level above a forgone conclusion.

> **Dominic:** *I can't stop thinking about you. I'm annoying the shit out of Joe because I thought I saw you come back in about ten times today.*
> **Thea:** *I'm sorry. I put my phone away for the after-*

noon. But no burn, and I've been in Pentier Beach all day so that wasn't me.

Thea: *And I've been thinking about you all day, too.*

Dominic: *We're going to make it this time, sweetheart.*

Thea: *What makes you so sure?*

Dominic: *Because I won't stop fighting for us until we do.*

He didn't have to fight for me. I was always his. Maybe it was time I stopped fighting *him.*

32

DOMINIC

"Does Joe know that you stole all his food?" A wry grin stretched Thea's lips as she held the door open for me to come in.

I gave her a quick kiss since my hands were full. I didn't plan on bringing three bags full of food, but when I started packing, everything I picked made me think of something else. I knew Thea wouldn't be picky about the food. As long as I threw a couple of shrimp on a plate she would be happy, but I was obsessed with making all of our time together perfect.

I was so fixated on details because I was afraid it would all end soon. The distance didn't scare me, although managing the new space would make it more difficult to come into the city and see her, but I was sure I'd find a way to work that out.

It was the flash of hesitation I kept seeing in her eyes. I wasn't worried that she didn't want to be with me or that she didn't love me. It was that she didn't trust me, and I didn't blame her. We went from being on the verge of moving in together to me slowly isolating myself from her and everyone else.

"It's not *that* much food." I set it down on the dining room table and ambled back over to her. My heart raced at the sight of her tight tank top and painted on denim shorts. She knew I loved her in shorts, so I took that as a good sign of things to come tonight.

"We *are* only two people, unless you planned on a party stopping by."

"And share you, tonight? No way."

I wrapped my arms around her and pulled her close to me, kissing her crinkled forehead.

"And it's not *all* Joe's food. I have some news."

"Well, don't keep me in suspense. What news?"

"Over the years, I saved whatever money I made at the pub for the most part. I had a small apartment and didn't travel or anything since living out here always felt like a vacation. Plus, I had some insurance money from my mom that I didn't touch. So long story short—"

"That would be a first." She laughed when I swatted her thigh.

"I'm an investor in The Beach Pub now, not just a manager. Which means the new space is mine too, I won't just be managing it."

Her eyes widened as she clutched my biceps.

"That's amazing! I'm surprised Joe let you do that. He always talked about being his own boss and not having to answer to anyone."

"He did." I cocked my head from side to side. "But he also realized that if he wants to renovate the pub and keep the new place going, he needs capital. He's still the main owner, but I get to share in the profits, too. So think of this as *my* mountain of food."

"I hope you brought champagne, too, we need to celebrate

this." She gave me a soft kiss as her hand drifted down my cheek. "I'm happy for you. You deserve this." Her big smile never made it to her eyes. I knew she was happy for me, but I'd bet watching me fit into Ocean Cove so well and putting down roots hurt her all over again.

"That's not the only thing to celebrate, tonight." I put my finger under her chin to make her look up. "I couldn't wait to see you. The day dragged on until I got here."

"I thought about you all day, too. Spending the night with you, having dinner, it seems like forever ago, and at the same time, like you never left." Her fingertips skimmed down my chest.

"Come here." I grabbed her hand, pulling her toward the couch. When she sat down, I crouched in front of her and took one of her hands in mine.

"I always thought about you. You were always right there, like a dull pang of something missing. I tried to move on, too, but it was always hollow. So many times, I wanted to reach out to you, but I'd hurt you enough. Coming after you seemed selfish after you didn't respond. Or...maybe I was just a chicken shit and couldn't face you."

"What hurt me the most, even more than losing you," her voice cracked before she sucked in a breath, "was that I knew how much you were suffering alone. Sometimes, I'd think if I'd pushed more, not let you retreat so far into yourself—"

"It wouldn't have worked." I shook my head. "I needed to work it out on my own. Want to hear a crazy confession?" I quirked a brow.

"The food may get cold, but yes." She smiled. "You can confess anything you want to me."

"Steve dragged me to this grief counseling group at the hospital she was in when she died. He said he needed to go, and he was worried about me. Then made sure to point out how Mom would want us both to go, so what choice did I have?" I huffed out a laugh. "They said if you have unresolved issues with a loved one that you didn't get to deal with before they passed, write them a letter. I only went once, but I think Steve kept going for a few weeks."

Thea stayed silent, her hand massaging my neck and encouraging me to keep going. Why had I been so full of self-loathing years ago that I couldn't let her love me like this? It soothed me to finally let it all out in front of her. She'd tried back then, but I'd snap at her and close off until I told her I needed to be alone, permanently. I shut my eyes, willing away the roll of shame mixed with guilt that felt a lot like nausea.

"Before I left to come out here, he gave me a huge note-book. He said he started writing to Mom, and it helped. Maybe if I did it too, maybe I'd start to come around. I took it and said sure, never really intending to do anything with it. One night, I drank alone in my apartment and just started scribbling. A whole bunch of shit came out. I stuffed it into my nightstand drawer like I was shoving it into a mailbox to heaven or something." I shrugged, darting my eyes around the living room.

No one knew about that notebook, and I never planned on saying a word about it to anyone. A grown man writing to his dead mother at night wasn't a great conversation starter.

"It was weird, but it did sort of make me feel better."

"I'm glad. I'm sure you had a lot to say," she said, her eyes glossy and sad.

"The more I drank, the crazier the letters became. Then one night, I stopped writing to her, and started writing to you."

She flinched back a moment as her eyes thinned to slits.

"You wrote to me?"

I nodded. "I wrote I'm sorry in about a thousand different ways. I even asked you to wait for me, because I could never do that in real life. That notebook was the altered reality my screwed up mind could handle at the time."

"You could have." She rolled her eyes. "I ended up doing it anyway."

"I didn't deserve that. Hell, I don't deserve it now. I still don't think it's right to try to get you back." I drifted my hands up and down her thigh. "But, I need you. I always did."

She rose from the sofa and climbed on my lap, sliding her hand across my jaw.

"I need you, too. You just scare me a little."

"I scare you?"

"It happens when you love someone too much. And I always loved you too much."

I cupped the back of her neck as I exhaled in a little relief at hearing the words.

"Sometimes," she whispered, looping her arms around my neck, "I pictured what would have happened if your mom hadn't passed away. I thought of us living together, having break-fast in the mornings, you sneaking in those old movie posters you'd plastered your apartment walls with when you thought I wasn't looking." A watery smile curved her lips. "Waiting up for you when you worked nights. It would have been amazing."

I moved her around on my lap until she straddled me on the floor and dropped my head into her chest. She had no idea how amazing it would have been.

But I had hopes that it still could be.

"At the risk of sounding like a total asshole, I think I needed to come here. It wasn't possible to grieve where I saw my mother everywhere. As lonely as I was without you, it felt like I belonged here. But, I like to think that maybe," I threaded my fingers through her hair, "the fact that you ended up here means I'm where I'm supposed to be. That my mother is helping us find our way back to each other."

"If Linda could, I'm sure she would," she cradled my face, running her thumbs back and forth on my cheeks. "Not that she would recognize her bearded, tatted-up son."

"Don't pretend you don't love it." I grabbed her hips and yanked her closer.

She laughed for a minute before her smile faded.

"I love *you*, Dominic. Then, now, and always."

She lowered her lips to mine with slow tiny pecks that made the blood sing in my veins. I glided my tongue along the seam of her lips, and they parted on a sweet moan. Instead of devouring her in a frenzied hunger like I did last night, I savored her slowly, reveling in how her body rocked against mine on the floor just enough for my growing erection to swipe at her core. The more she moved, the more her shorts inched up her thighs.

"Just one favor," she asked, chasing her breath after we broke apart.

"Anything, sweetheart." I weaved my hand around a fistful of her hair.

"Please don't break me again," she pleaded in a breathless whisper.

"Believe me when I tell you that I will never lose you again. You'll have to fight me off. "

She covered my mouth with hers, our kiss igniting as I fell back against the carpet. We pulled at each other's clothes as we wrestled back and forth on the floor, a mess of lips, tongues, and impatience.

"All I'll ever want is you. And you in these shorts—"

She straightened to peel her tank top off, throwing it in my face before she unhooked her bra and threw it behind her.

"And you still talk too much." She climbed on top of me and brought her lips back to mine. I rubbed my hands up and down her naked back and shut the hell up.

I finally had my girl back. There was nothing else to say.

33

THEA

Dᴏᴍɪɴɪᴄ ᴡᴀs ᴡʀᴀᴘᴘᴇᴅ around me like a hot, muscular vine. His arms were cinched around my waist and his head was buried into the crook of my neck. I used to have to elbow him in his sleep to get him to loosen his grip, but I didn't want to this morning. After all those mornings of waking up lonely —even when I hadn't been alone—I enjoyed having him all around me.

I settled into the pillow, smiling at his sigh of satisfaction when I scratched my nails up and down his arm. For the first time that I could remember in a long time, I woke up light and happy with a mix of joy and relief coursing through me, although there was still a twinge of guilt.

Last night had been the perfect opportunity to unload the burden I'd been carrying since that night in the emergency room, but I didn't want to ruin anything when things were so perfect.

Especially, when they seemed a little too perfect.

"Hey, why did you stop?" He moved his head and dragged light kisses over the nape of my neck.

"Because it's time to wake up." I managed to squirm

enough away from Dominic to glance at my phone on my bedside table. "It's almost ten."

"I have nowhere to be," his voice was husky and still full of sleep as his hand drifted up my torso to cup my breast. My nipple pebbled against his fingers as I leaned into the delicious poking at my back. "And neither do you."

"Yeah, but..." I lost my train of thought as my head sank deeper into the pillow. His hand drifted lower and settled between my legs. He groaned and hissed out a curse when he found me already wet. I never needed much prep time when it came to Dominic. He just needed to be there, and I loved that he was.

"There's my girl," he growled into my ear, my hips following the tiny circles he made around my clit, getting me wetter and harder with each go around.

"Aren't you hungry?" My legs fell open as I whimpered, both craving the release so badly my eyes teared but wishing it away so I could enjoy it.

"Starving," he growled, sinking his teeth into my neck. I traced my finger along the bite marks indented into my skin, hoping it didn't leave a mark.

"I can't go to work with a hickey, you animal," I tried to scold but the words came out in a needy, breathless whisper.

"Then I better leave the marks where no one can see." He cupped my chin and turned my face towards his, giving me a deep but quick kiss.

He lifted the sheets and climbed on top of me, setting between my legs as he trailed open-mouthed kisses from the middle of my collarbone, down my stomach, stopping right before the ache between my legs. I cried out when he sucked on the damp skin inside my thigh, knowing I'd have a big bruise and not caring in the least.

He raised his head, licking his lips. I glanced at the red

and swollen welt in the shape of his mouth and instead of being pissed off, I loved it. I looked back at him with a sleepy smile and speared my hand through his hair, grabbing the back of his head and pushing him toward where my body was almost screaming for him.

"Mine," he whispered, giving the growing bruise a quick lick before he dove between my legs, sucking on my clit with the same ferocity. I fisted the tangled sheets around me as my legs flailed back and forth, the rippling up and down my spine both too much and not enough.

I grabbed one of the pillows and held it over my face, screaming into it as I came apart on his tongue, every nerve ending from my hips to my toes sparking to life.

His deep chuckle vibrated against my stomach.

"Where's Thea?" He peeled my hands off the pillow and threw it behind him. "Did I make her come so hard that she had to hide?"

"Get inside me before you start annoying me." I sank my fingers into the firm swell of his ass and pulled him into me.

"Have I told you how much I love you yet today?"

He leaned over the bed and reached for the new box of condoms that was already half empty. We'd come back into each other's lives over a month ago, but last night and today felt like a true reunion. He felt like mine, and I felt like his, and I was so high on joy that I never wanted to leave this bed.

Eventually, I'd have to leave not only this bed but this town, too. But I wasn't worried. We'd come this far, and I had faith we'd figure something out.

He slid inside me and groaned as if he hadn't been there for most of the night. I hoped this was the start of making up for lost time on a lot of things.

"So good to be home," he said through gritted teeth as he inched in and out of me. Each time we came together it was slower, both of us shedding some of the fear that the other would disappear.

"Inside me is home?" I slid my hand to the back of his neck, my lips twitching into a smile. He winced each time he went deep, as if it was too good to be real.

"*You're* my home, Thea. Everything about you is home."

He covered my mouth with his until his body went rigid above me. I clenched around him, falling over the edge a second time as he pulsed into me.

"Eventually," I sighed, swiping the damp hair away from his sticky forehead, "we're going to have to get out of bed and get dressed."

"But that day doesn't have to be today. Maybe a quick trip to the kitchen for breakfast, only because I need fuel for round...whatever we're on."

"If you want me to make breakfast, all you have to do is ask."

"I brought breakfast. There are cinnamon rolls in one of the bags, we just need to heat them up for a few minutes. Then I can spend the rest of today licking the icing off of you."

"You need a cold shower, Gallo." I rolled my eyes, hiding my smile as I leaned over to my dresser to pull out a pair of underwear when he caught my wrist.

"No clothes." He quirked a brow and slowly shook his head.

"It's a little dangerous to cook naked." I stood and pulled my robe from behind the door. "At least put your boxers back on and come downstairs with me."

"Fine," he huffed and plucked his boxers from the pile of his clothes on the floor as he headed for the bathroom to get rid of the condom. "But once we come back up here, the clothes come off."

Shaking my head, I headed down stairs and shoved two cinnamon buns from the large paper bag of pastries into the toaster oven.

"We should sit on the deck later," Dominic said as he peered out the back door.

"You need clothes for that too, babe."

"Why? Who can see us?" He grumbled as he loaded up the coffee maker.

I pictured all our mornings like this: the both of us playfully bickering during breakfast after long, amazing nights together. I put the warm rolls on a plate and turned back towards the stairs.

"You can be naked again in just a few minutes, try to hold out."

He swatted my ass and looped an arm around my waist to pull me back.

"You *love* me naked. Get upstairs, lose the robe, and wait for me."

I climbed up the stairs as Dominic finished the coffee, my face and the rest of me flushing hot, and did what I was told until he came back into the bedroom balancing two steaming mugs.

"This is nice," he mumbled around a piece of cinnamon roll as he lounged on my bed.

"It is," I agreed as I sipped coffee under the sheets. "Like all those Sunday mornings back at your apartment in Queens. I don't know why we always ended up at your place and not mine."

"Because you were afraid of your parents seeing me leave in the morning, even though they were two blocks away." He leaned back to rest the back of his head on the iron headboard.

"Ah yes, I remember. Which was silly since they knew I was always with you anyway."

"Have you seen them since you've been out here?"

I shook my head as I ate the last bite on my plate. "Moira was here the one weekend, but I haven't seen them since I left. My mother's been after me to come home because she didn't like the idea of me out here alone."

"They don't like you out here alone with me, right?"

Once I told them that I was back with Dominic, I wasn't sure how they'd take it. They'd loved him at the time but hated how long it had taken me to get over him, or to be able to pretend in front of them I was over him.

I shrugged at the crook of his brow. "Yes and no, I guess. I told her that I didn't want to make the drive but, I was a little afraid to go home."

"Afraid? Why?"

I averted his gaze a minute before meeting his narrowed dark eyes. "At first, it was because I didn't want to lose the nerve to come back out here, but then I just didn't want to be away from you, even though I kept you at a distance. Stupid and silly."

"Nope, not stupid at all." He put his coffee mug down on the bedside table and pulled me toward him. "First, if you did lose your nerve, which you're too stubborn to do, I would have made the drive to Queens to get you. And second, I understand because knowing you were around, I never wanted to go too far, either."

He swiped a glop of icing off what was left of his roll and dragged it around my nipple.

"We are two sad and pathetic people, and I love it."

He leaned in to kiss me then dropped his head to lick across my breast. I squealed before my back fell against the bed, trying to squirm out of his hold when he pinned my arms above me.

"Dominic, stop!" I screamed before we both stilled at what I thought was a knock at the door.

"Did you hear something?" I asked before hearing it again only stronger.

"You didn't get the doorbell fixed, did you?" He dropped his head on my chest with a groan.

"Why? The only ones who visit are you and Caterina."

I shrugged my robe back on before I headed downstairs.

"You're calling maintenance again on Monday, or I'll fix it myself," he shouted after me.

"Yeah, yeah," I taunted over my shoulder before I peeked through the side window next to the door, spotting my sister and both of my parents.

Shit.

I glanced down at my robe, and realized how short it cut across my thighs, my *pantyless* thighs. Dominic was naked upstairs and it was too late to change what I was wearing or warn him.

Well, this was one way to break the news.

I clicked the locks open, shutting my eyes a second before I braced myself.

"Mom, Dad, Moira, hi! This is such a surprise."

My sister crossed her arms, laughing into her hand while my parents regarded me with matching crinkled foreheads.

"Did you know your doorbell doesn't work?" Mom said kissing my cheek before stepping inside.

"We thought maybe you were out, but your car is in the driveway." My father pulled me into a hug. I wrapped one arm around him and pulled down the hem of my robe with the other. "We would have been here sooner if not for the damn traffic."

I let the door slam behind my sister, hoping that would

send up some kind of signal to Dominic in the bedroom to put pants on.

"You are so busted!" Moira whispered from behind me.

I swiveled my head and glowered at her, attempting to cross my arms but stopped when I noticed how much that made my robe ride up even more.

"Shut up!" I whispered back, which only made her laugh harder.

"Like I don't know you, baby sister, and you didn't slam the door to send up some kind of code to tell Dominic to put his pants on."

"How do you know it's Dominic?"

She dropped a hand to my shoulder. "I knew Dominic would end up here before you did, honey. And to think, I complained they were dragging me out here early on a Sunday. This was too good to miss."

I jabbed her in the arm.

"Mom, Dad, do you want some coffee? I only have the one cup at a time machine, but I can make you some." I said much louder than I needed to, hoping my voice carried up the stairs.

"Why are you speaking so loud?" Mom asked. "We aren't that old." She chuckled. "How are you feeling? I knew you'd get a nasty infection while you were here alone." She *tsked*, shaking her head.

My father looked me over, his lips pursed and his nose crinkled, as if he knew what he was looking at, but didn't want to say it out loud.

"It doesn't look like she's here alone, Debbie."

"Could you excuse me a second?" I crept toward the steps in an attempt to escape. "Help yourself to whatever you want, I think there are some pastries left in the bag on the counter."

"Wait," my mother called after me after I made it to the second step.

"If you're headed upstairs, maybe you should take these with you." She picked my bra and tank top up from where they laid on the floor by the staircase and handed it to me, her eyes thinned to slits.

"Thanks," was all I could say before I sprinted up the stairs.

My face heated as I trudged into the bedroom.

"Listen," I started before shutting the door behind me. When I turned to Dominic, he was already fully dressed and sitting on the bed. He met my gaze and burst out laughing before rolling onto the floor.

"Oh my God, you think this is funny?" I swatted him with my tank top. "I greeted my parents half-naked and my mother just handed me my clothes that she found on the floor."

"I'm laughing at the signals you tried to send up here. Slamming the door, talking to your parents like they needed hearing aids." He folded over in laughter. "I love you so damn much, come over here." He pulled me to the floor. "We'll take them to the pub for brunch, they can't yell at you or beat me up there."

"Okay," I kissed him and shoved his still shaking shoulder. "It's still not funny, you big jerk."

"Hopefully, I can make it up to them eventually." His smile faded. "Hey, if I were them, I'd hate me, too. The important thing is that *you* don't hate me."

"I could never hate you. Even at the worst of it, I still loved you."

He pecked my lips and stood, holding his hand out to lift me up.

"Get dressed, Theodora. I'll wait for you in the kitchen."

"Bite me, Domenico."

"I'll have to wait until everyone leaves." He slapped my ass and made his way out the door.

Despite myself, my lips curled into a grin. I threw on a yellow sundress after digging for a bra and underwear when I turned to a knock on the door.

"I'll be right out," I called over my shoulder.

"It's just me."

I relaxed at my sister's voice.

"I figured being up here was better than the uncomfortable small talk in your kitchen."

"Ugh, I knew they'd be like that." I shook my head.

"Give them a minute, Thea. When I came out here the last time *you* were like that. So I guess you guys are back, all in?"

I nodded. "All in. I know you all don't agree with it."

"Thea, if you can make it work this time, I think that's great. I'm concerned, I won't lie, but for you to let him back into your life he must have proven himself. Mom and Dad will be a harder sell but what you feel is what matters."

"Thanks." I relaxed for the first time since they came in. "I appreciate that."

"I'm guessing he knows?" She leaned against the wall with her arms crossed.

"Not yet," I said, squaring my shoulders as I tensed up all over again.

"You need to tell him."

"Why?" My hands dropped to my sides. "So he can feel bad for no reason? It happened and now it's over."

I slipped into my flip flops and went to leave before Moira stepped in front of me.

"Thea, it's not over. If you don't tell him, you guys will never fully heal because it's still weighing on you. I'm afraid something will happen and it will just come out. You look happy, and I don't want to ruin that, but you can't wait much longer. Promise me you'll do it soon."

"I promise," I relented, but she still wouldn't let me pass.

"Look me in the eye and promise."

"I promise."

I knew I had to, and I knew if I didn't it would come out anyway at the worst possible time, but I loved the new bubble I was nestled in with Dominic.

I was afraid to test how easily it would pop.

34

DOMINIC

"WHAT IS WITH YOU, TODAY?" Jordan asked me as she waited for a pitcher of mimosas by the bar, squinting as she gave me a once over.

"What is with me, today?" I narrowed my eyes back at her. "I'm fine."

"You may want to tone down the dopey grin since you walked in," Joe whispered behind me. "I think the wait staff isn't used to seeing you this happy."

"Am I that much of a grumpy asshole every day?"

"Not *every* day." Jordan shrugged as she took the drinks and scurried back to her table.

"If there is one thing you could count on that girl for, it's the blunt and honest truth." Joe snickered as she sauntered away.

I had to laugh with him. I'd like to think I was a good manager, but even I knew I was moody at times. I had Thea back, so all the little things that irked me seemed too insignificant to give a second thought to. I even gave Ben a wave and good morning when I came in, although I pulled Thea closer when I did it.

"I didn't expect to see you today."

"I didn't expect you to see me, either. I planned on being at Thea's rental for the day until her parents surprised her this morning. I thought coming here would somehow make it less awkward."

I leaned against the bar and glanced over to Thea. She sat at the edge of the table, nodding at something her father said when she caught my gaze and smiled.

"That's probably what Jordan means. You're acting like you smoked something on the way in."

"Is it a crime to be happy all of a sudden? I didn't bother you when you first met Caterina and attached yourself to her hip."

He cocked his head to the side and rolled his eyes. "Yes, you did."

I reluctantly nodded. "Yeah, I did."

"Why is it awkward? I thought you got along with her parents."

"I did, but then I left and I broke Thea's heart. She's forgiven me, I hope, but her parents haven't given me more than one-word answers since I first saw them this morning. And her mother found Thea's clothes in the living room from last night, so that may have something to d—"

"I get it," Joe said, wincing as he raised his hand. "My parents dropped in for a random visit the summer I met Caterina and caught us...off guard like that. Granted, my parents thought it was funny—"

"And were probably relieved you weren't a hermit like they thought."

He scowled at me then shrugged.

"Probably. But, if one of Caterina's uncles had found us like that at the beginning, I would've had a broken nose and cracked jaw."

"Her father did look like he wanted to slug me, but I don't think it was because of that. I hurt Thea—a lot. It may take a while, but I'll get them to trust me again. I'm not going anywhere, so they'll eventually have no choice but to tolerate me."

"That sure, already?" He quirked a brow.

"I was always that sure. I was just a little messed up for a bit and forgot. Trust me, Joe. I'm never losing her again."

I pushed off the bar and headed to her table, sliding into the vacant seat next to Thea.

"When are you guys heading back?" I asked as I draped my arm over the back of Thea's chair. I peered down to the end of the table where her parents were, neither of them rushing to answer me.

"Today," Moira finally said. "Dad drove out here, and I'm driving back. They called me last night with the idea to surprise Thea." She smiled around the rim of her glass. "But we got surprised instead, right little sister?"

Thea glowered at her sister as she leaned back in the chair.

I rested my chin on her shoulder. "Did they ground you, yet?" I whispered.

She laughed and elbowed my side before turning to kiss my cheek.

"If they did, it would be worth it," she said, cupping my neck. I wished my original plan to stay naked and in bed with her all day had worked out.

I wanted her all to myself today, and for the rest of my life.

Our heads whipped toward the end of the table when her mother cleared her throat.

"Thea told us the restaurant at the hotel is opening soon. I know you've both been working on it all summer."

I rubbed Thea's shoulders and nodded, hoping that

maybe since Mrs. Kelly spoke directly to me, the ice was breaking.

"I've only been working on the restaurant, but she's been working on the entire hotel. Managing the budgets, keeping the timelines. She's amazing." I kissed her temple.

Her lips curled in a bashful smile as a blush stained her cheeks.

"I'm okay." She shrugged with a laugh. "Dominic won't only be managing, he's part owner of The Beach Pub."

When I glanced across the table, both of her parents eyed me with the same scrutinizing stare.

"Glad to see you've made a home here," Mr. Kelly said. Something about his tone had me on edge.

His daughter was my home, but I had a feeling telling him that would fall on deaf and bitter ears.

"It's a really nice area, Dad. That's why my company is investing here. Great tourism opportunities and a good place to settle. With The Beach Pub so popular, I think the new restaurant may do even better." She picked up my hand and slid her palm against mine.

"Hey guys," Caterina breezed over to the table, looking between Thea and me with a furrowed brow. "I thought you were off today."

"Change in plans," we both said at the same time.

Thea flashed a grin over her shoulder at me before she stood.

"Mom, Dad, this is Caterina."

"Nice to meet you." Caterina extended her hand. "I heard a lot of nice things about you from Thea."

"Same," Thea's father smiled and took Caterina's hand. "We were glad when Thea told us she had a friend out here. We were worried thinking about her here alone."

Caterina's smile faded, most likely picking up on the tension.

"I'm from Brooklyn, and my friends are still mostly there. I made fast friends with Thea, so I was glad when she came out here, too. If you'll excuse me, I'm going to sneak and get a mimosa while my six-month old is still sleeping in her carriage by the bar."

"I'd love one right now," Thea said, not hiding her heavy sigh before turning back to me. "Babe, do you want anything?"

That was my cue to follow her and escape this stifling tension, but I was never one to back down.

"No thank you, sweetheart. I'm good." I shook my head as her eyes pleaded with me to come with her.

"I'll come. I'm allowed one drink and I think it would come in handy, right now," Moira stood and followed Thea and Caterina.

I sat back down and rested my elbows on the table.

"Mr. and Mrs. Kelly, I'm sure I'm not your favorite person. But please know that I love your daughter very much."

"Did you love her back then?" Mrs. Kelly leveled me with a glare. "I hated thinking of her out here alone and all her old wounds opening up from spending time with you."

I nodded, trying to ignore the jab in my gut from thinking of her old wounds caused by me.

"Yes, I loved her then, too, but I was in a bad place. It's no excuse, and I've been sorry every day for years. I hate that I hurt her and I intend to spend the rest of my life making it up to her."

Mrs. Kelly opened her mouth to say something when her husband dropped a hand on her elbow.

"My daughter seems happy now, but I remember a time when she was devastated and alone. Do you know what it was like for her?" His chest rose as he took in a long breath. "You can understand why we're both concerned."

"I do, and I don't blame you. But I promise, I'm never going anywhere. I was beyond lucky to get a second chance with her, and I assure you I won't ever take that for granted."

I caught the both of them looking over my shoulder. Moira shook her head slowly at them both in my periphery and mouthed something to them that I couldn't decipher.

"Maybe we can stop by the hotel." Thea drifted her hand across my back and squeezed my shoulder before she sat back down. "It's not quite finished yet, but we can give you a tour."

Her hopeful smile made my heart sink. I had a weird feeling there was something she wasn't telling me. I knew how upset she was when we split up, but now it seemed as if maybe I didn't know the whole story. I understood her parents worry and reluctance at us being together again, but there was more to it.

I needed to get her alone later and find out what she was holding back.

"We would but we need to head back after brunch." Mrs. Kelly's smile was tight.

Thea pursed her lips at her mother. "You came to visit me only to spend most of the day in the car?"

"We were worried about you, but we see you're okay out here." Mr. Kelly said while holding his gaze on me. I wasn't sure if that was an olive branch or a warning.

Thea's hand slid under the table and squeezed my knee.

A couple of hours ago, I was floating high on Thea and our new beginning, not realizing the past may still be haunting us.

After her parents left I suggested taking a ride to the hotel. Thea was chatting up a storm, but for once I was the quiet one.

"I've never been here on a Sunday." Thea's arm slid through mine as we stepped into the hotel. "It's spooky without all the drilling."

Digging into my pocket for the key to the restaurant, my eyes lingered on Thea. She hugged my free arm and kissed my cheek. A brick in my stomach kept me from basking in her love tonight.

"Are you okay?" she asked, running her fingers through the hair at the back of my neck. "You seem a little tense. Did my parents say anything to you?"

"Nothing I didn't expect." I shrugged and pushed the door open.

"Wow, it looks awesome," she gasped. "It looks like a real restaurant. Of course, you hung up that picture."

She pointed to the framed poster of the Rat Pack under the Sands sign in old time Las Vegas.

I barked out a laugh. "Of course. I thought a couple of posters would give it a different feel. Joe and I agreed it should be the same but a little different."

"Smart." She wrapped her arms around my waist and kissed my chin. "Now, tell me what my parents said."

I tucked a lock of hair behind her ear before resting my forehead against hers.

"They're still angry with me because of how upset you were after I left."

"I know, but once they get to know you again, it'll all be water under the bridge." She ran her hands down the cotton of my T-Shirt. "I love you, and I'm all that matters." She cocked her head to the side. "Didn't you say that this morning?"

"I love you, too." I cinched my arms around her. "And yes, you're all that matters. But is there something that happened after I left that you aren't telling me?"

I noticed Thea flinch and try to shake it off.

"I told you, I was more or less broken, but I survived. You were suffering too, I get that now. Can't we just move forward?"

"I want to move forward more than anything, but we can't shake the past if we don't deal with it, right?" I tapped her chin to get her to look up. "You can tell me anything. You don't have to sugarcoat it or hold back."

"I know, but a little at a time, okay?"

"Okay," I allowed for the moment. "Because all I want is to move forward with you." I sifted my fingers into her hair. "But, I'm selfish and want you to stay. Stay with me, live with me, like we planned before life went to total shit."

"You do?" Her nose crinkled. "Don't you think that's fast?"

"Fast?" I chuckled, shaking my head. "I've wanted this for years. I want more of this morning. Your nails on my arm, breakfast in bed." I slid my hands down her back.

"I'd love that." She cradled my face. "I have to go back to the city next week. I'll be here when the hotel opens, but I have meetings, and they may want to reassign me in the meantime."

"You said you wanted to find something else, anyway." I turned my head to kiss her palm. "Stay with me, sweetheart."

"Why are you so hard to say no to?" Thea groaned.

"Because you belong with me. And I belong with you. We're together either way, my suggestion saves us a lot of gas and time on the highway."

Her head fell into my chest. We were robbed of so much time, I had to grab it back where I could.

"I have a surprise for you," I took her hand and led her over to the bar in the back.

"This looks like the bar at the pub, not as big but I like the lighter wood." She ran her hand along the counter.

I lifted a bottle of champagne from the shelf in the back.

"My father sent me this. Turns out we have a wine salesman in the family. Ricci is supposed to be a good brand according to him."

"I've heard of Ricci. Female-owned company, too. I guess this place is official if you have liquor stocked at the bar."

"True." I nodded. "This is for us, after closing time on the day this place opens. I want to celebrate what brought us back together."

Thea scrubbed her hand down her face.

"Do you have to be so damn charming? God, it's annoying." She grabbed the back of my neck and crashed her lips into mine. The kiss was long and deep, neither of us wanting to stop as her back hit the counter.

It was an unspoken promise and the beginning of things to come. After all these years on pause, my life was finally starting.

35

DOMINIC

"I'm starving. Shouldn't the owners get served quicker than this?" Caterina slurred.

Thea and I shared a laugh. Caterina's mother had come in for the weekend and offered to take Ava for the night so they could go out. 'Out' when it was this busy at the end of the summer still meant the pub, but we took a table on the patio and pretended to be customers on a double date. After her third RumChata shot, her speech was loud and slow.

"How about some water, baby?" Joe crooned as he brought the glass to her lips.

She took a sip while throwing him a scathing look.

"Our daughter cut three teeth this week, and I haven't slept this badly since we brought her home. I know you're keeping long hours too, but at least you have a break from all the screaming."

"Not completely," I said. "Jordan's boyfriend caught her making out with Tommy outside last night. We had to break up the fight before someone called the cops."

Caterina's mouth dropped open.

"You're kidding!"

"Not that it was a surprise. We called it in June." I snickered and scanned the crowd for them both to make sure they weren't anywhere near each other. We told them to keep their distance when they worked together since we couldn't alternate shifts with it this crazy. "My throat is still sore from yelling at them to break it up."

"I guess you're both dealing with screaming children these days," Thea chuckled. "And I suppose that's why you didn't talk much when you came over last night." She scratched her nails across my back. "For once."

"Do you think I want to waste time talking about those two? I have better uses for my mouth on your last weekend here." I buried my head in the crook of her shoulder and took her earlobe in between my teeth.

"You know we're both still sitting here, right?" Joe lifted a brow when we peered across the table.

"Like I haven't heard and seen worse from the two of you." I cringed as I took a long pull from my beer bottle.

"I'll be back. I'm not going that far." She rested her chin on my shoulder with her bottom lip jutted out in an exaggerated pout.

"I know, sweetheart. When they got together," I nudged my chin in Joe and Caterina's direction, "you would have thought New York City and Ocean Cove were in different countries."

"It was far enough at the time," Joe said, his eyes narrowed. "And keep that in mind when you're moping around here like a lost puppy after Thea leaves, like I know you will be."

"Aw, babe." Thea looped her arms around my neck. "You don't have to mope. I'll be back before either of us knows it."

"Damn right, you will." I leaned in to give her a kiss when I heard a familiar voice call my name.

"Dominic! I thought that was you! Wow, this place looks amazing."

I tensed up when I turned and recognized who it was.

We met April four years ago when I first came out here. She worked at one of the local bars and would always linger around while Joe and I were still building the restaurant from when it used to be a dive bar. I was out of my catatonic phase but was still mostly mute. That didn't stop her from trying to chat me up every day.

One night, Joe suggested we go have a drink to blow off some steam. We both woke up the next morning hungover with a load of our own regrets. It was the night I finally started to open my eyes. When I woke up next to someone who wasn't Thea, the realization of what I'd done and what I'd lost shocked me back to life.

"Hey April, what brings you back to Ocean Cove?" Joe asked as his eyes darted from her to me.

I hoped we'd make quick small talk and she'd be on her way. I could explain she was just a girl that used to live around here and leave it at that, although Thea would be smart enough to know there was more to it. I was certain that what I did wouldn't matter as much as *when* I did it.

"My cousin still lives a couple of towns over. We're the bachelorette party in the corner." She pointed to the group of girls at a large table inside. I recognized the girl with the bride sash as Kim, her cousin who'd worked with her in the bar and ended up with Joe that night.

"Tell Kim we said congratulations," I said, praying she'd take the hint and leave.

"Yeah," she exhaled a long breath. "She's the last one of us. I can't believe how you guys built this place up. Things are a lot different since that crazy night four years ago." Her eyebrows jumped and I sensed Thea stiffen beside me.

Fuck.

"Well, I'll let you get back to your night. Nice to see you guys, again."

April sauntered off, oblivious to the bomb she just dropped.

"Four years ago?" Thea asked. "I thought when you came here you were so out of it you and Joe didn't even speak."

"He was," Joe offered in my defense. "When he first came here, we spent long days knocking down walls and sanding down everything. I pushed him out one night to get a drink after a long day, that's all."

She sucked in a breath as she pressed her hands on the table.

"If that was all, then why did the two of you cringe when she came to the table?" Thea's voice shook and my stomach bottomed out in panic.

This couldn't derail us, but her ticking jaw told me that we were sprinting in that direction.

"And all this happened when you *first* came out here?"

I spied Joe wince as we all watched Thea put the pieces together.

"Thea," I started, but didn't know how to finish. There was nothing I could do or say, she was too smart to be lied to.

"Well, I'm glad you found a way out of your crippling grief long enough to stick your dick in one of the locals after a long day of dry wall." Her chair screeched as she shot up and grabbed her purse. "Goodnight, Caterina, Joe. I'm leaving."

Thea cut her way through the restaurant toward the parking lot. I ran after her, screaming her name but she either didn't hear me over the loud din of the crowd, or she was ignoring me.

I finally caught up to her, grabbing her arm and spinning her around to make her look at me.

"Thea, let me explain, please," I begged. "It was one drunken, stupid night a long time ago—"

I fell back when she slapped me across my face, the loud smack echoing across the parking lot.

"How could you do that? Do you know how long it was before I could even look at anyone again, much less let anyone touch me?" Her voice screeched as thick tears streamed down her face. "I cried for you every night, and I couldn't even let myself be mad at you because you were grieving for your mother." She swiped at her cheeks with the palm of her hand. "God, what a fucking idiot I am. You weren't out here a month I bet before you moved on."

"No! I never stopped loving you. Ever." I clutched her by the arms, panic and desperation filling me with the worst kind of dread. "That night I realized what a horrible mistake I made and tried to call you, but I was too late."

"Am I right? What was it, like a month?" Her nostrils flared as the tears continued to snake down her cheeks.

"I don't know. I didn't keep track of time back then. Maybe, I'm honestly not sure," I stammered, wondering when the hell I went from having all my dreams coming true to living my worst nightmare.

"Want to know what I was doing a month after you left?" She linked her arms over her chest, her hands shaking as she tried to bury them under her elbows.

"You said you were in the hospital for appendicitis when I tried to call you."

"I lied." Her jaw ticked as she stepped closer to me. "I did spend the weekend in the hospital after having emergency surgery. I lost our baby the month after you left."

The blood drained from my head as I fell back again, this time from my insides clenching and twisting as if I'd been shot. Everything was spinning around me and I couldn't breathe. I held on to the edge of the trunk of Thea's car to stay upright.

"Our baby? Thea, what are you talking about?"

My brain couldn't absorb what she was saying.

"I didn't know I was pregnant until I almost died from it. I grieved a baby I didn't even know about—by myself—because how could I come to you with another loss? But what about *my* losses, Dominic?" she bellowed, digging her finger into her chest.

She shook her head and backed away.

"I never should've come here in the first place."

She climbed into her car and sped away. My limbs wouldn't move as shock filtered through my body.

I promised I'd fight for us until we made it, but I thought we already had.

I was the fucking idiot.

36

THEA

FOUR YEARS AGO

"Come on, kiddo. One foot then the other." Moira smiled as she tried to make a joke.

I clutched her shoulder as I slowly lifted one leg into a pair of sweatpants that she held open for me on the floor. Moving any part of my body, even a centimeter, made my eyes tear up. Who knew that having abdominal surgery would be so painful all over? I craved some relief from the agony shooting across my stomach and squeezing my heart.

Exhaling when I slipped my other foot in, Moira gingerly pulled the pants up my legs and adjusted them at my waist.

"How's that, little sister?" Her sad smile made my eyes cloud up once more.

"Hey, don't cry," She kissed my forehead. "No shame in asking for a little help pulling your pants up. What are sisters for?"

I nodded, not uttering any words in reply. I hadn't spoken much since they wheeled me into the operating room.

Maybe if I hadn't been so out of it the past month, I would have realized something was wrong. I'd lost my appetite right after Dominic and I had broken up, but didn't suspect it was due to anything but bone-deep sorrow.

Dismissing what I was feeling as either a stomach bug or residual feelings from a broken heart, I cried into my pillow at night and somehow got out of bed the next morning and made it through work the next day. When the pain on one side of my abdomen shot up toward my shoulder, my mother forced me to come with her to the emergency room.

The baby I hadn't known I'd made with Dominic before he left over a month ago couldn't survive, and had to come out as soon as possible or else my life could be in danger as well.

Before I'd known it, I was signing consent forms and being wheeled off to surgery. When I opened my eyes after the anesthesia wore off, I searched for Dominic next to my bed, holding my hand and making me laugh. But that Dominic didn't exist anymore, and neither did the baby he'd left me with. The realization made me sob so hard, I hiccupped around the nose cannula giving me oxygen and had hardly uttered a word since.

Not suspecting I was pregnant until I was told it had to be terminated I'd decided was an odd sort of blessing. It hadn't made me love the baby I was about to lose any less, but at least I hadn't been teased with false happiness before I had to let it go.

Moira helped me with my T-shirt before we heard a knock on the open door.

"Dad? I thought you were picking us up in front of the hospital?"

"Your mother is parked on the corner in front. I wanted to speak to your sister for a minute before we left."

My eyes clenched shut. My parents had to be disappointed in me. It was one thing to look the other way at me going on trips with my boyfriend and spending nights at his apartment. They were intelligent enough to know I hadn't been a virgin in a long time, but it didn't matter. I was sure getting pregnant like this had disappointed them both, no matter if I was a twenty-seven year old adult or not.

I had so much to be sad about and be sorry for. The weight of all the emotions combined with the pain still ricocheting across my mid-section made it difficult to stand up straight.

Dad inched closer to me as he spread his arms wide.

"Let it out, little girl."

The sob I was holding in bubbled out of my chest until I folded, falling into my father's arms as I finally let the tears fall without trying to will them back in.

"I'm sorry, Dad."

He cradled my face and lifted it off his chest. "Honey, I need you to stop beating yourself up about everything. This is tough, yes, but it will get better. I promise you. I miss the light in your eyes, but I know it's just dimmed, not gone."

"At least one of us believes that," I coughed out a humorless laugh before clutching my stomach.

"Come with me," he helped me into the wheelchair the nurse left for me and rolled me to the window. "What's the sun doing?" He pointed at the horizon behind the row of tall buildings.

"It's...setting," I searched his gaze, wondering what he was trying to tell me.

"And what is it going to do tomorrow morning?" He arched a brow.

"Rise?"

He nodded and kissed my forehead.

"That means life goes on, Theodora. No matter what happens. And so will you. You'll love again and be happy. Maybe not for a little while, but it'll happen. Until then, you have three people staying at your apartment this week who love the hell out of you and will see you through this."

"All of you?" I let out my first real chuckle in what felt like forever.

His head fell back with a laugh.

"We'll take turns, although I think your mother is going to be a fixture there until you start feeling better. That may give you some incentive to push forward."

He grinned as he draped my jacket over my shoulders and wheeled me out of the hospital room.

There was an odd relief in hitting rock bottom with nowhere to go but up.

37

THEA

PRESENT

THE DRIVE from the pub to my rental was only a half hour. My angry foot stomped on the gas, and I arrived in what seemed like seconds since I slapped Dominic in The Beach Pub parking lot.

I didn't rush out of the car and into the house. While lingering in the driveway, I dropped my head back and shut my eyes as I remembered how happy I'd been this morning, and how it was all a huge lie. I'd overlooked so many things when I'd decided to give what Dominic and I had another try, reasoning that he'd been suffering too much to know what he was doing when we'd broken up.

He hadn't been suffering too much to fall into another woman's bed for a night. Knowing what I'd gone through when he'd done it, even though he'd had no idea, made the knife not only twist but slice me in half. I ran tonight not because I was a coward, but because looking at him after finding out had caused me visceral pain. He'd owned every single part of me from the very beginning, and I felt duped and devastated all over again.

I finally stepped out of my car and trudged up my outside steps.

But they weren't my steps, were they? This wasn't my house, and I didn't live here, even though I'd been figuring out a way to stay. That was over, too.

I didn't make it too far inside, sliding down the back of the door and slumping into a ball. Everything I was most afraid of had come to fruition tonight. Moira was right, I wasn't honest with Dominic. And it all spilled out at the worst possible time.

As I mourned the love we'd had and the baby that had been just as doomed as we were, he'd had sex with someone else. As much as I tried, I couldn't make an excuse for that. The love I had for Dominic would never die as long as I was alive, but for the very first time, we felt finished. This was the end of the line because there was no way we could come back from this.

I pulled my knees into my chest and dropped my head, crying so hard my ribs hurt. When I lifted my head toward the short flight of steps to the bedroom, I wasn't sure I'd be able to stand much less climb. Pulling my denim jacket from the hook on the wall, I gathered it into a ball and turned on my side, laying my head down and hoping the tears wore me out enough to eventually pass out.

My eyes closed only to pop open at a loud bang on the other side of the door.

"Thea! Let me in, please. We need to talk."

"There's nothing to say," I called back, my voice too hoarse to scream.

"Yes, there is. And I'm not leaving until you let me in. Call the cops if you have to, but I'm not going anywhere."

I used the little energy I had left to push off the floor and unlock the door. Still unable to look Dominic in the eye, I held it open then turned to go into the living room.

The lock clicked behind me as I fell onto the couch, hugging one of the pillows to my chest.

"I need you to look at me." I wouldn't turn toward the crack in his voice. My heart ached, but I couldn't let it cloud my judgment anymore. So, Dominic was suffering. *Good.* My quest to comfort him was over.

"I can't look at you."

"Fine." He sat on the floor in front of me. "I won't give you a choice. I want to know everything. Why didn't you tell me? I thought we talked everything out, especially lately. I figured out when your parents came in something happened when we were apart. I asked you, and you blew me off. I get that you're angry."

My head jerked up. "Angry?" A humorless chuckle fell from my lips. "I don't even know what to call what I am right now, but angry is a huge understatement."

He nodded. "I know that, too, sweetheart. But right now, let's start at the beginning. Why didn't you say anything?"

"Because it's a terrible story. You were already dealing with Linda's death back then, I didn't see a reason for upsetting you now. Why do you want to know all the details?"

"Because it happened to you because of us—because of me. You lost *our* baby, and I hate like hell that you couldn't tell me when it happened. Because I left you both," he whispered to himself as he rubbed his forehead. "You suffered alone back then, and I think you're still suffering now. Please let me help you through it like I should have. Tell me. From the beginning."

His dark eyes were rimmed with red as if he'd been crying on the way here. Once more, I folded where Dominic was concerned. I pulled my legs under me and sucked in a long breath.

"When we were together, I used an IUD for birth control.

You knew that." I darted my eyes to his and he nodded. "Sometimes, although I was told, rarely, it can cause an ectopic pregnancy. Meaning from the time of conception, it's not viable.

"You didn't think you were pregnant before that?" His eyes stayed glued to mine as he waited for me to continue.

"Something wasn't right," I admitted with a shrug. "I thought I had an upset stomach from *being* upset. I lost a lot of weight because I didn't want to eat. Occasionally, I'd bleed a little bit but at the time it wasn't too out of the ordinary. It wasn't until Steve tipped my mother off that she forced me to get checked out."

He flinched back, his eyes thinned to slits.

"How did Steve tip your mother off?"

"I came over to drop off a pot roast, my mother would send him food from time to time after your mother passed away, and that was when he told me you gave up your apartment." I dug the heels of my palms into my eyes. The resurfacing memories brought bile to the back of my throat.

"Go on," he whispered, his eyes glassy as they remained fixed on me.

"Anyway, when he called my mother to thank her, he told her he was worried because I didn't look so good. She was on me to see a doctor for days until the bleeding became heavier, and this weird pain started in my shoulder."

I reached up on instinct to rub at my shoulder, remembering the sharp pain that had come out of nowhere.

"My parents took me to the emergency room, and I had a sonogram. The doctor told me if I had waited two more days, it may have ruptured. I never thanked Steve for basically saving my life." I brought my gaze back to Dominic. His skin paled as he sank his teeth into his bottom lip.

"My God, Thea."

His face crumpled before his head fell against the cushion of the couch, his hands digging into my thighs as if they were some kind of lifeline. His shoulders shook and, on instinct, I brought my hand to the back of his head and sifted my fingers into his hair. As much as I hated it, I still had an innate need to take care of Dominic, even if he was the root of my own torment.

"Are you sure you want to hear the rest of this?"

"Yes. Go on. Please." When he raised his head, he wiped at his eyes with the back of his hand. "Please."

"I was rushed into emergency surgery and went home with my parents and sister after a couple of days. The official story is still appendicitis. No one knows other than my immediate family."

He rose from the floor and sat next to me.

"Was it," he began before his Adam's apple bobbed in his throat. "Was it because you were under stress? Did I do this?"

"No," I answered quickly. "This happened the moment we conceived, more or less. Just one of those things, probably from the IUD. I was actually grateful it happened this way."

He squinted at me, his brow furrowed. "Why were you grateful?"

"Had I thought I was pregnant and maybe actually looked forward to having your baby, and then lost it...?" I looked away and clutched the back of my neck. "When they told me in the hospital I was pregnant but it had to be terminated, it was like ripping off an excruciating band-aid but all at once. I didn't have a chance to dream about you snapping out of it when I told you you'd be a father, or picture a sweet, funny little boy with floppy dark hair."

My nose burned and I stumbled a moment. "Or a little girl who lights up around you like Ava does. In that respect, I was spared. I only had to dwell on how I wasn't what you needed—again. My stupid body couldn't even carry your baby the right way, and I couldn't love you the right way to keep you."

I covered my face as I cried into my hands, hiccuping for air like I had in the recovery room all those years ago.

Dominic slid his arm under me and pulled me onto his lap. I didn't fight him as I melted into his chest as it shook with his own sobs. He rocked me back and forth, muttering, "I'm so sorry," over and over again as he dropped kisses on the top of my head.

It didn't erase the rage or the hurt, or the constant feeling of being less than what he needed. But finally taking the comfort from the person I wanted it from the most, and the one who had as much vested in the loss as I did, spread a balm across the most broken parts of my soul.

"Since we're suffering tonight," I said, pushing off his chest. "Tell me what happened with April."

"There is honestly nothing to tell. I went out with Joe, had way too much to drink, I did that back then." He rubbed his eyes and shook his head. "I don't remember much at all to tell you the truth. Just waking up the next morning and not knowing where I was, as cliché as that sounds. For a second, I thought she was you," he whispered, brushing the matted hair off of my forehead. "I almost asked her to scratch my arm. Once I realized where I was and what I'd done, I left and never spoke to her again or stepped foot in the bar she worked at. I swear on my mother."

I never doubted that he was lost, but I'd always resent not being the one to bring him back.

"And, I was actually grateful for that night, if I can say that without being slapped again." He grimaced when he met my eyes. "It was like cold water dumped over my head. I woke up, or started to anyway. I should've driven back to see you when you didn't answer me and been there with you when this happened."

"Should'ves don't help us. You can't go back, and neither can I." I lifted a shoulder. "You're happy here, and you belong here. You've said it, and I can see it."

"I'm happy with *you*, and I belong with *you*. You'll never know how sorry I am or how much I love you. I tried to move on, and I never could. You can ask Joe."

He cradled my cheek. I shut my eyes, his touch bringing pleasure and pain, both of which overwhelmed me too much to think.

"Please tell me I didn't lose you again."

I reached up to grab his wrist, looking away as I didn't know what to reply.

"I think it's a good thing I'm going back now. I need time to think, and I can't do that around you." I slid off of his lap and sat on the couch, leaning forward to rest my elbows on my knees. "I'll always love you—"

"Don't say that! Don't start telling me goodbye!" He raked his hand through his hair. "There has to be a way. Something we could do. That *I* could do. I want to spend the rest of my life with you." He grabbed my hands. "I want the smartass little boy and the beautiful baby girl with freckles, and I want them with you. Please, Thea."

I drifted my hand down his wet cheek.

"If we spend the rest of our lives together, we can't carry around all this hurt. Well, I can't. I do believe you love me, but I don't know if I'll ever believe I'm enough for you. I'm scared I'll always have...reservations."

I stood. "I think we both need a good night's sleep, and I need to start packing. Though, I'll be back here next month unless they rent it out."

I swept my gaze around the living room. It really was a

nice little house. A family would flourish here. I hoped a happy one would.

"So this is it? I won't see you again before you go?"

"I'll be at the hotel Monday. I need a few reports from Violet, and I'll probably need you to sign a few things. I'll leave for Queens in the afternoon, and be back out here with my boss when the hotel opens."

"Next month." He shut his eyes, his head falling back a minute before he stood, gutting me with the pain etched in his features.

It was my turn to leave for my own good.

If we hadn't run into April tonight, we'd be upstairs right now, tangled up in my sheets and in each other while making plans for our future. I was tempted to ask him to stay, even if I was uncertain where we went from here. I'd memorize every inch of him with my mouth and my hands and hold it for safe-keeping on the cold and lonely nights without him.

I unlocked the door and held it open. Dominic grabbed my face, our mouths colliding in a desperate kiss that should have been goodbye but neither of us could let go. Each time I pulled back, he pressed harder as if to keep me from slipping away.

He picked up my hand and slid his palm against mine as he stepped back, his face falling when our hands dropped. I watched as he made his way into his truck, turning back inside when he started the engine.

Despite the reservations I said I had, I'd never be completely free from Dominic. He'd always be my other half, but maybe some people aren't meant to be whole.

38

DOMINIC

"I wish there was something I could do."

I wouldn't turn toward the pity I knew I'd see in Joe's gaze. When I'd come back last night, I'd headed straight upstairs to my apartment but couldn't sleep. For the brief time I managed to drift off, I was haunted by images of Thea in a hospital bed, crying into her hands until she gasped for air, like she had last night. I kept screaming that I was there and I wouldn't leave her, but she couldn't hear me.

After waking up in a cold sweat, knowing sleep wasn't coming back to me anytime soon, I showered and headed down to the pub to start setting up early.

Getting lost in work was the only thing that had ever helped me, but the dull pain in my chest never dissipated.

When I didn't respond to Joe's texts asking if everything was okay, and apologizing for his slip in front of Thea last night, he knew me well enough to figure he'd probably find me here before sunrise. After I told Joe what happened after I ran out last night and what I'd found out, he steered clear of me for most of the morning.

"There's nothing anyone can do. I knew when she came

back that I'd probably broke us beyond repair, but by some miracle, she actually gave me another chance. Now," I shrugged, scrubbing the same space on the bar counter for the umpteenth time since five a.m., "once that hotel opens, I'll never see her again."

"You don't know that, man. You said you'd fight for her, and you sound like you want to give up."

My head shot up. "Want to? Joe, I picture the rest of my life without her, and I don't even know how I'll breathe. My fucking bones ache from missing her, and she's not even gone, yet." I threw the towel in the corner and leaned over the counter, dropping my head onto the wood.

"Hey, guys." Caterina's tentative voice drifted in from the front entrance. Ava babbled with wide eyes as Caterina navigated the stroller to where we were standing.

"Hey," I whispered, unable to muster a better greeting than that.

"How are you holding up?" She asked as she climbed into one of the seats.

"I'm alive," I answered without lifting my head, knowing I'd see nothing but sympathy all over her face, too, and I couldn't handle it from either of them right now.

"Da Da Da," Ava bellowed around the squeaky toy in her mouth as she fixed her blue eyes on me.

"Did she just say Daddy?" I asked, my usual joy in seeing her chubby smile overshadowed by the pang in my chest.

"No," Joe huffed out a laugh. "I think she's saying 'Dom'."

I was surprised when a smile crept across my lips.

I wanted to think that if Thea answered my call and told me she'd lost our baby, I would have snapped out of it enough to be there for her when she needed me.

But I didn't know how I would've handled another loss. I was already withdrawn and barely functional at the time.

Those months after my mother died had been like being in a conscious coma. I'd been too riddled with guilt and sorrow to think and act as an actual human being, so I'd left the woman I loved more than anything to suffer alone.

If all I'd ever done was hurt her, maybe the only way I could love her now was to let her go.

"How was the beach?" Joe pecked her lips and scooped Ava into his arms. I had to look away when she cuddled into his neck. I could add sucky godfather to my list of offenses lately.

"I didn't go. I stopped by the bakery and had Maria's daughter babysit for a couple of hours while I went to see Thea."

My head whipped around at the sound of her name.

"Is she all right? Did she ask you to stop by?"

It was none of my business, but in addition to missing her so damn much, I was worried sick about her. She'd gone through so much—thanks to me—and relived it all last night.

"No, she didn't ask me, but I was concerned. I've only known her a few weeks, but she doesn't strike me as someone who reaches out when she's upset or needs help."

I nodded. Stubborn as hell and never asked for help, that was my girl.

Was my girl.

"I helped her pack a little and load stuff in her car for tomorrow." Her eyes darted away before they came back to mine, and there was the pity I'd been avoiding from Joe. I knew then that Caterina had heard all the awful details.

"How was she? I'm glad you went to see her. She's not ready to see me, again."

Or ever. After I signed a couple of forms tomorrow, any official ties we had this summer would be cut, and that terrified me most of all.

"She's the same as you are now." She sighed, shaking her head. "Sad, distant, and miserable."

"Thea's been through a lot, thanks to me." I huffed out a humorless laugh.

"I don't think that's why she's sad. She misses you as much as you're missing her, right now. My heart is breaking for both of you."

"Save your sympathy for Thea," I cupped my forehead, pressing my fingers into my temples and wishing I could run to her rental right now and beg on my hands and knees. She didn't have to miss me, I was right here if she wanted me. "I don't deserve any of it."

"You found out you lost a baby last night. You're allowed to mourn, no matter what the semantics are," Joe said as he rested Ava on his hip.

"I'm going to get a little nosy, but something doesn't quite add up to me." Caterina folded her arms and rested her elbows on the counter as she leveled her eyes at me. "Why did you leave Thea in the first place?"

"Because when my mother died, I couldn't handle it, and I became a zombie. She didn't need to go through any of that with me. I just wanted to be alone."

Her mouth turned down in a frown as if she didn't believe my answer.

"I get withdrawing, but if, God forbid, I went through a terrible loss like that, I would never leave Joe. I'd need him too much. Did you not love her or feel like you needed her?"

"Of course I loved her!" Now, her poking pissed me off. "I loved her *too* much."

She squinted at me and drew closer to the counter. "What do you mean by too much?"

"For the first year, she was all I thought about. I spent every minute I could spare with her and it still wasn't enough.

I wanted to marry her less than six months in. My mother was sick and I hadn't noticed a goddamn thing!"

I didn't realize how loud I was until Caterina flinched. She shot a side glance at Joe, who shut his eyes and nodded.

"So you felt guilty for missing the signs of your mother's illness while you were falling in love with Thea?"

"Yes, of course. What does that have to do with anything, Dr. Hunter?"

She pursed her lips. "I'm not a therapist, no, but I think that is it. Thea is thinking you left because you didn't love her enough, but you cut her off to punish yourself for loving her *too* much." She exhaled a long gust of air. "If you guys are going to have any kind of chance, you need to make her believe that."

"How? Maybe she's better off without me, anyway."

I rubbed at the back of my neck, trying to process more information I had no clue what the hell to do with.

"Love isn't supposed to be easy." She tilted her head with a sad smile. "You're supposed to cry, scream, and hurt. That's how you know your heart is in it."

"You should go open up a stand on the boardwalk with T-shirts. Tourists love that crap."

"Maybe I will." She raised a brow. "You need to think of a way to show her the real reason why you pushed her away."

I picked up my head as an idea ran through my tired brain. If Thea really wanted to see what had been going through my head back then, there was only one way. I never planned on actually showing anyone, but Caterina was right. The only way I'd get her back was for her to see the shattered mess I was four years ago and why.

THEA TEXTED me Monday morning to meet her at the hotel by ten. I packed a bag of food for her in the morning and arrived way too early, lingering in my truck until nine-forty-five. Strolling through the hotel, I realized I'd be working with daily reminders of Thea every day. If I lost her, I guessed I deserved the sentence of torture I'd have to endure as long as we leased the hotel space.

"Hey," I whispered, knocking softly on her open door.

When her gaze slid to mine, I could tell she was exhausted. The dark circles around her red eyes were a dead giveaway.

"You're early," she said with a tired smile and motioned to the seat in front of her desk. "There are only two forms for you to sign, and I noted exactly where so it should be quick."

She handed a folder to me and our eyes locked as I took it from her hand. It was only days ago I woke up with her in my arms, dreaming of the life we'd wished for but never got to have. I couldn't let all that go. Not yet. The yearning in her eyes gave me a little hope that maybe she couldn't either.

I signed quickly on the highlighted lines and handed the folder back to her.

"I brought you a bag of food to take with you. You said you were leaving in the early afternoon, and I assume you have no food at your apartment after spending two months out here."

Her eyes darted around the room, her mouth curving into a grin before her gaze drifted back to mine.

"That was thoughtful of you. Thank you."

"I need you to promise me something. Just one thing." I stood and lifted the bag by the handle to place on her desk.

"What is it?" She asked with a crinkled brow.

"You'll empty the bag as soon as you get home."

Her mouth curved in a tiny smile. "I wouldn't leave perishables in the car, but yes I promise."

"There's something in there I need you to see when you get home. I don't deserve anything from you, but I love you, whether or not you'll ever believe that. I'm asking you to wait until you get back to Queens, but promise me that you'll look."

Her jaw quivered as she stood from her chair.

"Okay," she whispered as she came closer. "I promise."

"I have to get back. We still have a straggler crowd. The rest of the furniture comes tomorrow so I'll be here early. Not that you'll know." I pulled at the hair at my neck, not wanting to tear my eyes away from Thea's, even though the pain in her gaze gutted me.

"Right. It all looks great, Dominic. I'm excited for you."

I cupped her chin and brushed her lips with a light kiss, stealing another quick one when she didn't turn away.

"Drive safe, sweetheart."

Her eyes clenched shut for a moment. I spied the roll of her throat as she swallowed hard.

"I will."

I nodded and saw myself out, my heart heavy as I moped out of the hotel and back into my truck.

If my mother was really watching from the other side, I prayed she'd give her foolish son this one last chance to make things right.

39

THEA

"Why don't you work from home tomorrow morning? You have to be exhausted from that long drive this afternoon."

I smiled at my mother's huff in my ear. She always hovered, but I swore she had surveillance on me at times. The minute I came through the door my cell phone buzzed in my purse. I appreciated the sentiment, but after all those hours in traffic with no stops, and the weekend I'd had, I wasn't up for talking to anyone.

Saturday night had aged me a few years, but the restless feeling I'd always had when I thought of Dominic and me finally ceased. I wouldn't have to wonder how he would react when I told him or think about how he was doing all this time.

I wished I hadn't gotten a glimpse of *who* he'd been doing, but even that didn't bother me as much as it originally had. I couldn't give him a total pass, but that wasn't the reason I'd asked him to go on Saturday and had only saw him briefly on business before I left.

"I have meetings in the morning. It's fine. I can unpack tomorrow after I get some sleep," I told her on a loud yawn. Being in my own space relaxed me, hopefully enough that I'd drift to sleep quickly and not have any issues sleeping alone. I only shared a bed with Dominic again for a short time, but nighttime was when I missed him the most.

I thought the time apart would clear my head, but he was never far from my mind.

"Eat something, then go to bed. I guess you're going back to see Dominic, right?"

I cringed at the sound of his name, my eyes drifting to the bag of food he'd given me still on my kitchen counter. I didn't know what was in there that he wanted me to see, but before I went to bed, I knew I had to find out.

Something told me eating or sleeping wasn't happening for me tonight once I opened that bag.

"I head back in a few weeks," I said, not wanting to acknowledge her tone when she mentioned Dominic, or whether or not I'd ever be going back to see him. "Listen, Mom, I'll talk to you tomorrow."

I said a quick goodbye and hung up, approaching the bag as if I were about to defuse a bomb.

Reaching inside, I pulled out a bag of muffins and cookies, a silver tray of something that managed to stay almost warm. My fingers wrapped around a metal wire at the bottom of the bag, and when I pulled at it, it was connected to a thick notebook with a black cover.

The edges of the pages were folded and frayed. When I turned the cover over and read the first page, my heart leaped into my throat.

Dear Mom,

Steve asked me to do this, so I figured appeasing him would appease you. Not that you'll know. Or maybe you do. After all those years in Catholic school, learning about heaven and the afterlife, maybe that's where you are.

Wherever you are, you aren't here and I hate that.

How did I not know you were sick? Looking back, I could see a ton of signs. But I was too damn distracted to see any of them. I was too busy planning trips with my girlfriend to take care of my own mother. I'm sorry, Mom. I'm so fucking sorry.

This was the notebook he told me about, where he'd written letters to his mother and, later, to me. I set the book back down on the counter for a moment to grab the half bottle of Pinot Grigio on the inside door of my fridge, not caring if it went bad or wasting time finding a glass. Grabbing the book and bottle, I headed to my couch and tucked my legs under me. My fingers shook as they drifted down the page, the marks of Dominic's handwriting so deeply ingrained it had poked through the pages, in places.

Something about the way he mentioned *planning trips with his girlfriend* made the tiny hairs on my neck stand up. Tone wasn't clear in the written word, but it almost felt as if he resented me or the attention he gave me for distracting him from early signs of his mother's illness.

I flipped through more letters, wondering how much he'd had to drink when the letters became messy and incoherent. A sudden lump in the back of my throat made it hard to breathe when I realized he ended all the letters the exact same way.

I'm so fucking sorry.

I knew he was upset they'd kept her diagnosis from him until we'd come back from vacation. I was always grateful that Linda gave us those few extra days to be young and in love with no worries, knowing how Dominic would react to the news, but he'd never seen it that way.

Page after page was more of the same. Guilt over not making her quit smoking sooner, second guessing all the times he thought she had a simple cold, questioning if that was the start of it. Furious that he'd gone days without seeing her and talking to her because he was "too busy with Thea." If he would have just noticed something, if he'd been paying more attention, he was sure he could have stopped it earlier, and she would still be alive.

No one loved their mother more than he did, which was why I'd been so nervous when I'd first met her. But I'd soon found out that I had nothing to worry about because Linda was one of the best people I'd ever met. She'd taken me in right away like I was one of her own. Her big heart would have broken at what her son went through after she was gone.

I'd known he was grieving, and he'd reiterated over and over how much he'd wanted to be alone, but I'd never understood how tortured he'd been. Because he'd withdrawn so far from me, I hadn't gotten a grasp on how deep his self-loathing went. Instead of being angry that he'd left, I thanked God that Joe had given him a place to escape to and had kept an eye on him.

My hand flew to my mouth at the next three pages. All were identical with one sentence scrawled down the middle and covering the length of three lines.

I deserve to be alone.

Lots of people lost parents they were close to, but didn't leave the person they claimed to love to grieve alone. After twenty-something pages of Dominic begging his late mother for her forgiveness, and citing me as the reason why he hadn't taken care of her like he thought he should have, I finally understood what had happened to us.

He'd felt guilty for being so happy with me and not paying enough attention to her. Therefore, in his mind, her death was his fault. He had mentioned a few, "I should've done this," or "Had I realized that," to me while she'd been in treatment, but actually losing her had made it sink all into his head so deeply he hadn't wanted to be a part of his own life or part of anything that made him happy.

That included me.

I turned two blank pages and moved on to the next letter, my heart seizing when I read my name at the top.

Dear Thea,

We aren't together anymore, and I honestly was too drunk to remember actually doing it, but I cheated on you last night. Or, at least, that's what it feels like. I woke up in someone else's bed, and almost threw up on her carpet when I realized she wasn't you. I'm the worst kind of person, and I never deserved you. I knew that when we got together, but I was too selfish. I still wanted you all to myself.

I'm really losing it. First writing to my dead mother and then my ex-girlfriend. I never thought I'd see the day when I'd call you my ex-girlfriend. What I'd give to have you nagging me to eat and sleep right now. I'd gladly take all your love and comfort and never be stupid enough to let go of the best thing that ever happened to me.

But I was, and I did.

I miss you so much I can't even think. I played an old video of us on my phone today just to hear your voice. I want to call you but I'm too ashamed to speak to you. I've hurt you enough and for that I'll always be so sorry.

It wasn't supposed to be like this.

No, Dominic. It absolutely wasn't.

Tears I didn't know I was crying dripped onto the pages as I read about our first date, about how he waited to tell me he loved me because he was scared I'd freak out at hearing it so soon, how the first thought in his head when he woke up was speaking to me. He wrote a ton of I'm sorries, but never mentioned trying to reach out to me.

Dear Thea,

Congratulations. I heard you're engaged. I didn't really expect you to wait for me, but in the back of my mind, I'd always hoped. I don't know who the guy is. My aunt is usually good with details, but she was missing that one. I hope he treats you right. I hope he gave you one of those over the top proposals, and it was everything you wanted it to be. When I was about to propose, there was no way I'd have the patience to plan anything like that.

You didn't know that. When we came back from Florida, the reason I was itching to leave you that day was because I wanted to ask you to marry me. I headed to my mother's house to pick up my grandmother's ring and planned on shooting right back to your apartment to ask you. I figured I'd call your dad afterward for his permission and pretend I hadn't asked you yet. I didn't want to be disrespectful, but I couldn't wait another second.

I'd actually wanted to ask you for months but was too scared. If you'd said no, I would've been destroyed.

I never wanted that weekend to end, or have one of us ever have to go home the next morning. I wanted you all the time, every single day.

My poor mother died thinking I was going to ask you. She was so thrilled when I told her you were the one. She handed me the ring right away, making me promise I'd have it cleaned before I gave it to you. Once I found out she had cancer, all my plans were blown to pieces. I thought once Mom was out of the woods and on the mend, I'd propose and we'd all have two things to celebrate. That never happened, so in the end, we had none.

Be happy, sweetheart.

There were only so many big reveals a person could take in one week.

I rested the book in my lap and covered my face with my

hands. I'd need to dig my inhaler out of my purse if my breathing didn't slow to a normal, human pace.

Adam had planned an elaborate proposal. He took me to a fancy dinner and put the ring on a silver dessert tray. Anyone else would have swooned their heart out, but I'd felt nothing.

Dominic running back to my apartment to ask me to marry him because he was too excited to wait would have been the greatest moment of my life.

I propped my elbow on the arm of my couch and rubbed my forehead. We were cheated out of so much. The unfairness of it all infuriated me.

I turned to the last page and found one more letter.

Dear Thea,

Unlike the rest of the letters in this book, this one was written in the hopes you'd actually read it.

I hadn't read through the letters myself until now. I'd scribble in anger and shove the book into the drawer, never giving them a second look. I think it's pretty clear that I was beyond messed up for a while and realized what I'd done when it was too late.

But maybe it's not. Maybe there's a reason that of all the hotels in the world, you ended up working at this one this summer. I promised I wouldn't stop fighting for us until we made it, and I'm not giving up, because we still can.

Come back to me, Thea.

I love you. Then, now, and always.

40

DOMINIC

"I AM so happy for you guys!" Caterina beamed at Joe and me, almost bouncing up and down.

We had finished walls, tables and chairs, and a state-of-the-art kitchen that made Joe almost drool all over his shirt. The Beach Pub 2 was three weeks away from opening for business.

I was also three weeks away from possibly telling the only woman I ever loved goodbye. That quelled any excitement I'd had over starting our new business venture. I still held out hope I'd hear from her before then, but each day without a word made it hard to keep it up.

"Violet said they already have reservations booked. And we'll be the only restaurant in the general area, so that's good news for us." Trying to sound upbeat was exhausting as hell.

Caterina came up to me and dropped a hand on my forearm.

"Still no word?"

"Nope. And I have no idea what else I can do but wait. Maybe reading the ramblings of a madman turned her off completely."

She shook her head. "Not possible. Give her a little time. It hasn't even been a week. I don't doubt she's coming back."

"She has to come back. She'll make sure the hotel is open and on budget then leave." I shrugged, gathering up the tools I'd been using all afternoon to hang things up and assemble some of the furniture. I made sure to spend every second of every day keeping busy so I wouldn't think about Thea, but it never worked.

"This place looks fantastic," Joe mused, scanning the dining area.

"It's the same as we talked about." I lifted a shoulder. "Little shinier than the original but not different."

"No, Dom. This place is you. Great things are about to happen, I know it." He slapped my back. "And I'm with my wife. Thea is coming back, and not just for the opening."

I wasn't giving up, I was just out of ideas. Grabbing her ankles and begging her not to leave when she was here was all I had left.

"You guys are a chain now." Caterina cracked a wide grin. "That's pretty freaking awesome." She wrapped one arm around each of us. "I can say I knew you back when."

"Make that your next marketing campaign." I laughed, despite myself.

She dropped her arms with a chuckle. "That's not a bad idea. We can talk about it at the next marketing meeting."

"Ugh," I groaned. "You're making me do that, too?"

She narrowed her eyes and strutted up to me.

"You're a partner now, so I'm your social media manager. How about Mondays at eight? We can figure out which restaurant each week."

"Wow, you're really selling it." I squinted at her, but couldn't hold back a smile. "For what it's worth," my voice dropped to a whisper, "whatever happens, thank you."

She squeezed my hand. "What are friends for? And I'm friends with both of you. She's coming back, Dominic. Have faith."

I squeezed back before I heard a knock at the door.

"It's probably Violet." I nodded to the fuzzy figure on the outside of the frosted glass. "She likes to peek in around this time and see the progress."

Joe padded to the front to answer, and I took a minute to look around. It really did look amazing, but it felt hollow to celebrate it alone.

"Looks like a real restaurant now," I said before I turned around, almost falling over when I noticed Thea standing next to Joe.

"It sure does," she said, a hint of a smile crossed her lips as the both of us stood in silence, like that first time I spotted her at the pub. There was so much I needed to say, but the words jumbled up in the back of my throat.

"I've been meaning to check out the deck," Caterina chirped as she pushed Joe toward the back door. "We'll be back, don't mind us."

"She's subtle," I told Thea. My chest swelled when her smile widened. "When did you get back?"

"This afternoon, I had a few things to take care of, and they took longer than I thought." She crossed her arms and stepped closer to me, the pounding of my heart echoing in the silence.

"I didn't expect to see you this soon. I mean, not that I didn't want to, but because..." I trailed off and scrubbed a hand down my face. "I missed you. A lot."

"I missed you, too. A lot." She inched even closer, her arms still crossed and my hands still at my sides. "I was reassigned this week. A new position with no travel."

"That's what you wanted, right?" My mouth was dry, and

my lungs fought to hold air. What was she here to tell me? That she was moving across the country and stopped here to tell me one last goodbye? I wanted to believe she wouldn't come all the way out here to say fuck off.

"Since I have experience with the area, and the hotel is opening on budget and on time, they wanted to know if I'd be interested in managing something bigger. They offered me a position with a rental home development near the beach, except this is scoped out for years not weeks."

"What beach?"

"Pentier Beach." Her lips twitched. "I'd have to move out here indefinitely."

The uptick in my heart almost made it burst out of my chest.

"What are you telling me, Thea?"

"That whether or not I was offered this job," she said, placing her hand on my chest, "I was coming back, anyway. I love you. We got a little sidetracked," she sputtered out a nervous laugh before biting her quivering lip, "but my home is with you. It's time, Dominic. It's finally time."

I was still too scared to feel the joy and relief filtering through me.

"Unless you don't want me to take this job? I can always say no and go back—"

I lifted her by the waist and crushed my lips to hers, burying my head into her neck holding her as tightly as I could without cutting off her air supply. I didn't deserve the woman in my arms, but I was never letting her go again.

"You aren't going anywhere. I'm so sorry," I put her down and weaved a hand into her hair. "I'm so damn sorry for everything."

"Stop. I'm sorry, too. I had no idea what you were going through," her voice cracked. "I'm glad Joe gave you somewhere to go. *I'm* sorry I never answered when you called." She rested her forehead against mine.

"And I'm sorry I didn't tell you when I lost our baby. I couldn't hurt you. You were already hurting so much. But I should've told you instead of resenting you for not being there when you didn't know I needed you." Her hands drifted up and down my arms. "I'm done looking back, and I'm ready to start the life we were cheated out of."

"Please tell me I'm not dreaming, again," I pleaded as I drew her closer.

"Nope, I'm real," she chuckled against my lips. "You can pinch me if you want."

"Later," I whispered, my grin so wide my cheeks ached as I threaded my fingers into her hair. "I love you. I was terrified I'd lost you for good, this time."

Her smile faded as she shook her head. "You could never lose me for good. Oh, I forgot to tell you the best part!" Her eyes widened as she clutched my biceps. "I can stay at the same rental. Part of my salary package." She wrapped her arms around my waist. "A perfect commute for someone who works at the hotel."

"I suppose it could be." I ran my finger along her jaw. "Are you asking me what I think you're asking me?"

Her smile faded as she fisted the collar of my shirt. "We missed out on so much. I refuse to waste any more time."

"We're getting the doorbell fixed."

She giggled against my mouth as I kissed her again, smiling at her hungry whimper as my tongue stroked hers. She mewled and slumped back against the wall, her nails digging into my back to bring me closer.

"Mine," I grunted against her neck as my hand slid up her thigh.

She ran her fingers down my back, goosebumps chasing her touch. Thea brought me back to life in every single way.

Her hand grazed across my hip and palmed my ass.

"Damn right, you are."

"I know we're not open yet, but I'm sure groping customers against the wall violates one of the health department codes," Joe teased from behind us.

We broke apart, and Thea buried her head in my chest.

"You guys would know."

Caterina shot me a scowl as Thea laughed. "You're lucky I'm so happy for you that I'm letting that slide."

"I hate to throw you out but I'm leaving with my girl, so..." I picked up my backpack and nodded toward the door.

"You're throwing us out, anyway. Got it." Joe wrapped his arm around Caterina's shoulders. "See you tomorrow."

"*Late* tomorrow," I called after them. I heard them both chuckle in the distance as they made their way out.

A giggle escaped Thea when I pulled her body flush to mine. I grabbed her face and searched her gaze.

"You came back to me," I whispered.

She smiled and kissed my cheek.

"I did. And I'm here to stay. We're going to make it this time. No doubts." She pressed her lips against mine. "No reservations."

I shook my head. "Nope. None of that ever again."

"Ready to go home?" Thea wrapped her arms around my waist. The corners of her eyes crinkled as her lips curved with an easy smile.

"Ready? I've waited *years*, sweetheart."

I'd been in love with her for so long, it was hard to remember a life without her.

Because there wasn't one.

She was right, it was finally time.

EPILOGUE
ONE YEAR LATER

Thea

"Babe, it's not a big deal."

I rubbed Dominic's shoulder as he drove us to dinner. Tonight was the first anniversary of what he called our first date, even though I still counted that night at the bar all those years ago.

"I wanted the same table outside. And now it's a monsoon," he huffed, literally huffed, as each pellet of rain on the windshield seemed to piss him off all over again.

"The restaurant inside is just as nice, and we could always go another time. I don't care where we are, you know that."

"I know, sweetheart. Getting coverage so that I could take a Saturday night off wasn't an easy feat, and tonight is important to me, all right?" He grabbed my hand and entwined our fingers, his hold tighter than usual. His frustration was adorable.

"You're cute when you're having a tantrum."

The Halston Hotel was a huge success and had reservations booked months in advance. A full hotel meant a busy restaurant, and Dominic pulled long hours until he built a staff he could trust enough to watch things if he took a night off. Both Beach Pubs were killing it this summer, and I loved watching my boyfriend in his element.

In fact, I loved it so much that Joe had caught us in Dominic's tiny office behind the bar more than once. We'd been so happy this past year, it was almost spooky. But all the ghosts were gone—well at least at a comfortable enough distance to not affect us.

"I may have gotten you an anniversary present," I told him as I tried to rub away the tension in his neck.

"Did you?" I spotted the side of his mouth curve up. "Is it you naked on our deck?"

I let my head fall back against the headrest as I rolled my eyes.

"Like I keep telling you, we aren't having sex on the deck, Dominic."

"Well, not in the rain, although you wet and riding me would be hot as *fuck*. We can wait until it clears up. Another reason this weather sucks."

"Since when are you an exhibitionist? The neighbors are too close by."

"I've never had a deck before. I want to make the most of it." He reached over to squeeze the inside of my thigh as we pulled up to the restaurant.

"I guess I'll pull the umbrella from the back," he said on a sigh, his frown so low I thought it would droop past his chin. I wondered what was up since he wasn't the type to obsess over a silly detail like that. That was more Joe than Dominic.

When he walked to the back of the truck, I pulled out the envelope I had for him, smiling when I took a peek inside. I couldn't care less where we sat. This night was already perfect.

DOMINIC

"THIS ISN'T SO BAD," Thea tried to reassure me as we strolled to the front of the restaurant. The rain came down in buckets as I held the umbrella over us, the wind making it difficult to open the door to the front entrance.

This was what happened when you tried to make elaborate plans. Nothing cooperated.

When we finally got inside, Thea giggled as she shook the rain out of the ends of her hair. She'd even worn the red dress I'd asked her to wear last year, when I'd brought her here in a desperate effort to get her back and make her stay. Now, she was mine and was in my bed every night. *Our* bed. Although, sometimes I didn't come home from work until the early hours of the morning.

I didn't mind working twelve hour shifts with Thea waiting up for me every night, although most nights she still passed out before I got home no matter how hard she tried. Waking her up was something else I could look forward to every night, too.

"Sorry, the patio is closed, but we have a great table for you by the window." The hostess smiled and motioned for us to follow her.

"Wait, nothing in the back?"

I felt Thea's eyes roll next to me. Yes, the window had a view of the water, which you couldn't see through the heavy rain and dense fog, but I wanted some privacy. I wasn't worried that things wouldn't end up the way I wanted them to, but I didn't want that moment to belong to anyone but us.

"Babe, it's fine," she sighed and slipped her arm in the crook of my elbow. "It's fine. A table by the window sounds great. I'm starving." She smiled at the hostess before giving me a narrowed side eye.

I smiled as she waved to some of the patrons she'd recognized on the way to our table. She'd always teased me about being too social, but since working so often with the residents of Pentier Beach and going back and forth to Ocean Cove, she knew more of the people here than I did. She had a beautiful personality to match the rest of her. As difficult as it was I tried not to tease her about all the new friends she'd made in a year.

"Why did you want a table in the back?" Thea crinkled her nose. "Looks dark and gloomy."

"It's not important." I said, feeling an onslaught of nerves as I pushed in her chair. I blew out a long breath and sat down, my lips twitching when I caught Thea's widened eyes as she searched the menu.

"I don't actually remember what we had last time, but it all looks so good."

"I don't remember what we ate either, I was more focused on convincing the sexy blonde in the red dress to come home with me."

She looked up, a blush staining her cheeks. "Sexy blonde? Glad I kept it like this. And anyway, now I live with you, so we can focus on the food. I'm thinking the big shrimp appetizer if you're up for it. I'm *so* hungry."

"Anything you want, sweetheart."

She tilted her head as she met my eyes. "Are you okay? You're acting a little weird tonight."

"I'm fine. Some things didn't work out like I would have liked but, the whole point is to celebrate the best year of my life." I picked up her hand and laced our fingers together. "Details aren't important."

"Best year of my life, too." She flashed a wide grin. "Living with you hasn't been as taxing as I would've thought."

I laughed as Thea smirked around her water glass.

"I'm a dream to live with. At least I don't talk in my sleep."

"I do *not* talk in my sleep."

"Yes, you do. And it's funny as hell." I snickered. "I'll record it next time."

The waitress came over to take our order, and I had to decide if I wanted to do this now or later.

After the waitress left, Thea averted her gaze a moment before turning back toward me.

"We've come a long way in a year. I love every minute of our life. I hope you know that." Her lips curved in a watery smile.

"So do I," I whispered. "Even when you say no to sex on the deck. But I think you'll come around."

Her eyes widened as she glanced around the room.

"Keep your voice down."

I scooted closer to the table and leaned in. "You licked my collarbone in the parking lot and almost ripped off my shirt the last time we were here. Why can't I talk about sex on the deck?"

Her lips pursed as she leaned back in the chair. "I couldn't help it. I'm a sucker for a black button-down." She motioned with her chin to the shirt I wore tonight, top button opened on purpose.

"Right, I remember." I rose from my seat and made my way to her side of the table. "You looked at me like I was on the menu, probably why you don't remember what you ate."

"Maybe, I—what are you doing?"

Instead of crouching in front of her like the last time, I sank to one knee and fished the ring box out of my pocket.

The same box I'd had for years. I hadn't given it to her when I'd wanted to, but it had always belonged to her.

"This is why I wanted to be outside." I felt dozens of eyes on us as I spoke as softly as I could. "But details don't matter. All I care about is that you're mine forever. From the second I saw you at the bar, you owned every single part of me. I was right in calling you an angel that night, because that's exactly what you are."

Thea said nothing as tears snaked down her cheeks.

"Don't cry," I crooned, swiping her tears with my thumbs. "I love you so much. Please marry me, Thea."

She dug into her purse as I waited for an answer. No didn't seem like a possibility before but her hesitation made my heart drop into my stomach.

"I have a present, too." She reached into her purse and handed me an envelope.

Not knowing what to do, I set the ring box on the table and opened the plain white envelope. It looked like an x-ray printout with Thea's name at the top and an $8w$ in the bottom corner.

"It's a sonogram picture. I see you eyeballing it." A laugh bubbled out through her tears. "That's our baby, Dominic."

"It's...what?" My hand flew to her stomach. "Is it...?" I pressed on her still flat abdomen, not able to voice the loud question in my head.

"It's fine. Perfect so far, they said. I had a feeling but was afraid to find out, at first. Then I was afraid to tell you until I saw the doctor after..." She trailed off with a shrug. "That's my present. I'm sorry I didn't get a box."

I grabbed the back of her head and kissed her so hard she almost fell off the chair.

"Our baby is okay?"

She nodded. "I want you forever, too. I always did." She

framed my face. "You, this, it's my every dream come true. I love you." She kissed me and dropped her forehead against mine. "Sorry, I kinda stole your thunder there. Ask me again."

"You kinda did, but I'm too fucking happy to care. Thea, will you marry me?"

"Dominic," she sniffled, her beaming smile taking my breath away, "yes, I will."

I kissed her too long and too hard for public eyes, but it didn't matter.

I was a lucky bastard to get not only one, but two, second chances.

Thea's head fell into my chest as my gaze drifted out the window. The rain had cleared up, and a few stars poked through the clouds, twinkling as if someone was winking at me from heaven.

I rested my chin on top of Thea's head and winked back.

THEA

My son's mouth was going a mile a minute. His dark eyebrows furrowed as he glared into the mirror behind his rear-facing car seat. I couldn't stop laughing when his babbling got louder and faster as he pointed his stubby finger at his reflection.

Just like his daddy, Luca was never at a loss for words.

He was still at it after I pulled into a spot in the Halston Hotel parking lot and reached into the back seat to lift him out of the car.

"Three shots at the doctor and a long drive, and you're not the least bit tired." I sighed, kissing his forehead before I fastened him into the stroller. He met my gaze with a raspy laugh that always melted me into a puddle.

The two men in my life had me wrapped around their fingers, and I loved every single second.

I wheeled Luca into The Beach Pub 2, smiling at the hostess before we took our usual booth in the back. He strained his chubby little body against the restraints and kicked his feet. My son hated being still. The first thing he did when I parked the carriage was try to escape.

"Yes, little guy. I know you want out."

He grunted when my fingers didn't work fast enough.

"Give Mommy a minute."

I unsnapped the safety harness and lifted him up, covering his cheek with kisses before he squirmed again in my arms. The only way Luca would sit still was if I turned him around so he could see everything. I slid into the booth and planted him on my lap, brushing his thick black locks off of his forehead.

"Can I get you guys anything?" Dawn, one of the waitresses who had been here since the hotel opened, asked.

"An iced tea would be awesome, thank you." I dug through my bag for Luca's bottle, releasing a relieved breath when I found it. He happily gulped his milk as he surveyed the dining area.

I often wished Linda was still with us—for so many reasons. Lately, I would have loved her advice on how to deal with a baby Dominic.

"Is the boss around?"

She laughed and shook her head. "He took a walk at lunch." She glanced at her watch. "He said he'd be back in an hour, which was like forty minutes ago."

Luca leaned back and sighed around the nipple of his bottle. I adjusted him in my arms so that he was still facing front but nestled into the crook of my arm.

"My big boy," I whispered, brushing a kiss on his soft cheek as his heavy eyes drooped. He was like a six-month-old old man, not wanting to miss a thing. "You were so good for the doctor. Why don't you take a little snooze before Daddy gets back?" I only had to rock him a couple of times before his mouth fell open, and the bottle dropped from his lips.

I smiled and sank into the soft vinyl of the booth. My mother had scolded me more than once needing to put babies in the stroller or crib once they fell asleep, but I lived for these quiet moments of pure love. From the second I'd found out I was pregnant, Dominic and I didn't take a single thing for granted.

"Wow, he's actually out."

I smiled at my husband's whisper beside me. He pecked my lips and pressed a light kiss to his son's forehead.

"You gave Mommy a break for a change."

"He only *just* conked out." I chuckled. "What's this one still doing up?"

My daughter gave me a toothless, sleepy grin from where she hung in the carrier on Dominic's chest. Luca had wanted no part of the baby harness, and Lyndee only liked it when it was attached to her daddy. She was as stocky as her brother and running out of room in that little thing, but I wouldn't dare mention it. The day she outgrew it, both their hearts would break.

"Everything go okay?" He bent so I could kiss Lyndee's cheek and sat across from us.

"He was a trooper like always. You know how he only cries at the doctor if his sister cries." I nodded to my little girl.

Bringing twins for shots at the same time wasn't for the weak. It didn't matter who went first. Both of them would cry for each other until they were inconsolable. Separate trips to the pediatrician weren't exactly convenient but saved us a huge hassle in the long run.

"He has to look out for his little sister."

I leaned back and rolled my eyes. "He's only two minutes older."

"Older is older." He shrugged. "When his grip gets better we'll start lifting weights." He slid his pinky into Luca's hand

and gingerly wiggled it up and down. "She looks just like her mother, so I'll need help keeping boys away."

Lyndee's head rested against Dominic's shoulder, her light complexion seeming even paler against Dominic's olive skin. She crinkled her freckled nose before her lips widened in a loud yawn.

"Shh," he crooned and rubbed her back. "Go to sleep, princess."

My heart swelled as I gazed at them both. He was never going to let her out of that carrier, never mind let a boy come near her.

When my morning sickness had gotten out of hand and I could barely stay awake, Dominic dragged me to the doctor to get checked out. We were so thrilled to be parents but full of anxiety that we never wanted to address. When I'd had another sonogram, they told us the babies must have been standing single file the first time as I had two, not one, healthy embryos. There wasn't anything wrong. My body was just doing double duty from growing two babies.

When the technician and doctor left the examining room, Dominic and I had met each other's gaze with widened eyes before we both burst into tears. Biologically, it wasn't possible, but we believed that the baby we'd lost had come back to us. While we were still overwhelmed, the influx of gratitude and joy rushing through our veins warded off any impending panic.

We were married on the beach in back of the hotel with our immediate family and friends. A big wedding seemed like a moot point, and officially starting the rest of our lives together in the place that brought us *back* together was all that mattered to us. Our families didn't care. They were just as focused on the babies as we were. Although, we'd put every-thing together quickly, I was already busting out of my dress when I walked down the sandy aisle to marry the man of my dreams.

Luca shifted in my arms as his mouth opened and shut as if he were having an argument in his sleep.

"He is *so* you, I can't take it sometimes," I said to Dominic with a sigh. "Even when he's passed out, his lips keep moving."

"*You're* the one who talks in her sleep, not me." Dominic reached over to glide his thumb over Luca's crinkled forehead. "This is why they can't share a crib. Lyndee sleeps like a log and doesn't move." He nodded down to where she was in a dead sleep, mouth hanging wide open.

I gave my husband's body a shameless perusal. He was still all bronze skin and lean muscle, and watching him with one of our babies in his arms did things to me—things I couldn't cash in on anytime soon.

We managed to survive on short spurts of sex, but I ached for the old days when he'd sneak me into his office after lunch and have me for dessert.

"You stop that," he growled in a husky whisper.

"Stop what?" My shoulder lifted in an innocent shrug.

"Looking at me like that. Keep it up, and you'll pay for it later."

"Promise?" I raised a brow as I eased Luca's pacifier into his mouth when he started to fuss in his sleep.

He stood and leaned over the table to kiss my lips. We couldn't full on make out while we were in his restaurant, especially with the babies between us, but I still groaned when he sucked on my bottom lip and let it go with a nibble. If this was how I was going to pay for it, I was totally on board.

"Oh hey, you're back," Dawn said when she came back to the table, smiling as she tilted her head to where Lyndee slumbered on Dominic's chest.

"Things seem pretty quiet this afternoon, I'm going to take my wife and babies home. Anything comes up, text me." He shot her a grin, and she nodded.

The whole exchange gave me goosebumps; the "let's get out of here" look in his dark eyes, the way he said "his wife and babies," and the pure happiness that radiated off of him all the time, even when our children wore us out to the point of exhaustion.

We gingerly loaded Luca and Lyndee into each other's cars and headed home. I peeked in the rear-view mirror at my sleeping son, hoping he and his sister stayed out for at least the next hour. She loved her naps, but Luca always wanted to skip his, like he did this morning.

Dominic beat me home and had already laid Lyndee in her crib. She was still sleeping peacefully with a hint of a smile on her face. I laughed to myself as I carefully set Luca down, feeling Dominic's eyes on me from the hallway as I made sure they were asleep and crept out of the room, easing the door shut behind me.

I exhaled a long, quiet sigh as my gaze slid to Dominic, but my smile quickly faded. His narrowed eyes were dark and full of wicked intent.

He closed the distance between us before I could even blink, cupping my ass with both hands and pulling me close.

"Is this where you make me pay for it?" I breathed out, hooking my fingers into the waistband of his pants.

"I told you, sweetheart," he rasped, backing me against the wall. "Teasing me in public." His hand slid to the back of my neck as he raked his hooded eyes up and down my body. "Looking like that." He slanted his mouth over mine, licking inside with a desperate hunger that made my knees buckle.

The fact that sex had to be fast somehow made it that much hotter. We were like gluttons, devouring each other before the crackling of the baby monitor made us stop. We needed to get our fill as much and as quickly as we could.

"Frazzled turns you on? Good to know," I whispered as he dragged his lips across my jaw and down my neck, the wet heat of his mouth drawing a whimper out of me.

He draped his hand over my mouth and backed me down the hall to our bedroom, nudging me inside before he shut the door.

"Your son could hear a pin drop on a marshmallow." He shook his head before peeling off his shirt.

I salivated at the sight of my husband's bare chest. My eyes traveled lower as he unbuckled his pants and let them pool at his feet before kicking them across the floor.

"I love when you're loud, but with the two of them," he motioned next door with his chin, "it'll be over before it starts. And I'm not done with you, yet." He grabbed the back of my head and attacked my lips. All the hunger and heat reignited quickly as he fisted the hem of my sundress and broke the kiss just long enough to rip it off of me. He came back to my lips, almost tearing my bra in two before yanking down my underwear. I wanted him to both slow down and hurry up.

"So fucking beautiful," he murmured around a nipple, sucking and biting and making me crazy with the sweetest pain.

My body was different after having the babies. Most of the weight had dropped off quickly due to lack of time to eat, but I was much softer and curvier. I still didn't quite recognize myself and had felt self-conscious at first, but Dominic still looked at me as if was the sexiest woman in the world. Maybe even more so after the twins were born. The quantity of sex wasn't as much as we'd like, but the quality was out-fucking-standing.

"How do you want me?" He knelt and dragged his tongue

over the soaked skin between my legs, tracing figure eights over my clit until my legs shook. This question had multiple correct answers, but we only had time for me to choose one.

"I—I—" I stammered, grabbing a fistful of his hair as his mouth tortured me. "On top. Deep. Really deep."

His growl vibrated down my thighs before I backed away and climbed on top of the bed, spreading my legs wide as he kicked off his boxers. I laughed when he almost leaped onto the bed, covering my mouth with his as he eased into me. The first two thrusts were slow, but he pounded into me once I dug my nails into his back. Our widened eyes locked at the loud creak of the bed. I lifted my hips, not wanting to lose the rhythm but hoping to lessen the mattress impact.

"I can't help it, sweetheart. I want more of you. I need to be deeper," he grunted, sweat dripping down his forehead. "I can't stop."

"Don't stop, babe," I begged, framing his face. "Give me more—" My orgasm hit me hard, the tremors traveling down my spine all the way to my toes as my mouth opened with a silent scream. Dominic fisted the sheets over my head as he spilled into me, collapsing onto my chest with a contented sigh.

"Are we getting faster, or are they sleeping longer?" He lifted his head to glance at the video monitor.

"Maybe a little of both." I chuckled and kissed the top of his head. "I love you so much," I said, running my fingers through his damp hair. "You have no idea how hot you look with that baby carrier on your chest."

He burst out laughing. "Is that the reason for eye-fucking me in the restaurant?"

"You're a good daddy. Your babies love you."

He smiled and lay next to me, drawing me into his side.

"I love my babies. Even if I won't sleep a full night for the next decade. As long as we get to have naptime," he brushed my lips, "I can deal with it." He threaded his fingers through my hair. "Your babies love you, too. The last time I took Luca for his shots he wouldn't stop crying. With you, he's fine. He's already a mama's boy."

I nudged his shoulder. "No, he's not. And, in case you haven't noticed, it's getting a little tight for Lyndee in that carrier."

A sad smile crossed his lips as he nodded. "I know. It was nice to carry her hands free for a while."

"Or you could put her down."

He replied to my lifted eyebrow with a shrug. "I could, but I don't want to. And I wasn't knocking my son. I don't blame him for not wanting to leave your side since I never want to, either." He tightened his hold around my waist and kissed my temple. "Besides, I reveled in being a mama's boy. Still am." His eyes drifted to the ceiling. "I wish she was here."

"Me too. For so many reasons." I rested my head on Dominic's shoulder. "I was thinking of that today. What would she have said about Luca being your mini-me?"

His shoulders shook with a chuckle. "A kid of my own who's just like me? She would have told me it served me right." He rolled on his side and cupped my cheek. "Lyndee is all you. Probably why I can't put her down."

I shook my head and groaned into the pillow.

"When you say things like that, I want to give you ten more babies."

I laughed when he flinched. "I appreciate that, sweetheart, and maybe one or two more would be nice in the future, but let's focus on the two we have for the moment."

I pressed a kiss to his chest and ran my nails up and down his arm, smiling at his heavy sigh.

"I wish we could spend the afternoon naked, but one of us needs to get some clothes on." He leaned in to kiss my lips.

"We have a few more minutes—"

One wail followed by another pierced through the quiet.

Dominic stood, shaking his head as he scooped his boxers off the floor and slipped them on as he made his way out of our bedroom.

As I searched for my clothes, the crying ceased. When I stepped inside their door, Dominic held both babies, a head resting on each of his shoulders as he sang softly and rocked them back and forth. I slumped against the doorjamb, the sight in front of me obliterating my ovaries. Both of my children were under their father's spell, just like I always would be.

I should have run to snap a picture on my phone, but I didn't want to miss a second.

"Shh, it's okay," he told them, swaying back and forth before he caught my gaze. A wry grin split his mouth. Even after all this time, I loved this man more every day.

"If Mommy could stop ogling Daddy for a minute, we could get your bottles together." His brows jumped as his gaze stayed fixed on me.

"I'll go." I narrowed my eyes but couldn't help the smile spreading my lips.

"Thea," he called out when I turned to go. "I love you. I love you so fucking much. Oh, sorry guys, Daddy said a bad word," he whispered, his gaze still fixed on me. "And maybe three more wouldn't be so bad." He pursed his lips then went back to rocking the babies.

Who needed to sleep? When life was this good, why waste a single second with your eyes closed?

ACKNOWLEDGMENTS

All my books are special, but this story will always mean a lot to me.

When life as we all knew it changed in New York City and around the world, Dominic and Thea gave me something to look forward to every day. They were one of the few bright spots in my life as I tried to get used to my new normal of full-time work at home, remote learning for my fourth grader (common core math and I got used to each other, but I wouldn't call us friends), and isolation under a heavy blanket of uncertainty. I hope their journey brought as much joy to you as it did to me.

To my betas: Jodi, Julia, Bianca, Ariadna, Rachel, Marley, Jeannine, and Lisa, thank you for always believing in me enough to push me to be my best. This book is something I'm proud of thanks to you.

Christine, thank you for all you've taught me, and for saying this book is my very best. From you, that already makes it a huge win! You kick my ass every book and I love you for it.

Laura, thank you for doing such a great proofing job in such a short time. And bust vs break was my favorite debate in a long time.

Kaitie, thank you so much for loving my stories and for always doing a final pass.

Najla Qamber, after so many covers, I'm sure I make you nuts but you deliver perfection every time. This cover is so amazing and spot on, I get chills whenever I look at it. You're nothing short of spectacular.

Give Me Books, you guys are always amazing. Thank you for putting together an amazing release event.

Beth, for all the graphics born from my stick figure drawings, for an awesome cover reveal, and for being one of the most amazing humans ever. Thank you for everything.

Ariadna, you're like one of those prizes you never thought you'd win in a million years and when you do, it's even better than you imagined. I'm blessed to have you as a friend.

Jodi, I have no clue how I got so lucky to have you in my life, but I'm not going to question it. You keep me on track and not let me fall into a self-doubt spiral while making me smile and laugh every single day (We're never leaving TikTok), I love and admire you so much. Knowing you have my back and I can think of endeavors in author life in *we* not *me* terms because you're always right there means more to me than you know.

To the Rose Garden, I love how we've grown and how much your excitement fuels mine all the time. It's my happy place with my favorite people, thank you for being there through every release and making me feel your support and love.

To all my close author friends who support and guide me through this crazy book life, thank you for being friends to lean on and to aspire to.

To all the readers and bloggers who took a chance on me, I try to get better each book and I pray I delivered with this one. I appreciate every download, every share, and every message I get that someone loves my words. That is a pure joy that I am humbled and privileged to experience and it never gets old.

Finally, to my husband and son: the big guy who had to show up every day to his job at the Post Office and be essential during a terrifying time and the little guy who had to acclimate to homeschool and a temperamental teacher he called mom, you're both my heroes. All I do is for the both of you.

ABOUT THE AUTHOR

Stephanie Rose is a badass New Yorker, a wife, a mother, a former blogger and lover of all things chocolate. Most days you'll find her trying to avoid standing on discarded LEGO or deciding which book to read next. Her debut novel, Always You, released in 2015 and since then she's written several more—some of which will never see completion—and has ideas for hundred to come.

Stay in touch!
Join Stephanie's Rose Garden on Facebook and sign up for Stephanie Rose's newsletter at www.authorstephanierose.com

Follow Me on Book+Main @stephanierose

BOOKS BY STEPHANIE

The Second Chances Series
Always You
Only You
Always Us, A Second Chances Novella
After You
Second Chances Standalone Spinoffs
Finding Me
Think Twice
The Ocean Cove Series
No Vacancy
No Reservations
The Never Too Late Series
Rewrite
Simmer
Pining
Standalones
Safeguard
Just One Favor

Made in United States
North Haven, CT
05 March 2022

16816962R00178